Novels by the author

Islands of Dark Miracles

Morgan's Knot – A Serial Fantasy
Episode VII

By

Eric Thomas Stiller, Jr.

For Cory

Islands of Dark Miracles
Morgan's Knot – A Serial Fantasy
Episode VII

A woozy Zepallo gazed around the restricted ward in which he was the only patient. The sheets were white. The ceiling, walls, and floor were white. The *orbs* illuminating the room in soothing pools of cool blue spilling across the foot of the bed, banks of monitoring systems, and the floor just inside the door, cast the rest of the room into soft gray twilight. The effect reinforced the clinically sterile ambiance and grated on his testy disposition.

He struggled to sit up, as The Doctor rushed into the infirmary, a brilliant and determined renegade scientist, with a shock of white hair falling over a pallid complexion, dark deep-set eyes, and a white smock that almost brushed hygienic white booties covering his shoes.

The Dark Lord held up the bandaged stump of his right arm, "So our experiment bears fruit?"

"We are fortunate that the Masters chose you to father the next generation. Although we only have three specimens that qualify as a complete success, we have plenty of spare parts," replied The Doctor with clipped hints of a German accent.

"You can harvest a hand, my hand?"

"Of course, it will be your hand, with your fingerprints. The only difference is that your new hand will be young and it will develop the strength of a young hand." The Doctor smiled, "and we've added some new...options that you might find useful."

Zepallo scowled.

The Doctor continued, with due respect but unabated, "The only frustration is that our ability to generate new life on an accelerated schedule leads to rapid aging. We're working on the problem but our first generation is years ahead of what we consider a normal chronological scale. Your hand will suffer the same progression."

"So, the hand will have to be replaced again?"

"Yes. We're estimating ten to fifteen years."

"How quickly are my progeny aging?"

"Our latest calculations indicate that they are growing at approximately three times the normal rate. They'll mature at four or five, certainly before the year is out, and they'll have the size, weight, mental capacity, and physical prowess of a legal adult before the age of seven. At twenty-five, they'll qualify for retirement."

"What of the next generation?"

"We're confident that our success rate will increase dramatically and, through a manipulation of the genes that control aging, we hope their maturation will be slowed to about double the normal rate."

"How many new citizens might we hope for?"

"In the next group, I would expect, perhaps, one hundred."

"And the next?"

"We're anticipating ten times that number," replied The Doctor, with a confident smile, "but, in spite of learning and adapting over the last few years, there are challenges to be met."

"And each will be exactly the same as the next?"

"They'll be identical…carbon copies of our Dark Lord."

The patient settled back into his pillows, as The Doctor inserted a hypodermic into the intravenous tube feeding into the Zepallo's veins. The chemicals would take effect within a few moments and the operation could begin.

"This process could conceivably continue indefinitely. The seeds have been sewn for an endless source of reliable, dedicated, and lethal agents to lead the planet to unification under the Dark Powers…"

Chapter 2

Adrian hovered a foot above the ground, eyes closed, hands resting on his knees, palms open to the sky. It was cool in the shade of the huge oak tree draped over the edge of the vegetable garden. A gentle wind wafted in off the ocean tussling the blond hair, hanging in soft waves around his tanned face, like the lazy branches of a willow tree…moving with the breeze and then falling back against his stillness.

The words of his three-hundred-year old self kept echoing through his head, *"Life is filled with joy and wonder. It is everywhere and in everything. It's in every child's smile, every animal that you encounter, every day that ends without a battle, and every calm moment that you will enjoy. Looking back on it all, I'd say that you should be thankful for every normal day. Those days when nothing happens, when you could be bored, when things are confined to everyday routines, those are most precious."*

A smile rippled through is mind. The last three months had been calm, allowing time with the people he loved the most. He could honestly say that he found days when he had been bored, in spite of endless chores around the House of the Four Seasons, his work with Alius and the texts at Ponte's observatory, and days when he got to play in the sunshine, like a normal boy, with his friends. The wound on his chest healed enough to dive with Raffe and help with the construction of the first dome. In spite of missing most of the final semester of classes the previous year and having to make up the work, he had enjoyed his first real summer vacation since he left the little house on the bay.

His Mother told him that the tailors would be shutting down the seamstress shop within the next month. Once everyone was fitted, they would only need to repair or replace diving suits that were damaged or outgrown. Almost everyone on the island completed their training with Soule and Amy and the anticipation of exploring and joining this new undersea world inspired the entire population.

The first dome would serve as the primary interface connecting the dry world with the wet. It would also be the new, though temporary, home for the upper school students, because the old school building on the ridge was bursting at the seams with students overflowing every classroom, flocking into the canteen in ravenous waves during extended lunch hours, even packing the playground and the athletic fields during breaks and after classes. The Headmaster, Dr. Carringsworth, demanded that the first undersea dome be dedicated to providing facilities for the senior school to relieve the congestion. Thus, all of the classes for the upperclassmen, which now included Adrian, Alius, and the twins, were transferred out of the old building.

The new classrooms were completed the day before the start of classes, although some had yet to receive the finishing touches or final cleaning, but each had an open view of the sea. Most of the students felt that the younger children should have been moved into the new dome, allowing the older children to finish their schooling in the building to which they had grown accustomed. It was a change that disrupted tradition and, although most young people rebel at such things, they still sought to use any change to their advantage in their eternal quest to rile the elders.

~

Each evening after dinner, Adrian joined the twins to watch the international news on the *messenger* in their bedroom…he, for the World view, and the twins for a continuing assignment from their political science teacher, Mrs. Hammon, who insisted that her students stay attuned to the political, economic, and social changes happening across the globe. She was known for her pop quizzes posing in depth questions on the latest maneuverings in Washington or Peking, the current political attitude of the oil producing countries, or the impact of an election in some minor country…and this year, they were to pay special attention to the effects of the children's campaign against war, against the savagery that adults wage upon each other for reasons beyond any child's comprehension.

Adrian turned to his cousins, "Do you realize that, other than terrorists who prey on common citizens for their own weird political purposes, there aren't any wars happening anywhere in the world?"

Megan piped up, "I think they have you to thank for that!"

"Oh, I can't take the credit or the blame, I just spoke the truth and the children of the world did the rest."

"It's too bad that President Bartlett can't run for another term. He was a good president and a true world leader. I wonder who will take his place?"

"The election is two weeks off and the political reporters say it's dead even," said Molly.

"I wonder what he'll do after he leaves office," pondered Adrian.

"Did you feel that the guy we see on the *messenger,* was the person you met?"

Adrian smiled, "He's shorter than he appears on the news but much stronger and even more in command than when he's in public."

"Did you like him?" asked Megan.

"Yeah, I did. I thought he was extremely intelligent and polite, genuine in an old-fashioned sort of way. He listened to our tale and didn't act as if we were just children telling stories and he does have a sense of humor. I'd like to show him the island, especially now that we have the first dome completed. Who knows, maybe after he leaves office, we could convince him to come for a visit."

"Yeah, like the Secret Service is going to place the security of an ex-president in the hands of a bunch of children and people they can't trace, on an island that doesn't show up on their radar, let alone their maps!" laughed Megan. "That'll never happen."

"Do you know how to get in touch with him?" asked Molly.

"Sure," replied Adrian. "I know his personal Internet address."

"Then you should invite him before he leaves office. I'll bet he'd come!"

"I might just do that...just to prove a point to your Mrs. Hammon. She'd have to give you a passing grade if you brought a president to class," smirked Adrian.

"That might be the only way to get a good grade in her class!" laughed Molly.

"I want to take your class," said Megan.

"Yeah, me too."

"I'm going to be a hard grader because I want all of you to grasp the potential of the Powers in everybody's lives. You don't have to be a *seer* or a Keeper to find new ways to use this energy. I think most people on the island have a vague understanding of how it works and they enjoy the benefits but what if everyone really understood it? Then we'd have hundreds of different viewpoints seeing things that none of us might have considered," said Adrian.

The two *seers* had been tasked with teaching a class together on The Powers. After consulting with Ester and Mary, who knew far more of their history than anyone else, other than Orana, they decided to confine their lessons to those adventures that might serve as examples for the rest of the children to use in their everyday lives. Dadeus and Ponte were working on a new curriculum that involved the use of the Powers with marine life in the ocean but the *seer's* class took a far more human approach.

Their first lesson generated more than a bit of trepidation. They were still students with the other children for the rest of each day but they were the instructors during this one hour and wanted to give their friends something more than they received in most of their other classes.

After long discussions, they decided to start with something that Shambala said before Adrian's speech to the United Nations. "We teach our children that if you truly believe that you can do something…say fly…you might not have the ability now but your belief will drive your curiosity and that will lead you to find a way to make it real. Taking it to its finest level, belief is enough to create reality."

On the first day of classes, Adrian and Alius allowed their students to enter the classroom, which was on the third level, before levitating through the door behind them, flying over their heads, and hovering above a small riser at the front of the classroom.

The students were awestruck, standing motionless, their mouths agape.

The young teachers descended to the floor and Alius said, with complete confidence, "Why don't you sit down and we'll tell you about The Powers?"

The smiling students took their chairs without a word.

Adrian stepped to the front of the little stage, "Our demonstration wasn't intended to show off our powers for your amusement. It was my personal reminder that, until a year and half ago, I didn't know that I had any special talents or that I might be called on to do the things that I've been asked to do. I was a normal kid, just like every one of you."

He looked around the room at the students, who were enthralled with his every word. "The point is that each of us has a unique set of powers and talents. Every one of you is capable of doing at least one thing that I couldn't possibly accomplish and, yet, they've become second nature and you do them with ease."

Pointing to Eloise, a pudgy girl with dark curly hair, a pale complexion, and lips that curled into a most beautiful smile, he said, "Eloise, you can play the flute. You can make absolutely beautiful music. That's a talent that none of the rest of us has. And Hector," He pointed to a small boy with red hair, blues eyes, and an impish grin, "You can run faster than any other kid on the island. No one can catch you. Almy, you get the best grades in the school. The rest of us try to complete but you always come out on top."

"Do you see what I'm saying?" He paused. "Each of you has talents and abilities that make you unique and special. Be proud of those gifts, work hard to develop them, and use them well.

"We have no proof...but we believe that some of the things that we've learned to do, could be done by anyone. Some of these seemingly magical talents are not confined to those who are born a *seer* or study to become a Keeper."

Alius interrupted, "We talked and talked about how to present our view of The Powers to you in a way that would make sense and help you to reach for your own potential. We agreed that our lessons should be based on something that a friend of ours told us…and that was, that you might not be able to accomplish everything that you dream of doing, at least not now. But, if you truly believe, that energy and determination will lead you to pursue your dreams and, perhaps someday, allow you to find the path to fulfillment. She said, 'Taking this idea to its finest level, belief is enough to create reality'."

With that, Simian strode into the room, dressed in a beautiful yellow sash with a floral pattern that wrapped around his upper torso. He wore blue pantaloon pants made from the same material that Sara and Morgan bought from his little stall in Jamaica, during their trip to the Island of Children, and bright pink shoes that curled up at the toes. His little glasses hung precariously on the end of his broad nose and his goatee seemed whiter than before he returned to Jamaica, after Adrian's speech.

The old Jamaican carried a bundle of goose feathers in a rough woven shoulder bag, which leaked white fluff that floated to the floor, trailing a wispy veil in his wake. He smiled at the students, "Good afternoon, I'm pleased to be here with you!"

Alius took Simian's arm and said, "Many of the things that we've learned came through the instruction of our friend Simian, a master *seer* from Jamaica."

Simian turned to the students with a huge smile, "I want to talk with you about the power that lives inside seemingly inanimate things. There's energy in everything around us…the trees, the rocks, the ocean…" He turned and waved at the spectacular view of sunlight streaming through the water behind him. "The ocean pulses with its own rhythm. Certainly, the tides are governed by the movements of the moon and the waves are the product of the winds but, if you look beyond the obvious scientific explanations, it is the home, the origin for all life. Our ancient ancestors crawled out of the sea, onto the shore, where they changed and evolved over the eons to become us!

Everything has its own energy and we're affected by the energies around us. Each of you gives off a charge that is unique to you. We call it an aura, an energy field that surrounds everything and everyone…but that is another lecture!"

He pulled a large white feather from his bag and held it on the flattened palm of his hand. "This feather has no weight."

He blew hard and the feather leapt into the air and spiraled to the floor. "It is in its nature to fly!"

Retrieving the feather, he held it up to the class. "This feather lifted a heavy bird into the air and carried it for hundreds, if not, thousands of miles. It is strong and sturdy, ingeniously crafted to flex in several directions without breaking, and perfectly curved to provide lift. It wants to fly, even if there is no wind."

He concentrated on the white feather in his hand and, slowly, it began to flutter, rising several inches above his palm to fan his face, before returning to rest on his fingertips. The students stared in wonder.

Simian smiled and said softly, "It was not my energy that made it fly. That energy already exists inside the feather. I merely gave it permission."

Everyone laughed, as Simian moved from one desk to the next, plucking feathers from his bag and handing one to each student. He returned to the riser at the front of the classroom, with a wink to Adrian and Alius. "I want each of you to hold your feather on the tips of your fingers and then blow on it gently, give it just enough air to provide lift."

The students puffed at their feathers, which flew into the air, a blizzard spinning down to the floor, as if some giant goose had fluttered through the room, shedding soft downy snowflakes.

"Now let's see whether each of you can allow the feather to show its true character. Don't try to make it fly…allow it to use the air. Hold it on your palm. Concentrate on the fact that it wants to fly. It's in its nature and the only thing holding it back is your hand. Set it free!"

Most of the feathers spiraled to the floor but every child picked them up and tried again and again. There were fierce stares, as they concentrated on the essence of their feathers but none showed any frustration, when the experiment did not supply instant gratification.

Simian spotted Eloise at the back of the room and her feather floating just above the palm of her hand, as she whispered and coaxed it into the air. "Ah, I see that one of you has found the magic. The young lady with the dark hair in the back, everyone look, she's done it!"

The rest of the students gathered around the flautist. "I thought that maybe there was a musical tone that would fit with my feather, so I started humming to it, trying to find the right vibration, and suddenly it started to rise, all by itself!"

There were comments and whispers throughout the group, "If she can do it, then I can too!" and several more made their feathers fly, before the young tutors had to dismiss the class for the day.

Simian raised his hands for the attention of the students, "This is a preliminary demonstration. With some practice, more of you will master this challenge. I'll come back and we'll learn a bit more the next time."

The students applauded and reluctantly moved on to their next classes.

Adrian and Alius hugged their friend, "That was brilliant!" said Alius, "I think we were both reminded of our hesitation and disbelief when you first taught us about levitation. We really appreciate your help."

"Ah, it is my pleasure," laughed the little Jamaican. "What's brilliant is that the authorities in this school have allowed you to conduct this class! The rest of the students will certainly benefit from the things that you've experienced."

"How's Sammy?" asked Adrian.

"He's fine. In fact, he's at the observatory, as we speak. He has a long list of questions for the Professor and Nanchez, and now Dadeus, about using the vectors to supply electrical power. Although our country is modern in many ways, there are many poor people who live in conditions that are shameful at best. They lack power and fresh clean water, let alone a sewer. He wants to construct a small experimental network to help those people."

"That's wonderful," commented Alius. "The Powers should benefit the common people, not the rich corporations!"

"I believe that he'll be successful but we'll have to find a way to construct this network without raising the suspicion of the authorities. They might wonder why shanties have lighting without being connected to their grid and accuse these poor people of stealing their precious electricity."

"I can see the problem," said Adrian. "It was hard for me to believe that *orbs* could provide light without being connected to wires or batteries or whatever, that cars could move along the paths without proper engines, or that the three-dimensional images we see on the *messengers* are not available in the rest of the world. All of it is still rather amazing."

"I agree," said Simian. "Considering some of what we've learned from Dadeus and the other Keepers, I might guess that we're only using a small part of the potential of the Crystals."

Adrian laughed, "As Ponte always says, 'There's always more to learn about the Powers!'."

Simian smiled knowingly and placed his gnarled hand on the young *seer's* shoulder, "We all know he speaks the truth."

~

Zepallo inspected his new hand. It was young. The skin was taut and unmarked. The long slender fingers extended and flexed smoothly, his knuckles a series of well-lubricated gears, and it was a youthful mirror image of his left hand. He was amazed by the thin red line around his arm, above the wrist, that marked the junction between his old body and his new appendage.

The Doctor wrapped a bandage around the healing wound, leaving the hand free and unbound. "It will take several weeks to regain your normal strength and coordination. You'll begin your therapy this afternoon and you'll also learn how to use several new devices that we've incorporated for your added...protection."

"I don't understand."

"For several years, I've been working on a personal weapon that could channel the Powers through the human body. After all, every function in our bodies is controlled by electrical impulses and they are the result of chemical reactions. The energy of the Crystals is very much the same as the energy that controls us. I've merely adjusted the frequency."

He took the Dark Lord's new hand and extended the index finger, pointing it towards an eye chart on the far wall. He pressed the first knuckle and the tip of his finger glowed the bluish white of a superheated flame. An electrical charge surged across the room, with a piercing crackle, shredding the paper into tiny fragments that showered the shiny floor in flames.

"You'll learn to use this by merely thinking about it. Obviously, we would rather that you not indulge your curiosity, until we have had a chance to work with you and to fine tune the instrument."

Zepallo stared at The Doctor. "That's incredible. I felt the surge flow down my arm and out through my finger!"

"I thought you might enjoy the…convenience."

"You said 'new devices.' What other options did you add?"

"Well, the other obvious improvement is that we've made some modifications to the tendons and ligaments that will allow your right hand to be several times stronger than your left," smiled The Doctor. "Please do not experiment with it yet. Just as you learned to use your original hand and developed your strength and coordination through a series of repetitive demands over time, we will teach you to reach an optimum level in short order."

"I'll try to be patient…but tell me about the charge. I want to understand it."

The Doctor smiled modestly, "As my modest demonstration showed, it's very similar in intensity to the blast that you might fire from your ring, with a range of perhaps twelve to fifteen meters but, in my experiments, I predict that, when it is used in close combat, it will leave no mark on the skin."

"That could be very useful."

"A charge of this magnitude, applied to the chest would result in violent fluctuations of the rhythm of the heart muscles or total paralysis, without leaving any evidence on the surface."

They both inspected the raised hand with a reverence reserved for a magnificent piece of sculpture. The Dark Lord stared at his physician, "I want to see my offspring."

The Doctor smiled again, "I've been wanting to share them with you for quite some time but I felt that it would be better, after they completed some of their initial training, and…your mere presence would disrupt our research. Now, I believe that time has come. Are you feeling up to a short stroll?"

Zepallo put his feet on the floor and stood up. He wavered for a moment as he adjusted his sense of balance, which suffered as a result of the anesthetics and his confinement. He arched his back and stretched, before placing his new hand on The Doctor's shoulder, "I've shown great restraint since the program's inception, because you must learn how to develop the children to achieve their potentials but I must admit that I've been anxious to see the results. Shall we go?"

The doctor took his patient's elbow to guide him through the sterile white hallways of the complex that had been nestled into the corals beneath an uncharted island in the Savu Sea along the southern archipelago of Indonesia. Research, development, and living quarters were attached to a central ring encircling a hub that contained a giant Black Crystal. To satellites that photographed every square inch of the planet as they swept through their orbits every ninety minutes, this facility appeared an integral part of a corral reef.

The Doctor said, "We chose this spot because it is easy to maintain the necessary temperatures for our production, without excessive cooling or heating. As we learned, pearls and human embryos require similar conditions. Our systems filter and purify millions of gallons of salt water, which provides a perfect medium, and our test facility is kept at a constant 98.6 degrees Fahrenheit, the temperature of the human body."

He tapped a code into a tiny *messenger* on a wall and the door slid back to reveal a glass tunnel to a darkened circular control station with a three-hundred and sixty-degree view. Clear aqua water sloshed around the glass sphere and thousands of bulbous tubes, each pulsing with an iridescent green glow swayed with the gentle rhythm of sea grasses in a modest current. The Doctor waved his hand around the circle at the giant incubator. "At the moment, these embryos are in various stages of development and, when we've perfected our program, we can easily expand to produce ten times this number."

"And all of these came from a small sample that was taken from me all those years ago?"

"Yes, we've replicated your DNA many times. That information is introduced into a fertilized egg that is grown in perfect conditions in our facility. After nine months, a child is born and moved to our nursery. They are cared for by trained nurses and gradually introduced to our educational program, which is still under development. As I said earlier, their progress is rather astonishing, maturing at three times the normal rate. Our first subjects would be about twelve or thirteen now. As you will see they are not like most twelve-year olds."

"I believe this qualifies as a miracle, a dark miracle."

They walked back to the corridor and turned into another glass tunnel open to sunlight streaming down through the sea. The two men entered an observation deck above a pod that had been constructed for the youngsters. Their vantage point offered an overhead view of the living quarters, a small classroom with multiple *messengers*, laboratory equipment, a library of books, and a large gymnasium that rose two stories, with ropes, wires, and climbing walls, as well as an interface to the open water.

Five divers emerged from the ocean and walked up a shallow ramp. The two larger divers were obviously instructors. The shorter three, although well-muscled for their age, pulled off their helmets to reveal identical features. Long dark hair framed the pale skin of a slender face. High cheekbones made intense blue eyes appear recessed slightly into their skulls. A fierce, ominous glare sparkled in the shadows beneath their eyebrows as each stopped to stare at the darkened observation pod.

Zepallo's jaw dropped open. He recognized those eyes, those faces from a lifetime of staring into a mirror. They were exactly as he had been when he was twelve...physically...and he could feel their energies probing his own. "What do you call them?"

"Alpha, Beta, and Gamma."

"Are they truly identical?"

"Physically, yes, but each has a slightly different personality. Alpha is the first to step forward, when there's any sort of challenge. Beta is a bit more standoffish...he likes to size up the situation, before deciding on a course of action. Where Alpha might rush into a hasty decision, Beta would have thought the problem through and come up with a reasonable response. Gamma is quiet, a bit withdrawn, and far more emotional and organized than his brothers."

"Considering that they all came from the same genes, they have lived together and received similar treatment and instruction, why would they be different in their manner?"

"One simple answer might be sibling rivalry. Put any group of subjects together in a confined space, especially under adverse conditions, and they'll establish, without prompting, their pecking order. Who is the strongest, who is the weakest, and who claims those places in between? It is the law of nature and each adapts to their role."

Zepallo stared at the clones. Each of them an exact copy, yet each was different, unique. He considered his past and realized that he could have been any of them. Alpha, standing ramrod straight, his hands moving as he talked...from his manner, it appeared that he was giving instructions. Beta was relaxed, his weight rested on his right leg, while his left was slightly bent, his foot tapping absently. He leaned back and hooked his thumbs into a strap around the waist of his diving suit, with a look of mild amusement in his eyes and the curve of his slender lips. Gamma, was bent over, arranging the equipment lying on the platform, ignoring his brothers. He would willingly work with the others but he would make conquests on his own.

"A leader in battle, a tactician, and an organizational genius. Each useful in their own unique way." The Doctor smiled, "They possess your gifts but each will make use of an individual set of talents that will define their identities. I thought that you would be pleased."

"Are they equal in all other ways?"

"Yes. They're all extraordinary students, each excelling in different areas but brilliant none-the-less. Although Alpha is physically dominant, Beta focuses and tames his enthusiasm, while Gamma maintains an equilibrium and controls everything in the background. They're a team and, when our next generation is born, I think that we should consider organizing them into family groups like this. Having grown up together and being trained as a unit, they'll work seamlessly, probably without even talking to each other, which should prove to be extremely useful."

"You're a genius!"

The Doctor bowed.

"I'd like to see them in the field and I think I might have the perfect test subject for them to execute the skills that you've taught them. We'll need some bait to draw him out of his sanctuary," smiled Zepallo, holding up his new hand like a trophy.

~

Sir Jonathon retired to his study, after a rather spare but splendidly prepared dinner of filet of sole, Au Gratin potatoes, and fresh asparagus. He sat alone at the head of a long formal table capable of seating sixteen comfortably, staring intently at a massive eighteenth-century oil painting of red and black cavalries charging down opposing hills, under clouds of dense smoke from barrages of canon fire on the ridges, to certain carnage and defeat. He shook his head, reminded that there is no glory in slaughter and death, no matter the cause or justification.

The secure room was his sanctuary, the place that held all of his secrets, communication with agencies across the world, his trophies, and his memories. Few had entered this room since its construction thirty years ago and, for the sake of several governments, it was probably better that way.

He sat down at the large maple desk in the center of the room, surrounded by walls of books. Two leather wing chairs rested on a plush Persian carpet facing the desk, a small French game table between them with a vase of white lilies from the little garden at the rear of the house. Turning to a credenza behind him, he poured two fingers of brandy into a snifter, opened a beautifully inlaid wooden box and withdrew a cigar, which had been smuggled in from Cuba, and reached for a file that had been locked in the top right-hand drawer along with a small caliber pistol.

The green glass globe of the brass reading-lamp on the desk cast a soft glow around the room. His awards and honors were displayed with subtle, almost humble design. A medal with colored ribbons laid casually on an end table. Honoraria bound in simple frames and a small model of one of the submarines that he commanded were nestled amongst the books. It was a masculine room yet there was nothing boastful about its character. It held the history of his life...or, at least, his previous life. He had dedicated his energies to his duty and career but he had neglected his private life...his wife and his children.

There was always another mission, another crisis, and time slipped away. He stared at the photograph of his children sitting on the corner of the desk, all teeth and smiles. He provided for them but he had not given of himself those things that they needed. He carried the guilt of his professional life with quiet dignity but the pain in his heart for all that he missed would surely follow him to his grave.

The amber light spilling across the desk beneath the lamp illuminated the title on the cover of the file, DARK FORCES – EYES ONLY. He was aware that the Prime Minister and the president had met secretly to discuss what Bartlett referred to as a clandestine international force. Had it not been Bartlett who broached the subject and made the inference, no one would have believed it and the matter would have been tossed into the bin reserved for the conspiracy theories of lunatics and fanatics.

There was nothing fanatical or insane about the outgoing president. Sir Jonathon knew of secret internal investigations being pursued by at least three governments. To those who had been assigned to look into these matters, it could only mean that the upper-levels of intelligence had been breached by the tentacles of the Dark Forces. The question had become…how deep?

The old man leaned back in his chair and opened the cover to reveal the first page. It was stamped with a large red seal, <u>TOP</u> <u>SECRET</u> - <u>EYES</u> <u>ONLY</u>. He flipped to the second page, adjusted his reading glasses, and scanned through a dozen paragraphs at high speed until he came to the phrase,

President Bartlett stated that he has photographic evidence of the infiltration of allied governments at the highest level by agents of this force, led by the man we know as Palloze. He also claimed that this group has mastered the power of mysterious giant crystals and built expansive facilities scattered across the globe.

The combined intelligence of the Western powers does not support his contention, although numerous inquiries have been raised and pursued concerning Palloze. Despite a concerted effort through every available channel, very little is known of his background or his connections and there is no information on his location. He appears and disappears, seemingly, without normal conveyance. There does not seem to be a financial trail or a visible organization behind him, yet he has entrée and access to the leaders of the second and third-world countries. Intelligence has no records of communication by any means between Palloze and anyone else.

Questions have also been raised about the young man who spoke to the United Nations. He and his friends appeared to fly through the chamber and he also spoke of powers that are unknown to the scientists of the world. The effect of his speech, on the children in every country, has raised questions about mass hypnosis or subliminal messages buried in his talk. Review of the tapes of the speech revealed nothing unusual and no information is available on the boy or his whereabouts.

Sir Jonathon closed the file and placed it on his desk, held the snifter to his nose, inhaling the deep earthy aroma before taking a sip of his brandy. He puffed on his fine cigar, and watched the smoke rise slowly through the warm glow of the reading lamp on his desk. "You fools don't know that half of it. That young man is my grandson."

Since before the confrontation with the New Coalition and Adrian's speech to the United Nations, he had overseen quiet inquiries into Palloze and The Powers. Officially, they turned up no new information and he passed those findings along through the proper channels…but there was more. There was always more.

His son John arrived, unannounced, on a cold autumn night last fall. Jonathon had been overjoyed because the last word that he had received was that the Sparrow was missing and his contacts found no trace of the boat or his son and daughter-in-law, Sara.

They sat in this room and John talked of their voyage, of their rescue, Adrian's battle with the pirates and the most recent efforts to connect the nodes. He relayed the history of The Powers and his son's place in their world…and, finally, he sought his father's approval for leaving a proper job and a normal way of life to pursue something that seemed far more important to him.

Sir Jonathon had taken a long draw on his cigar, a short sip of his brandy, leaned back in his chair, put his feet up on the desk, and smiled the smile of a father who is proud of a child's accomplishments.

He looked John straight in the eye, "I'm very proud that you've made the right choice. I knew that you'd follow in my footsteps, given half a chance! Now you're living in the shadow world!" The old man roared with laughter. "Your brother wouldn't have the guts and your sister is, I hate to admit, far too spoiled to venture farther than her favorite salon or their beach house."

John was laughing so hard he couldn't speak. His brother, Ralph, had become a corporate attorney, chasing deals and attempting to forge a reputation in the business world. John loved his brother but honestly felt that, other than working constantly to enhance his own significance, he was of very little use to humanity. His sister, Margaret, married rich, had two kids, a husband who lusted after women but not his wife, a fancy house, a fast car, and nowhere to go. She dropped out of school, used her beauty to snare her husband, and settled into a very comfortable but boring existence.

Finally, his father leaned forward, his elbows on the desk, the smoke of his cigar rolling up through the light to surround his face in a gray cloud. His dark eyes sparkled, as he gazed at his son, "So the Powers really do exist. There's another world and no one ever noticed?"

"I think the fact that the Powers and these opposing civilizations have existed, since long before the beginning of written history, has made it easier to hide these forces from the general population. They influence the very best and the very worst of our world and it's all there in the history books, if you read between the lines. There have always been stories, rumors, legends and myths but no one knew where to look. It was right under their noses all the time!"

"But traveling from place to place, levitating in the air...it's all real?"

"Of course, it's real. My son can levitate from one home to another around the island. He can move through the vectors from city to city or between continents in moments. He possesses powers that I don't understand and he hears and feels the energies of the world that are beyond my comprehension. He understands the messages in texts that have existed for thousands of years and very few have inherited the talent that he got from his mother. I'm in awe of his abilities and, at the same time, terrified because he's still just a boy," whispered John. His mood changed from pride to fear in the time it took for him to say these few sentences and the old man felt his pain…joyfully.

"There are parallel planes that exist in the same time and the same space as our reality. Some are used by the Dark Forces, and I think that we're only just learning about their potential. These things are real and so is the threat of Zepallo and the Dark Forces."

The father stared at his son, his mouth was hanging open and a small wisp of smoke escaped from his nose.

John sat back in the wingback leather chair, sipping his brandy. "Zepallo poses the gravest threat to the future of the world as we know it and, I fear, my son is the only one who can stop him. He won't turn back and I have no choice but to do everything I can to assist and protect him."

"You don't need my permission to do with your life what you think best. I'm proud of everything that you've done, your talents as a student and an athlete, your abilities with a boat in any weather, your career and your family…and the strength of character that you possess. It's your lot to stand with your son and help him hold back these Dark Forces. For the rest of mankind, I beg of you, do not allow Adrian to fail."

Sir Jonathon was jarred from his thoughts by a cold blue whirling light that erupted on the Persian carpet before the two wingback chairs. A tall dark form materialized and stared down at the old man, who rose behind his desk. He glanced at the handle of the pistol that was partially concealed in the drawer, "Who are you and what are you doing in my study?"

The black cowl of his robes concealed a sallow face but the blue eyes glowed, "I believe that we have a common friend. You are Sir Jonathon, Master of the Underworld…beneath the sea and the darkness of the world of secrets. You are also Adrian's grandfather, are you not?"

"May I ask who you might be?"

"You, of all people, know who I am. You released your spies to investigate me and there was nothing to find. I am not of your world."

"I believe the name is Zepallo or Palloze or a hundred other aliases."

"You are correct. We, collectively, are also known as Legio Obscurum, although that's a useless bit of information at this point."

"How may I help you?"

"You can help me by dying," sneered the Dark Lord with a sinister laugh.

In one smooth movement, Adrian's Grandfather reached for the gun, aimed it at Zepallo's heart, and fired. The bullet flew straight and true but, to his astonishment, moved in slow motion, and the Evil One lifted his new right hand and plucked the bullet from the air, holding it up like a prize. "Your weapons can not hurt me. Your jails can't hold me. Your armies can not defeat me and, sooner or later, all of you will bow to my power. In the meantime, I need our grandson out in the open for a little educational demonstration. What better emergency than a funeral?"

Sir Jonathon stared into the blazing blue eyes and realized that, behind the evil glare, they were familiar. He tried to move but there was no escape as the Dark Lord stepped forward, leaned across the desk, and touched the old man squarely on the chest above his heart with the index finger of his right hand.

Chapter 3

Simian's presence triggered visions of the lessons of Adrian's time with Orana. There had been no opportunity to return to the cave in the plane of the animals but every few days, the young *seer* would find a quiet time to focus his senses out into the world, to trace the vibrations that revealed the state of the planet. Since his speech to the United Nations, the world had changed… had he been an adult, he might have used the word matured. The rebellious children demanded peace, fairness, equality, and hope for all the people and animals on the globe. The governments of the rich and powerful nations were shamed into working with the nations of the New Coalition, to rewrite treaties and trade agreements to accommodate the needs of all participants. Warring countries and tribes were persuaded to begin negotiations, when thousands of children marched onto the front lines in the killing fields, into government offices, and tribal headquarters, in noisy demonstrations and confrontations that disrupted any chance of continued senseless slaughter.

He knew that the calm could not last forever. His older-self told him as much but he could only hope that events happening across the globe would inspire the population to overcome their fears, to join together to put an end to the pillaging of the riches of the Earth, and to learn to treat each other with the love and respect of brothers and sisters, committed to the wonders that might be shared by everyone. There was only one force that could hold back the Dark tide and that was the unity and strength of the vast majority of the population of the planet. They had to learn to stand together for their own salvation.

Zepallo vanished after their battle over the fields near the village. As far as Adrian knew, no one had seen or heard of him since. He failed to appear as spokesman for the countries of the New Coalition and there had been no indications on the *messengers* of any large-scale movements in the vectors. The Keepers were monitoring activity around various Black Crystals and plenty of information passed into their systems but none of it seemed threatening to the progress being made for the common good.

The prickly itch crawled over his skin, on detecting a faint grating in the background of the reassuring hum rippling through the vectors…a faint whisper in a windstorm, far away, almost indiscernible from the noise of life…yet, distinct in tone and rhythm, in an odd way, for he felt that it was a message directed at him…that the balance of the planet had been disrupted by something small but hardly insignificant.

Today, there was something else, something dark, evil, and close to his heart. That familiar chill raced up his spine and a dull ache clamped down at the base of his skull, an agonizing reminder that the battles were far from finished. His three-hundred-year-old voice reverberated through his mind, "You have only begun the fight!"

He opened his eyes to view the garden, a golden sun setting over his left shoulder painted fruits and vegetables in vibrant flashes of orange and yellow. Beneath a large straw hat, with a brim that reached past her shoulders, Elsie tended her crops, gathering vegetables for dinner in a wicker basket, while pulling the occasional weed and whistling to the sparrows chattering along the fence. A cloud of butterflies fluttered around her like a gust of pastel fairies and tiny hummingbirds chased through the plantings, darting this way and that, stopping in midair to hover above a flower and drink of its nectar.

Bees swarmed around the entrances to their hives, as the last of the workers returned with a deposit from the fields. He mused on the ability of these tiny creatures to work in perfect harmony for the common good, if only humans could adopt that philosophy, that ethic.

He settled back to the ground as his mother walked over and sat down beside him, "What are you feeling today?"

Adrian smiled and bashfully stared at the ground, "Sometimes I wonder why everyone can't hear what I hear and feel the vibrations that surround us. Maybe, over time, we've learned to tune it out. It's always there, a constant hum in the background but maybe there's too much noise around us, too much commotion in our own minds, which makes me wonder whether, at some point in the distant past, humans had more senses...like this ability to feel the world around them. Does that make any sense?"

Sara wrapped her arms around her son and pulled him to her. He was beginning to grow and put on a little weight. His shoulders felt hard, taut muscles replacing childhood softness. She hated the idea that he was beginning to change from a child into a young man but realized that, in many ways, he made that transformation almost two years before, when he accepted the responsibilities of a *seer*. She kissed the top of his head, "Have I mentioned that I'm very proud of you, rather awestruck by some of the things that you can do, all that you've accomplished, and that I love you more than anything?"

Adrian returned her hug and buried his head in her shoulder. She was the living motivation for everything he believed in, everything he fought for, and he made a point of spending time with both of his parents, during the calm of the past few months. He knew that the tranquility spreading across the planet, like a warm blanket on a winter's night, was nearing an end.

"You didn't answer my question," said Sara softly. "What are you feeling today?"

"I haven't learned Simian's talent for seeing along the vectors. Instead, I listen and I hear a hum. It's soft and gentle and it pulses and ripples with a tempo all its own. I think it's the rhythm of life, the energy of every living creature merging together to create a harmony of tones. There are different parts or notes in the wall of vibrations...like the sound of new life...it's rapid, excited, and high pitched, while the sound of aging is slow and the tones are deep. There's also the sound of evil, conflict and anger, and of war and death."

"Lately, I've heard two different sounds. One is a calm that has settled over the world, since the children started their campaign to put an end to war and suffering...but there's a new sound. It's very faint, very far away, like the sound of the dark vectors but I sense that it's a warning of something evil that's lurking, growing, and I know this moment of peace can't last. The Dark Forces will see to that."

"You're frightening me."

"I honestly don't feel that it's an imminent threat. It's more like a seed that's been planted and it's growing."

"Then this is the time to enjoy the peace together."

Adrian smiled, "Yes, I told you about my conversation with my older self. I still don't quite know how to refer to that person...anyway, he told me two things that I've tried to remember every day. The first was that the fight and the war are far from over, there will be more confrontations, but the other thing he told me was that I should be thankful for every normal day, every day when I could be bored or lazy. Every day that I got to spend with the people that mean the most to me, because that's why I have to do the things that I have to do...for all of you."

His mother couldn't restrain the smile, "How could any mother be so lucky?"

They turned to the bang of the kitchen door flying open and Adrian's father staggered onto the little porch. He looked around the yard, eyes wide with panic, his tanned face a pasty shade of gray, before he spied his wife and son sitting beneath the old oak tree.

He ran down the steps, across the yard, and fell to his knees next to Sara, who asked, "What's wrong?"

She wrapped her arms around him, as he stammered, "It's dad, he's dead."

"Oh, my," whispered Sara. "I'm so sorry. He was such a wonderful man."

Adrian joined the hug and cried with his parents. His grandfather had been a proud naval captain, renowned for his many missions as a submariner during the war and, before his retirement, as the Liaison for Counter Intelligence. He was equally at home in the depths of the open sea or the secret world, where information was gathered, synthesized, and turned to his country's benefit, and he had been knighted for his efforts.

They visited the grand house in Washington several times and Adrian had fond memories of Sir Jonathon. He was a tall man, broad-chested, and quick with a smile and a joke. He wore his silver hair long, with waves flowing over his ears and down around his starched collar. Adrian wondered whether he alternated between secret missions on submarines and directing the world of spies. He always seemed prepared for either.

Sara leaned back and wiped the tears from her eyes with the cuff of her sleeve and touched John's cheek gently, "We have to go, you have to be there."

"I know," whispered Adrian's father. "It's just such a shock. He always seemed to be more fit than anyone else."

"What was the cause?"

"They said that it was a heart attack. Sudden. Massive. Lethal."

"At least he went quickly. He wasn't the kind of man who would have done well, wasting away over the years. I think he would have wanted it this way," said Sara quietly.

"He was something, wasn't he?"

"There won't be another like him…"

Adrian pulled away from his parents. The odd sensation that he felt suddenly made sense, "I could get you there in minutes."

Sara leaned over and hugged her son, "No. This isn't about The Powers. We have to arrive by conventional transportation…like an airplane and a taxi. Besides, we'll all need some new clothes for the funeral."

Adrian hugged his father, thinking, *There's far more to this than a heart attack.*

In the distance, he heard a loud "caw" echoing across the fields, golden in the west, tall in the south, and a vibrant green blanket crawling across the bluff to the east.

~

It had been a long time since Adrian's last flight on a commercial airliner. He had forgotten how tedious the security screenings could be. He placed a small suitcase on the conveyor, removed his shoes, and emptied his pockets into a little plastic bowl, all of which was run through an X-ray machine. After walking through a magnetic detector, a guard went over his entire body with a handheld scanner. No one paid much attention to his ring.

Perhaps this was one of those times, when being recognized might not have been a bad thing. What amazed him was that any *seer* could just materialize on the other side of the barrier and continue on his way. He was half-tempted to vaporize before their eyes but knew that might not be appropriate at the moment, considering the purpose of their trip. Traveling along the vectors was so much easier and he would avoid this form of transportation, given the choice.

Trains were another matter. He remembered a train trip through France, when he was younger. He had been entranced with the idea of spending the night in their own little compartment, with fold-down beds, and he liked having tea in the dining car, where the waiters wore white coats and served their food very formally. It all seemed a great adventure and he knew that he would find a way to ride on an overnight train again.

They reached the gate but their plane had yet to arrive. The sign at the counter said that they would be delayed for at least an hour, so they walked over to a coffee shop and sat down at a small table. Sara went to the counter to order drinks and some donuts to tide them over and returned with a small tray.

A matronly old woman was seated at the table next to the window, with a little dog that she had removed from a tiny kennel, and Adrian could feel her staring at him. The dog began to bark and, if the woman could have understood what the dog was saying, it would have made matters worse. The little dog was shouting, "That's the boy on the television, the one who spoke at the United Nations. It's him, I'm sure of it. Oh, you must say hello to him. He introduced the world to The Balance…but then, you're a sweet lonely dunce, who doesn't have a clue about The Balance, but say hello to him anyway!"

Of course, the old woman couldn't understand her dog and Adrian was glad of it. He turned and whispered to his mother, "I think that I should excuse myself. The woman by the window seems to have recognized me and I don't think this is the time for that."

Sara turned and looked at the woman, who smiled and started to lean towards their table. She turned back to Adrian, "Well, at least it's a good thing she can't understand her dog!"

John stood up and picked up the tray, attempting to lead his family away from any confrontation, when the little dog started barking again, straining at the end of his short leash. Several other people were staring in their direction, curious about the commotion. The old woman could not contain herself and leaned a bit too far out of her seat, when the chair slipped out from beneath her and she sprawled across the floor like a beached whale, shrieking, "That's him, I know that's him!" The food and drinks, which had been sitting solidly on her table, rained down on her with a mighty clatter, bouncing and splattering all over her clothes.

Sara hesitated for a moment, her instinct to help the poor woman almost overwhelmed her common sense, before she led Adrian and John through the entrance and back to their gate.

He couldn't help himself and leaned over to his parents, "It would have been easier to travel through the vectors."

"That will be enough of that, young man," replied his mother, who could hardly contain an impish grin.

His father didn't seem to see the humor in the situation, at the moment, so Adrian whispered, "I'm awfully sorry about being recognized."

John gazed down at his son, "I don't think this will be the last time we'll have this problem."

The young *seer* tried to maintain a straight face, "Well, maybe I could grow a beard or something!"

His father exploded with laughter. The cups in the tray jiggled this way and that, splashing the drinks onto his hands and wrists. Adrian wrapped his arms around John's waist. It was the first time that John seemed to relax, since word had come of the death of his father.

Over his shoulder, he heard a girl's voice, "That's the boy! He's the boy who can fly!"

Adrian looked up, as his father's grin sagged. There was no place to go, their flight would be boarding in the next few minutes. John put the tray down on an empty seat, picked up their bags, and walked over to stand in line near the gangway to the airplane. Adrian and Sara followed.

Unfortunately, a small mob of curious people also moved to stand in line and the girl's mother, a rather portly woman who was wearing a pink headscarf, a tight pink knit blouse, Bermuda shorts with a garish pattern, and purple flip-flops on her bare feet, asked, "Are you that young fella, who talked on the television and flew through the air?"

Adrian did not know how to respond. On the one hand, he had been taught to be polite and to answer questions honestly. On the other, he remembered the comment that his older self had made about people always wanting to touch him or to be touched by him, because they thought that he could save them or bless them or make their lives better. This was going to be the first of those experiences.

Adrian looked the woman directly in the eye, "We all know that people can't fly."

The woman scoffed for a moment, unsure of how to respond, but her daughter couldn't restrain herself, "I'm sure it's him, Mama, go on ask him again."

"You're just foolin' with me, aren't you? You're that boy, the one who talked at the United Nations in New York. Everyone I know liked your speech. No one wants to be afraid, do they? You were right and we're all better for what you said. Now you take my daughter, Alissa, here...she used to be afraid of everything. Heck even the curtains in the night turned into ghosts and goblins and night creatures...but since your appearance, she hasn't been afraid of anything or anyone. She stands right up for her little self and tells people what for...not that I always agree with her, mind you, but you made a difference in her life and we're thankful for it!"

Adrian stared at the woman and honestly did not know how to respond. Finally, he said, "Thank you," very quietly and turned back to his parents.

"Now, I do have one more question, Sonny. How come, if you can fly, you're standing here in line with the rest of us? That's a fair question, isn't it? I mean after all, if I could fly, I sure wouldn't be standing in this line or going through all that nonsense at security. I'd just fly through the air and be where I wanted to be right now." She turned to an older man, wearing a dark suit, standing behind her, "Wouldn't you?"

The man pushed his dark glasses up his nose with the index finger of his right hand, "I'd have to agree with you, Ma'am. No one in their right mind would put themselves through this ordeal if there was any other choice."

Behind him, a young woman was carrying a baby in her arms and she leaned over to Sara. "My baby is sick. I'm taking him to a specialist in Washington. Would your boy bless my son? I know it would help."

Adrian and his Mother exchanged looks, "I don't think that my son has to power to heal."

"Your son has magical powers. We all saw him on the television. If he can fly, then surely he can pass along his blessing to my son."

Adrian stepped up to the young woman, "I'm sorry that your child is sick. If there was something, anything that I could do to help, I would...but I know nothing of medicine and the things that I spoke about were not about magic or religion. They were about the powers that each of us already has...the power to love one another, to care for and help each other. I wish you well with the doctors, I know they'll do their best for your baby."

He turned back to his parents, just as a crackling loudspeaker announced their flight. They showed their tickets to the attendant, who stared at Adrian. "You are that boy. Please, stand over there for just a moment."

She picked up the telephone on the desk and spoke into it. Another uniformed woman approached Adrian and his parents. "Please follow me," she said, leading them down the tunnel to the airplane. They entered through the front door and she stopped in the First Class section. "Your tickets have been upgraded. Please, sit here," she pointed to three seats across the front of the cabin.

She leaned over to Adrian, "It will be easier on your parents, if we can keep people from bothering you and there will be less disruption for our crew during the flight."

The young *seer* smiled, "Thank you. I'm sorry if that was getting...out of hand."

"Don't worry about it. We understand that being a celebrity includes certain... inconveniences. There are many people in the world, who would like to thank you for saying what you said. I'm one of them. Enjoy your flight." With that, she turned and marched out of the cabin.

Adrian took a seat next to the window and watched as the baggage handlers moved luggage from several small trailers to a conveyor that fed up inside the belly of the airplane. Virtually everyone who boarded stopped to stare at Adrian and the people in the line leading to the rear of the plane took a long time finding their seats. Other than the stewardess greeting passengers, as they entered the front door, with a pleasant "Good Morning!" no one said a word until they passed into the rear section of the plane.

John sat down next to his son, "Well, at least we'll be the first off the plane. Maybe that will be easier than getting on."

Adrian leaned his head against his father's shoulder, "I'm sorry about all of that. I hope I didn't embarrass you."

"Embarrass me, no." replied his father. "I'm very proud of the things that you've accomplished and I've always wished that there was more that I could do to help you. I just wish that you...we could enjoy our anonymity."

"I think we should return on the vectors," whispered Adrian.

"You might have a point," laughed his father.

The final passengers trooped through the doorway and down the aisle. The last person to board the plane was tall, with dark hair and a fair complexion. He was dressed in a long black coat and, as he passed, he locked eyes with Adrian, with a strange cocked smile. There was a strong negative energy about the young man that grated up his spine and his aura was dark gray cobalt.

~

The taxi headed northwest along the Potomac from the airport, past the Pentagon and then the National Cemetery. Adrian noticed his father staring out the left-hand window and followed his gaze to the rows and rows of white granite headstones that marched up one hill and down another and seemed to go on forever.

"Is that where granddad will be buried?"

"Yes," replied John, solemnly. "If anyone deserves those honors, he does."

"Here, here," whispered Sara, wrapping her hand under her husband's arm. "He was quite a gentleman."

"That's probably the kindest compliment that you could offer. He always said that the highest honor for anyone of our gender was to be referred to as a gentle man."

Adrian mused, "That's interesting, considering his adventures."

"I know he didn't reveal the gentle soul in the rest of his life," replied John with a sad smile, "but, perhaps, in his heart, that was his greatest aspiration."

"I think I understand how he felt," said Adrian.

John hugged his son, "You've seen more than your share for your age and there's a lot of him in you."

Sara called to the cabbie, "We need to stop to get some proper clothes for a funeral. It's been a long time since we last visited, do Garfields or Woodward and Lothrops still exist?"

The Indian cab driver looked in the mirror and said, "Garfields has been gone for some time and Woodie's merged with Hecht's. Heck, they've got Hecht's all over the place but the main store is still at G Street and 12th."

"Could you take us there please?" inquired Adrian's mother with a smile.

"Oh course, Ma'am," said the cabbie, as he turned north across the Potomac.

The young *seer* gazed out the window at buildings and monuments drifting past in the gray mist hanging over the city. Light rain drizzled on shiny pavement and the windshield wipers made a rhythmic 'whap-whap' as they brushed the raindrops off the glass.

They passed the Lincoln Memorial and he could not help but remember Alius' confrontation with the Capitol Police, when she visited the site to install the ruby crystal. That seemed a very long time ago.

He felt that cold shiver run up his spine and a sharp pain jolted the base of his skull. This was not the moment to explore the vibrations but he could feel the power of the Dark Forces nearby. Perhaps, that should not have been surprising, considering Washington was the political capital of the western world. Power and influence were the currency of this city and Zepallo's representatives had probably been installed in positions deep within the system. Adrian wondered what the president found after their meeting, as they had not spoken since.

The cab pulled up to the curb beneath a big sign that read "Hecht's Department Store." Adrian looked up and down the street and realized that the storefront stretched an entire city block beneath a huge office building. The windows were filled with mannequins wearing fall fashions, the latest children's wear, and handsome suits and shoes for men. His mother took him by the hand and walked through the front doors, while John convinced the cabbie to wait for them with a twenty-dollar bill.

Several overly made-up women greeted them from the cosmetics counter as they passed, before John caught up, "The cab will wait."

"Good," replied Sara, "Now you two go over to the men's department and find black suits, white shirts, subdued ties, socks, underwear, and shoes. You'll probably need at least two shirts. I'll be in the women's department."

Sara wandered off and Adrian followed his father through the maze of displays to the men's department. A distinguished looking man in a pinstriped three-piece suit greeted them, "How may I help you?"

"We're here to attend a funeral and we'll be needing suits, shirts, ties, and shoes," replied John. "Unfortunately, we have to be at the funeral home this evening, so we'll have to find clothes that don't have to be altered."

"Step right this way," smiled the salesman. "You look like a 42 regular and you, young man, well, we'll just have to take some measurements."

They stopped at a long rack of black suits. They all seemed the same, except the sizes grew larger as they walked down the aisle. The man took two suits from the rack and held them up to show Adrian's father the different styles. "This one is a bit more modern, double-breasted with a narrow lapel, and this other is more traditional."

"I think we should lean toward the traditional. This is a funeral, not a wedding."

"Then simplicity and elegance are the order of the day," said the salesman, as he put the two suits back on the rod and pulled another, holding it up. "The finest wool, perfect for any season. A modest lapel and a single button, the pants are pleated with a cuff. What is your pants size? I'd say a 34 regular."

He checked the tag. "Perfect. Go try these on in our changing room, just there," he said pointing to a doorway between two large mirrors. Turning to Adrian he said, "Now, let me see."

He measured around Adrian's neck and chest, from the middle of his shoulders to his hands, his waist, and the inseam of his pants. "You are at that awkward stage where little boy's clothes are too small for you and men's clothes are too big. Come over here, I might just have something that would fit."

The salesman marched to the far end of the racks, pulled a black suit from a circular rack, took the jacket off the hanger and held it up for Adrian to try on. The young *seer* slid his arms into the sleeves of the jacket. The fabric was lined with a silky material that felt cool and slippery. The man turned him around and buttoned a single button of three down the front of the coat and lifted his left arm to check the length. "Perfect!"

He turned the boy around so he could see himself in the mirror. Adrian stared at his reflection. He was so used to wearing normal clothes and his robes that he felt uncomfortable in this fancy suit. The salesman reached around to unbutton the jacket, and handed him the pants, "Now, go try these on and see how they fit."

Adrian walked over to the alcove, just as his father emerged from the changing room wearing the black suit. He had to admit that his dad looked handsome and sophisticated, even if his shirt didn't go with the new jacket. "Wow, you look great!"

John turned in front of the mirror, "Getting dressed up is fun."

Adrian skipped down the hallway, found an empty room, and changed into his new pants, which were just a bit too long but with normal shoes, they would probably be all right. He ran down the hall to stand in front of the mirror and the salesman held his jacket for him. "Nice suit," said John. "We'll be needing a couple of shirts each, and banker's ties, and some dress shoes and dark socks."

The man led them to a display with beautiful ties, then to a bin where he picked out four white shirts in two sizes, then several pairs of socks for each and two black belts, before ending in the shoe department, where he showed John a pair of black wing-tips and Adrian a pair of black loafers. A younger man measured their feet and brought back several boxes of shoes. The salesman used a shoehorn to slip John's shoes on and tied the shoelaces, then slipped a pair of loafers on Adrian's feet, while John walked around to try his new shoes. He wandered back and forth, sliding the slick soles across the carpeting. "I think they're too loose," he said to the younger man, who reached for a box and produced another pair of the same shoes in a smaller size.

"Here let's try these. You have narrow feet." This time the shoes fit perfectly.

Sara appeared, "Have you found what you need?"

John and Adrian smiled, "Yes, I think that we're well cared for and how about you?"

"Oh, I picked up a couple of black dresses and a few other things. You know us women and our little black dresses!"

John laughed, paid the cashier, and led them out into the cold autumn afternoon. The cab was waiting just down the street with the motor running. They were each carrying several packages and the mist had turned to a light rain, so the cabbie pulled the taxi up to meet them just outside the door. As Adrian ran to the curb, he stooped to retrieve a large black feather lying on the pavement. It was, perhaps, a foot long and its deep color glistened in the gray light, changing from blue to purple to dead black as he moved it.

He dropped the feather on the pavement and looked around at the people passing on the street, in the automobiles that were not moving, and to the tops of the tall buildings. There was no sign of a raven, but there was a tall man, with a long dark coat and a cowl covering his head, walking quickly along the pavement at the far end of the block. It could be that he was just someone trying to get out of the rain but Adrian could see his cold blue aura and feel the dark energy.

Adrian followed his parents into the car and loaded their boxes and bags in a pile on the floor. "It's been a while, since we all had some new clothes," said Sara with a grin.

"Yeah, but the only time that we'll ever use them is for a wedding or a funeral," said Adrian, "and, besides, I'll outgrow mine, before they're needed again."

"It won't hurt you to be properly dressed for tonight and tomorrow," scolded Sara. "After that you can put your normal clothes back on and I won't bother you about it again."

"Alright," moaned Adrian. They rode in silence to the northwest, Sara holding hands with both her men, and John guided the taxi driver to the secluded mansion hidden behind a solid gate and a tree-lined drive off Shepard Street. John rolled down the window and pressed the call button on the post outside the gate.

His brother's voice answered, "Who's there?"

"It's John, Sara, and Adrian."

"Ah, John, family hero come to pay your respects?" replied Ralph, slurring his words. "I guess we'll let you in."

Adrian's father sat back in his seat and rubbed his hands through his hair, "I'd hoped we could avoid this but family traditions must be carried forward!"

The iron gates swung open and the taxi rolled down the path under a tall stately portico with stout white columns camouflaged by dense green ivy. Before they could get out of the cab, the ornately carved front door flew open and Ralph appeared, drink in hand, teetering on the top step. "Welcome home!" he bellowed, toasting.

John paid the cabbie, grabbed their packages and bags and marched up the steps, pushing past Ralph's open arms, into the front hall. There were boxes stacked in rows through the entry. "What's all of this?"

Ralph grinned, "Never too early to begin dividing up the bootie!"

Adrian had never seen his father lose his temper before but, in one swift movement, he grabbed his brother by the collar and pushed him up against a wall, the glass with his drink crashed to the floor, ice cubes skittering across black and white marble tiles, "You will put everything back, exactly where you found it and you will do it right now!"

Ralph seemed to be having trouble focusing. His lower lip quivered, "What, don't you think you'll get your share? You always were a bully!"

"I said put it back! Put it all back now! This house will be filled with people this evening!" John released his grip, "Where's Margaret?"

"Oh, she and Mikey are upstairs going through his clothes," mumbled Ralph as he slid down the wall, coming to rest in a heap on the floor, the fine material of his pants absorbing the puddle that had been his drink.

"Is there no reverence for the dead? He's not even cold and you two are pillaging through his things! Let's get him buried and read his will before we start dismantling his life!"

John charged up the stairs and Adrian could hear the screams of his aunt as his father chased her and husband, Michael, out of Sir

Jonathon's bedroom. "Get out," he yelled, slamming the door and following them down the stairs. "Where are your children?"

"Oh, they're in the clubroom looking through his gun cabinet," replied Margaret, innocently.

John charged through the entry and headed down the corridor to the back of the house. Presently, Adrian's cousins, Sam and Julie, came running through the hallway, screaming for their mother. "Uncle John has lost it!"

Adrian's father returned to the entry, "Have all of you lost your minds or perhaps just your sense of common decency? Unpack these boxes and put everything back where you found it. Nothing will leave this house until we've finished with the funeral and his attorney has read the will. Do you understand me?"

Ralph, who was still collapsed on the floor, nodded his head. Sam and Julie stood wide-eyed, gaping at their uncle and both seemed stuck in the same, rather odd, position…leaning forward on their toes, with their arms extended slightly behind them, their mouths hanging open, as if they were trying to fly into a heavy breeze while singing, "Ahhh." Margaret clung to her husband, Mike, who was the only one who looked mildly ashamed.

"I'm not kidding. Put it all away, right now!" shouted John, as he reached down and pulled Ralph to his feet. The five of them started opening the pile of boxes and carrying items towards the back of the house.

John marched across the hall and jiggled the door handle to the Sir Jonathon's study. "I trust that none of you have been inside the study?"

"None of us could find a key," replied Ralph, as he stumbled down the formal passageway.

"Good. Now get to work!"

Margaret whined, "We're all supposed to be at the funeral home at six o'clock to finalize the arrangements."

"Then I suggest you get busy, because no one is going anywhere until this house is put back the way you found it!" yelled John, as he grabbed two suitcases and marched up the stairs to the spare bedroom next to his father's.

Sara and Adrian followed him up to the balcony and then to the right. In spite of the drab skies outside, the bedroom was bright and cheery. The walls were painted a Tuscan yellow with a warm white trim. Rusty red curtains gathered at the sides of a pair of French doors that led to a tiny balcony overlooking a small formal garden installed in the courtyard at the back of the house. A large four-poster bed was flanked by French step-tables that served as nightstands and a fold-out bed was discreetly hidden in a large sofa that faced a small fireplace. There were logs but no fire.

Sara put her arms around her husband's neck, "Did you always fight like cats and dogs?"

John took a deep breath and smiled, "No, there was a time when we acted like a real family…before Mom died, I guess. After that, it all kind of fell apart. Dad was always gone. Ralph got into drinking with his high school buddies and Margaret went looking for a rich man. I left for school the following year and then went on to the Navy. I never really came back."

"Well, I'm embarrassed for them. They should know better."

"Don't be. That's who they've become. The best we might hope for is getting through the next few days, while avoiding any major confrontations. I'm sure that Dad left a will."

"Who was his attorney?"

"Tierney. Colburn Tierney. They went to college together and have been friends ever since. Dad said that he was one of the only people in Washington he could trust to keep his word and his mouth shut."

"That's high praise in this city," laughed Sara.

"I've got to call him before things get totally out of hand."

"I'll unpack, while you call."

Adrian stood at the window, staring at the reflections in the little pond at the center of the garden. The ripples were perfectly concentric, moving from the center, in expanding rings, to the edges. A dark purple light pulsed beneath the surface in rhythm with the strange reflections. He realized that there was no way the wind could cause the movement in the water and he doubted that Sir Jonathon had installed a dark *orb* to light his little pond.

This was a signal…an invitation, a challenge…and there could be no doubt about its origin.

Chapter 4

The long black limousine pulled to a stop beneath the portico of the grand old house. Thick ivy climbed the walls of the red brick mansion, weaving around black shutters aside white window frames, across the porch, reaching for the slate roof that hung heavy and gray on this cold misty evening. Two men dressed in black uniforms stepped out of the car, and touched their white gloved hands to the brims of their tall black hats as they held the doors while the family entered the car. One walked around the vehicle and got into the driver's seat. The other removed his hat, climbed in behind Sir Jonathon's heirs, and settled into the seat at the back with Sara and John.

Adrian's father looked at the man and said, rather indignantly, "Do you mind?"

"I'm sorry to bother you, sir, but I am Robert Montague, Sir Robert Montague, representing several governments on this most unfortunate occasion. I apologize for intruding at a moment like this but I would hope that you understand that there are certain…considerations in the events and ceremonies of the next few days."

The family members settled back in their seats without responding. Ralph's chin was resting on his chest and Adrian was surprised that he wasn't snoring. Aunt Margaret and Uncle Michael were not speaking to each other, let alone anyone else, and his cousins, Sam and Julie, had not uttered a word or looked him in the eye, since the scene in the foyer of grandfather's house.

Sam was a bit older and had a faint shadow across his upper lip…as if he was trying to look like he needed to shave. He had dark darting eyes and his mouth naturally curled down at the corners, making him look eternally unhappy. His dark hair was slicked down with something greasy and some of it rubbed off to stain the collar of his suit jacket.

Julie wore a black velvet dress with a white, schoolgirl collar that helped to distract from her mature shape. Her auburn hair, tied in a white satin bow, fell down across her shoulder in soft ringlets. Adrian noticed that she was wearing just the faintest hint of rouge on her cheeks, a pink lipstick, and a touch of gray makeup around her eyes, giving the impression that the poor girl had not slept in several days. Everything about her appearance made her look younger than her fifteen years and, certainly, worthy of sympathy and attention.

Adrian tuned back into Montague's clipped English accent, "Obviously, representatives of our governments will be in attendance and will want to pay tribute to Sir Jonathon. We are many in his debt. For security considerations, we were hoping that you would allow us to arrange for the service to be held in the Bethlehem Chapel rather than the High Alter. Unfortunately, that would severely restrict the number who might attend."

John looked at Ralph, who was barely conscious, and then at Margaret, who was staring at the bright red polish on her fingernails and frantically chewing a large wad of green gum, as if the clacking might drown out the conversation. He turned back to Sir Montague, who seemed genuinely concerned with the family's wishes. "That would be fine with us. We understand that our father was involved in programs that were not public knowledge and those relationships must be given due consideration. There are several other members of the family and a few friends who will probably want to attend but the rest is up to you."

"Thank you," replied Sir Robert Montague with quiet reverence. "I'm sure that you'll approve of the arrangements that will be made. A rather subdued service and memorial to a valiant warrior, who served several governments with honor."

"We appreciate your kind words and your help," said Sara.

The limousine crept up the drive to the entrance of the funeral home and Sir Montague climbed out of the car, donned his black brimmed hat, and stood erect at the door, as the family members trooped up the steps and into the building.

The funeral director, Richard Moressy, was waiting, as two attendants guided the family through the foyer. He was certainly going bald but his thin dark hair seemed to be combed from the side of his head over the top, perhaps to hide the shiny dome. He wore tiny glasses that sat on the end of his bulbous nose with a tiny gold chain attached to a button on his vest. The plump man took John's arm and whispered, "You have several guests in the viewing room. Most of the arrangements have already been made and I'm sure that you will approve, but, when you have a moment, there are some papers that need to be signed by a representative of the family."

"I appreciate your help and I'll meet with you as soon as I've had a chance to greet our guests."

Moressy bowed and extended his hand to the central viewing room, which was directly across the ornate lobby. Sam and Julie led the parade, followed by their parents, with Ralph, who was listing slightly to the left, staggering along behind.

Warm lights glowed beneath urns in alcoves around the curved walls of the room, silhouetting several people standing just outside the illuminated pool of a spotlight over the casket, which sat on a raised marble dais for better viewing. Adrian's Great Aunt Lucy sat alone in a straight-backed chair next to her brother's body, her feet barely touched the floor. She was ancient, her parchment skin deeply wrinkled, her white hair tied in a tidy bun on the crown of her head, the fabric of her black dress fell limp around her tiny frame, and those sad dark eyes…eyes that always seemed to see through you, were filled with tears.

John walked over and knelt down beside her, took her hands in his and kissed them.

Lucy attempted a weak smile, a tear ran down her cheek, "We've both lost someone dear."

"I'm so sorry," whispered John.

"Perhaps it was just his time," mused the old woman, reflecting on the journey from a tiny Scottish village, after their parents died, "but considering the life he led, I'm not convinced that it was…"

Her nephew looked confused for a moment. He just accepted the message that he received and it had not occurred to him to inquire further. He stood next to the coffin and hesitated for a moment, before he looked down at his father's face. Adrian walked over to stand with him and Sara came up between them to place an arm around each.

It was Sir Jonathon's face but it wasn't. Someone applied makeup to make his skin look warmer, his lips redder, and his eyelashes darker and more distinct with mascara. Waves of white hair fell across his ears, which made him look distinguished in his formal white uniform, laden with ribbons and medals.

Adrian was curious about the honors his Grandfather received and allowed his eyes to wander from one ribbon to the next, until he noticed the gemstone in the golden pin, that held the ribbon of his Medal of Honor, was a large, perfectly cut, black diamond.

~

Lorraine, Sir Jonathon's cook, hustled between the large commercial stove and the prep table, where her daughter, Angela, and her niece, Audrey, were chopping vegetables and putting the finishing touches on three trays of canapés. Two waiters, in starched white coats, passed hors d'oeuvres and drinks to guests overflowing the main floor of the old mansion.

Adrian sat on the staircase, sipping a soda, which were scarce and treasured on Morgan's Knot, and watching the guests arrive at the front door. He realized that many of these people lived in that shadow world of intelligence and counter-intelligence. He picked out five or six languages and recognized several faces from the news. No one seemed to notice him and he felt that it was probably for the better.

His parents were solemnly greeting guests, as they arrived. Sam and Julie had disappeared upstairs and Mike and Margaret were mingling, separately, in the crowd. Adrian could hear the bellow of his Uncle Ralph's drunken voice, over the din of conversation, from someplace at the back of the mansion.

Suddenly, a lady in a dark business suit and a gray pearl necklace appeared at the foot of the staircase, holding a drink in both hands and staring at Adrian, "Do you remember me?"

Adrian focused on her face and realized that she was the president's secretary, who brought a tray with ice water, when he and Alius visited the White House, "Yes, I do. I'm sorry…your name was…Natalie."

"That's right! Very good," she laughed. "May I sit next to you? I see these people all day, when I'm working, and, sometimes, it's nice to not be a part of it for a little while. Does that make any sense?"

"I think so," replied the young *seer*, as he scooted over to make room for her to sit on the stair next to him.

"I don't understand why you're here," smiled the president's secretary. "Were you related to Sir Jonathon?"

"He was my grandfather."

"Oh, I'm so sorry," said Natalie draping an arm around his shoulders. "He was a very special man."

"How did you know him?"

"I was his secretary for several years before he retired…well, he didn't really retire, he just gave up his office and moved to his study," she said, pointing to the closed and locked door across the hallway.

"Small world."

The woman laughed and touched her glass to his in a toast, "To a great man…to all great men!"

"How's the president?"

Natalie smiled, "It's kind of sad that his second term is nearing the end. I think that he definitely qualifies as a great man on so many levels and I'm privileged to work with him. He's very busy trying to finish up as many bills, initiatives, and executive orders as he can before time runs out. No matter who wins the office in the election, they'll have a hard time filling his shoes." She stared into the moving crowd for a moment and then turned to face Adrian with a serious expression, "He thinks very highly of you and your friend…Alius was it? You impressed him and not many children can claim that honor."

Adrian blushed. "I hope we helped."

"Oh, you helped all right…although not as many might have hoped…but the world is a calmer, quieter, more peaceful place for the moment and I think we all have you to thank for that."

"I just told the truth," replied Adrian quietly.

"You also exposed the Dark Forces and, in a way, pointed to the fact that their spies are buried deep in the bureaucracies of most governments. The president wants to leave office knowing that the leaders of the rest the countries of the world have been advised of the danger. There are many who don't want to believe what you told the president and the world…or, perhaps, they want to use that knowledge to their own advantage."

"I can't explain how, but…I know that this calm won't last for long. The Dark Forces will rise again and, each time they do, they'll chip away a little more at the goodness of the world. The New Coalition might not become the third world power they envisioned but they gained allies, support, and legitimacy. Zepallo, or Palloze as you know him, won't stop, until he rules the world. That's his goal."

"Are your parents very proud of you?"

Adrian blushed again, as she rustled his hair.

"My glass is empty and I'm hungry. Let's go see what Miss Lorraine has prepared for dinner."

~

Adrian escaped through the French doors off the dining room, after an awkward meal with the president's secretary, balancing plate and glass while standing amidst a jostling throng of bodies. Two people passed him, as he stepped outside and the doors closed behind them. For the first time, since they left Morgan's Knot, he was alone.

The garden was quiet. He could hear crickets and cicada in the foliage and a tree frog singing near the little pond. A short boxwood hedge framed two long formal flowerbeds that extended beyond the pool to the back of the house. Lights, hidden in the garden, illuminated the plants and cast long shadows rippling up the ivy on the walls, while floodlights, hidden in the canopy of the trees, poured an eerie blue brilliance over a manicured lawn stretching into the darkness of a forest.

The young *seer* wandered over to the pond and stared into the water, noticing the concentric ripples flowing from the center to the edge of the pool. They were backlit by the purple glow of a dark *orb* nestled in the rocks. The hairs on the back of his neck prickled and the familiar chill ran up his spine, loosing a burst of grating vibrations inside his brain.

He turned to a faint whoosh, in the open space at the back of the garden, where four dark figures materialized. Three of them were about his size, while the fourth could only be Zepallo.

His deep voice called out, "I do hope that we're not imposing at an awkward moment."

Adrian levitated several feet into the air and raised his right hand, his ring pointed at his enemy.

"We just stopped in to offer our condolences for the death of your grandfather, he was such an admirable soul."

"Did you know him well?"

"Oh, no…we met just once, although his reputation as a spymaster preceded him. It was a tragic and memorable encounter but I'm afraid he did not survive it."

"I knew it was you," hissed Adrian.

"Of course, it was me, we left an obvious trail for you to follow. I needed to create an excuse for you to come to me!" laughed the Dark Lord, gesturing with his right hand, "I want to introduce my progeny…Alpha, Beta, and Gamma. I'm sure you children will find an opportunity to play together very soon."

"How could you possibly have children?"

"You underestimate me, my young friend. There was a time…" He paused, "Soon, I'll have hundreds, if not thousands, of offspring and each will be just like me!"

The three figures flipped back their cowls to reveal identical faces, with Zepallo's long dark hair, pallid complexion, cold piercing eyes, and powerful build. They looked exactly as he must have when he was their age. Adrian was dumbfounded, "How is this possible?"

"It's one of the wonders of science! Unfortunately, the scientists of your society are restrained by morality and long discussions about the possible horrid repercussions of this technology. We have no constraints and our people solved the theoretical problems long ago, hence my young protégés!"

The three dark *seers* rose into the air and bowed, very formally, to Adrian, before flying at an incredible speed and spinning around him with the force of a human tornado. It took every ounce of restraint to remain calm, to avoid reacting in any way, and he stayed absolutely still but the distinct features of each of the faces of Zepallo's clones, flicked by one at a time like stuttering frames in an old movie, and their eyes glowed cold blue in the darkness. Although their features were identical, their auras were different colors. One was fiery red, another a cool blue, and third a cold gray. They might be triplets but they were not identical.

Zepallo's voice called out, "That will be enough boys. We must remember our manners, especially at a time like this. There will be plenty of opportunities for you to get to know each other within the next few days!"

Alpha, Beta, and Gamma, returned to hover with the Dark Lord, who touched the tip of his cowl with the fingers of his right hand, and, a moment later, they all vanished in a swirl of gray smoke.

Adrian lowered himself to the brick path between the boxwood hedges and took a deep breath, his heart pounding. A woman's voice said quietly, "That took a lot of restraint."

The young *seer* turned to find Natalie standing on the steps just outside the door to the dining room. "How long have you been standing there?"

"I saw you leave and decided that talking with you was far more interesting than people repeating the conversations I hear every day. I saw you fly on the tape of your speech at the United Nations and, I'm afraid, I thought that it was some kind of trick. You know, the way they make it appear that people can fly in the movies."

"This isn't a movie."

"As I now understand. Who were those…people?"

"That was Zepallo…or Palloze, as you know him."

"And who were the young people?"

"I believe they're his clones."

"Clones? But they've only succeeded with animals."

"The science community that you know has only done it with animals. The science of the Crystals and the planes is…different."

"Then the president was right. There really are other…realities."

"That's what we tried to tell him. I wasn't sure he believed us," said Adrian quietly.

"Oh, he believed you. The problem is finding a way to prove your story."

"Where I come from, we know the truth. We live it every day. I believe that one part of it is as close to living in Eden as modern man might get, yet the other part is as dark and evil as your worst nightmares. Our mission is to show the people of the world what might be…and, at the same, hold back the darkness for as long as we can."

"That's a lot of responsibility for someone of your age," said Natalie, gently.

"I didn't choose the responsibility of a *seer*, I've only known for a year and a half. It's one of those things that you accept or you don't. Once you do, there's no turning back. It's what I've become."

"And the rest of us are the better for it," she said, walking over to put her arm around his shoulders. "Are there others…like you?"

"Yes…but not enough to take on an army of clones."

"You believe he was telling the truth?"

"He murdered my grandfather, just so he could reveal the next nightmare I'll face…that we'll all face, if I don't find a way to stop him."

"Is there nothing we can do to help?"

Adrian pondered the question for a moment, "At this point, I honestly don't know what anyone can do. I need to talk with the Keeper of the Powers on Morgan's Knot. He knows more than anyone on the planet about the Powers."

"I'm positive that the president would be more than willing to offer any assistance you might need and his resources are vast."

"I appreciate that but, at this point, I don't know enough to know what to ask for. Conventional military power is useless against their weapons and defenses. Besides, the next skirmish will be between those three and me. Zepallo wants to test his newest weapon against the only person who's ever defeated him in battle. He's looking for revenge."

"You fought against that man?"

"Several times. I was lucky. I won."

"Tell me a little more about his forces," instructed the president's secretary, as she led him to some chairs near the pond.

"I guess the only way that I can explain it is to tell you that he has vast armies drawn from an invisible civilization. We've destroyed three of his command posts but there are more scattered around the globe inhabited by a population who believe in his vision of a dark future. When he invaded the island that I come from, his troops flew on giant ravens, surfaced in miniature submarines, and used weapons unknown in your world. They attacked in three waves and, if we had not been prepared, they would have defeated our meager forces with ease. We had a lot of help from the animals but someday we won't be enough."

"You're a brave young man."

"I'm not so sure that bravery has anything to do with it. As I've learned, I have to do what I have to do. There is no other choice. This war has been raging for thousands of years and it will continue, until one side finally defeats the other or we destroy the world in the process."

~

Adrian felt scratchy in his new shirt, shoes, suit, and tie, constricted by the tightness of his collar and clunky shoes, and wished that he could have slept during the night but haunting visions of the triplets swirled through the darkness. He saw no reason to tell his parents of the visitors, they had enough to deal with and there were people in the house until they all fell into bed.

He wanted to talk with the Professor but, other than a telephone, he had no way of making contact. The special glasses, that Dadeus provided for their venture to connect the Crystals, were sitting on the desk in his room at the House of the Four Seasons. Surely Ponte would be able to offer his wisdom and experience but the phone did not seem a secure solution to his problem and he would not send out a premature alarm to his fellow *seers* until he understood the logistics of the threat.

He felt confident of his abilities in a battle with Zepallo, in spite of his wounds, but he was intimidated with the speed of the clones and there was no way of knowing their level of sophistication. It probably stood to reason that they were trained by their best combat forces and, if he was going into a confrontation, he would have to arrange the setting or find something he could use to his advantage.

The limousine arrived at the front door and the family trooped down the steps in something less than orderly fashion. Margaret walked stiffly, holding Sam's hand for support. Her husband held his daughter's arm. None of them seemed to be talking to each other or anyone else. Ralph followed, haltingly, one step at a time, and there could be little doubt that the effects of his overindulgence the night before were still in full blossom. Sara held her husband's hand and Adrian could feel the pain flowing from his father. There would come a moment when he might tell him the truth but it would have to be after the ceremony.

As the car approached the drive into the Cathedral grounds, John turned to his son, "The plans for this cathedral were first proposed in 1792 but actual construction didn't begin until 1907. At three hundred feet, the tower is the tallest point in the District of Columbia and the structure is the sixth largest in the world. The Church is Episcopal but it's also the chapel for everyone in the country, all of which seems appropriate because your grandfather was Anglican to his core…despite the contradiction of his occupation." He smiled sadly.

Adrian felt completely guilty for what had not been said. He just could not interrupt the mourning and replace it with anger. He held his father's hand and stared out the window at the enormous chapel peeking through trees showing hints of red and yellow. As the car came to a stop, he noticed beds of roses showing their final burst of color for the year and was reminded of his last long look at their house on the mainland. His mother planted pink roses that were just blooming the day he left for Morgan's Knot.

The limousine parked at the bottom of a very wide staircase and Adrian stared up at the steeple rising into a gray sky, reaching to the heavens with solid assurance. He always wondered why the architects of the great churches designed them to be so imposing and frightening, rather than creating a structure that invited the people to come into God's house. The words, of his older self, echoed with that shrewd smirk, "Fear. It's all about fear."

"It's fear and control," he thought. The Darkness and the Light, the chance for mankind to walk in the sunshine or fall into a dark abyss. The children offered the world a glimpse of the power of the Light, the strength and wisdom of the innocent, and the promise of what they might create for themselves and each other.

The Bethlehem Chapel's pointed arches soared from solid stone columns rising out of the floor into an intricate geometric pattern, that reminded the young *seer* of a stonemason's interpretation of a spider's web. Hidden lights illuminated the curves of the structure and long shadows accentuated the shapes, making it feel as if a stone ribcage might be breathing.

Adrian followed his parents down a long aisle between rows of red chairs to the front row on the right, where the entire family sat in silence, staring at the beautiful alter that echoed the curves of the arched ceiling.

The deep tones of a pipe organ rumbled through the chapel and everyone stood, as Sir Jonathon's casket was wheeled down the aisle. Six uniformed officers, representing the United States Navy, the Royal Navy of the United Kingdom, Special Operations of both countries, and two officers wearing unmarked black uniforms, which represented secret operations, escorted the coffin to the alter. A single trumpet sounded, slow notes reverberating through the chamber like a lost soul wandering, searching for a path into heaven.

The Reverend Malcolm Cousins stood before the congregation of mourners and motioned for them to sit. "We are gathered here to celebrate a life, to commemorate the passing of a brave warrior, a patriot, a defender of freedom and liberty, a father and a grandfather…and to ask the question, 'Why is Sir Jonathon not with us today?

In every way, he was larger than life. He was a great student, an extraordinary athlete, a fearless skipper of sailboats and submarines, leading his crews on clandestine missions all over the globe. He left the service and joined an elite group, who served the interests of all the Western Powers for more than a quarter century and, even in retirement, he was the pulse and the center of the lifeblood of our security…knowledge, connections, and information.

He was a father to John, Ralph, and Margaret. He was a grandfather to Sam, Julie, and Adrian. He was brother to Lucy. He was a friend and colleague to many of us and he will be missed.

I asked the question, 'Why is Sir Jonathon not with us?' He was always there, when he was needed, always fit and brimming with energy, raising the possibilities instead of the dangers, always making those around him feel as if they had found the solution, or accomplished the deed, or saved the day…when we all knew that our success was the result of Jonathon's talents and insight. He was always bigger, stronger, smarter, better prepared, and more comfortable in his own skin than any of the rest of us…whether you were a seaman or a resident, a prime minister or a secretary, he treated everyone with the same courtesy and polite confidence, softened with just a touch of his wry humor.

I don't know, and perhaps do not care to know, the most secret and dangerous missions that he was involved in, but I find it amazing that life offered him so many opportunities to meet his death when, in the end, he greeted it in the study of his own home, his sanctuary, his safe haven."

The minister's eyes roved around the audience until they found Adrian. He hesitated for a moment before saying, "I read from Isaiah 40:31, 'But they that wait upon the Lord shall renew their strength; they shall mount up with wings as eagles; they shall run and not be weary; and they shall walk and not faint.'"

The deep tones of the pipe organ rolled over the last words and a stout little woman sang "On Eagle's Wings" with a voice that filled the chapel.

'You who dwell in the shelter of the Lord,
Who abide in His shadow for life,
Say to the Lord, "My Refuge,
My Rock in Whom I trust.
And He will raise you up on eagle's wings,
Bear you on the breath of dawn,
Make you to shine like the sun,
And hold you in the palm of His Hand.

The snare of the fowler will never capture you,
And famine will bring you no fear;
Under His Wings your refuge,
His faithfulness your shield.
And He will raise you up on eagle's wings,
Bear you on the breath of dawn,
Make you to shine like the sun,
And hold you in the palm of His Hand.

You need not fear the terror of the night,
Nor the arrow that flies by day,
Though thousands fall about you,
Near you it shall not come.
And He will raise you up on eagle's wings,

Bear you on the breath of dawn,
Make you to shine like the sun
And hold you in the palm of His Hand.

For to His angels He's given a command,
To guard you in all of your ways,
Upon their hands they will bear you up,
Lest you dash your foot against a stone
And He will raise you up on eagle's wings,
Bear you on the breath of dawn,
Make you to shine like the sun,
And hold you in the palm of His Hand.
And hold you in the palm of His Hand.'

Based on Psalm 91

As the song ended, the minister walked to the side of The Alter and sat down with several other priests. The congregation stood, as two men strode down the center aisle, their heels clicking on the marble floor, and stopped to bow before the alter, then to the clergy, and finally climbed the few steps to a podium.

President Bartlett smiled and waved his hand, "Please, be seated." The mourners sat down. "I wish that I could say that I...or we are pleased to be here. That is not the case. Sir Jonathon was a colleague and a friend."

Prime Minister Langdon spoke, "There are many words that might be said to describe the character, the bravery, and the dedication of Sir Jonathon. He was a man who moved freely in the twilight, that thin space that separates our nations' friends and our enemies, and he was a man of honor. He was one of us...and he was one of you. Born of my country and a living pillar, supporting the very concept of liberty, in yours. Our governments will miss his talents and his expertise...but we...you and I will miss the man that he was."

The Prime Minister stepped aside and the President moved to

the microphone. He gazed around at the people in attendance and his eyes stopped on Adrian for a long moment. There was something odd about the look in his eyes, perhaps it was that he recognized the relationship between Adrian and his grandfather. It was not even that he looked surprised… he obviously would have spoken with his secretary, Natalie, but the young *seer* felt Bartlett's energy reaching out to him, like fingertips barely touching…an invitation, a request for conversation.

The president turned back to the audience, "I look around this room and see testament of Sir Jonathon's ability to touch everyone with whom he came into contact. It didn't matter whether you worked with him or for him or were merely graced with his presence and his humor…we were all affected by him. Sir Jonathon was not merely a colleague, he was a friend to each of us. His accomplishments are legendary, his achievements were grounded and justified by most sincere beliefs and that, my friends, is why we're all here to mourn this hero."

He turned to the family, "I must offer my personal condolences to his family…his sister Lucy, John and Sara, Margaret and Michael, and Ralph…and the grandchildren Sam, Julie, and Adrian. I say to each of you that your brother, your father, your grandfather led his life to the very best of his abilities. It was a life that could easily be written as fiction and he would be the hero…fighting for what is just and right." He paused and stared at Adrian, "If any of us or any of you might follow in his footsteps, live by his example, and carry on with his legacy, our world will be a better place for it."

The two men walked over and shook The Reverend Malcolm Cousins' hand before descending to two red chairs in the front row on the left side of the aisle. Adrian leaned forward to watch them take their seats and the president turned to meet his gaze with a sad smile, as he sat down.

Reverend Cousins led the congregation in hymn and prayer, offered communion, sprinkled holy water on the casket and walked around it with the blessing of smoke. The six uniformed officers returned to escort Sir Jonathon out of the chapel and the priest barely whispered, "Let us all go in peace."

The family followed the coffin to the back of the church and as soon as they passed through the doors, a Secret Service agent walked over and whispered something to Adrian's father, who turned around and smiled at his son. "It seems that the president would like to have a moment of your time."

"Would it be rude to miss greeting all the people who will be coming out?"

"I think, in this case, your absence would be acceptable."

Adrian followed the Secret Service agent, who wore a dark blue suit, dark glasses, and a little earphone, out to a long black limousine. He opened the door, allowed Adrian to enter, and then closed the door behind him. The president and the Prime Minister were seated on the back seat, so Adrian took the bench seat.

Bartlett smiled, "We can't go on meeting like this!"

Adrian relaxed.

The Prime Minister spoke and his words sounded like a speech that might have been written by his press secretary days before. "Ms. Natalie informed us of your skirmish last night and of your suspicions about Zepallo's plans to populate his forces with clones of himself."

"He showed up last night with three boys about my age, who looked exactly as he must have looked when he was a boy. There could only be one possibility and he confirmed it."

"Did he give you any indication of how many of these…children were in existence?"

"No. As far as I know there are only three."

The president inquired quietly, "What's your feeling about this new insight?"

Adrian reflected for a moment, "I think there's nothing to stop the Dark Forces from using any scientific technique to make themselves more powerful and producing clones certainly fits into that goal. Zepallo wants to rule the world and what better way to do it than to install himself in every seat of power in every government, every religion, every center of commerce, everywhere? It would be like running the entire planet by remote control and all he'd have to do is think about something and his clones would instantly react to his inspiration."

The Prime Minister seemed astonished, "Do you really think that he could just...think and they would understand?"

"Of course! *Seers* can feel each other over great distances..." He turned to the President, "Do you remember my friend, Alius? Well, she and I can tell what the other one is doing when we're not together. The first time that I realized it could happen, she sent me a thought about eating chocolate ice cream and I could taste it!"

"That's amazing...but it hardly supports your theory that he could use telepathy between himself and his...offspring," commented the Prime Minister skeptically.

"It was only an example. I can send out a thought that I need help and my fellow *seers* will hear it and show up, wherever I am. I'm a novice compared to some of my teachers but I can feel the vibrations of the world and my friend, Simian, can see along the vectors."

The Prime Minister seemed a little exasperated. The President leaned forward, his elbows on his knees, the fingers of each hand just barely touching, "There's much that we don't understand about your world but, no matter how we look at it, Zepallo's plans will affect everyone. What can be done to stop him?"

"I'm not sure that your armies could wage a successful battle against the Dark Forces. They have weapons that are...different and more powerful than anything your forces might use. I think the only way to change the course that he's chosen is to find the laboratory where they're growing the clones and destroy it. Your equipment will never detect it, just as your radar doesn't see Morgan's Knot. The Keepers of the Powers are the only ones who have the ability to find that lair."

"Then might we ask that you keep us informed of what your people find?"

"I could do that."

"You have my email address?" asked the President.

"Is it the same as the one I used the last time we met?"

"Yes...and I've learned more about those damned machines. I can turn mine off and on and find the files or addresses that I'm looking for!"

Adrian laughed and started to get out of the car, "Then I'll be in touch when I know more."

Bartlett reached a hand to restrain him, "There's one more thing. Natalie told me that Zepallo and his...children, said that they'd be back to see you before you left the city. Is that true?"

"Yes. I expect them to show up at any moment."

"And you're willing to take on four of them?"

"I have no choice."

"I wish there was something that we could do to help."

"I think the only ones who can help are my friends and fellow *seers*...but having an audience might convince the world about his true character."

The Prime Minister looked concerned, "Then now might be a good time to send out that call. The ceremony at the grave site won't take long."

"I appreciate your concern," said Adrian quietly. "I don't really know this city but I passed by the Lincoln Memorial, yesterday, and noticed that there's a long open space in front of it. If I get a chance to choose the place where the battle will be held, that will be it."

"I'll see what we can arrange."

"Thank you, I'll be in touch, as soon as I know more."

"Thank you for coming and be careful." The president smiled, "I think I should have suspected that you might be related to your grandfather."

The boy replied, "I appreciated your kind words and I'll do my best to live up to his legacy." He paused, "There is one more thing."

"What's that?"

"My cousins were wondering whether you would consider talking to their political science class, after you leave office?"

"I'd be honored but I don't know where you live."

Adrian grinned, "It's one of those places that you can't get to from here!"

Chapter 5

Adrian found it hard to concentrate. Everywhere he looked there were perfectly aligned rows of white gravestones, marking the thousands who gave their lives in defense of their country, stretching for as far as he could see in every direction. There was no ideal to justify the tragedy of war, of sending the young to fight old men's battles. Yet here, in spite of the warm autumn colors on the old trees that seemed to bow out of respect for the fallen, he was reminded that the victors always claim that crusades are mounted to rid the world of a scourge threatening all that is right and true, whatever is right and true for the government of that time but rarely for common citizens. His grandfather was the first victim of the next confrontation.

Seven uniformed Special Forces officers fired three rounds in unison as tribute to a fallen comrade. American and British flags were folded carefully and presented to Aunt Lucy, who wept, and Adrian noticed the tears rolling down his father's cheeks. Reverend Cousins closed the ceremony, "May each of you go in peace."

One by one the family walked past the coffin. Some just touched it, others dropped a handful of dirt on it or a single rose. Most rushed through the drizzle to the limousines but Adrian could not just walk away. It felt as if there was something more that needed to be said but he had no idea of what it might be. He wished there had been time to know his grandfather better but family visits were usually limited to a long weekend or several days during the holidays and he could only remember a few times when they actually spent time alone together.

Adrian smiled to himself, *"There's much that I could have learned from you. I wonder whether you ever knew about the world that we live in?"*

John put an arm around his son's shoulders and guided him towards the limousine, "He knew about your talents and the Powers. He was impressed."

Adrian looked up at his father. His eyes were sad and knowing. "There's something that I haven't told you."

"That it wasn't a heart attack?"

"Yes…and that Zepallo killed Grandfather so he could test out his newest weapon."

"First, I think I knew the truth in my heart from the beginning. I just didn't put it all together, until Aunt Lucy said something about it last night at the funeral home. What is his newest weapon?"

"Three clones who are about my age. He wants to see how they stand up in battle conditions against the only person who's ever defeated him."

John slowed to a stop, knelt down, and stared into his son's eyes, "And that would be you?"

"Yes."

"Is there anything that I can do to help you or protect you?"

"No. The president and the Prime Minister asked the same question and the answer remains the same. This will be a demonstration and the only thing I can hope to control is where it will be fought."

"Where?"

"Over the reflecting pools in front of the Lincoln Memorial. It's a long, narrow space and easier to defend, if I can keep them in front of me."

"You don't have any weapons."

Adrian held up his right hand and the ring that Dadeus had given him not so long ago. I wish I'd brought my sword and a shield but I honestly didn't think there would be any need for it. I do have this and I have my belief in the Power of the Light."

"You'll need help."

"I know but there isn't time. I'm sure Zepallo and his friends will show up at the first opportunity."

John put his arm around Adrian's shoulders and started to the waiting car. The door was open and he could see Aunt Margaret's high-heels and the hem of her black dress. The young *seer* stopped at the sound of a loud "caw" in the distance. He turned as the misty gray sky molted into a dark churning surge tumbling through the heavens amid great claps of thunder threatening the living and the dead. Lightning rippled above the white stones on the grave covered rise to his right, silhouetting Zepallo and his clones, hovering on the backs of giant ravens.

"I think this might be the first opportunity," whispered Adrian, as he loosened his tie, peeled off his new jacket, and stepped out of his shoes.

Sara knelt down and wrapped her arms around her son, "No, please, not now! We've just buried your grandfather and you're not going into battle!"

"I don't think there's really any choice," said Adrian. He leaned over and kissed the top of her head. As he started to pull away from his mother, the deep sound of the movement of air made him spin to his enemy. The wings of the four ravens moved in a slow rhythmic dance that propelled them at an astonishing speed within a few feet of the people standing next to the limousines.

Zepallo called, "Care to join us?"

Adrian leapt into the sky, his hands before him, the ring pointed at the ravens and their riders but they were all flying too fast for a clean shot. He realized that he was at a disadvantage but he also knew that he would survive to be that three-hundred-year old man.

As he chased his enemies across the Potomac towards the Lincoln Memorial, flying at top speed, he realized that they were headed directly for the spot he would have chosen for this battle. Could Zepallo have the same strategy?

The ravens flew past the Lincoln Memorial, across the reflecting pool, and circled around the top of the Washington Monument. Adrian hovered in front of the statue of President Lincoln and concentrated on the four dark *seers* suspended one-hundred feet above the reflecting pool. He felt as if there was someone watching him and turned to stare into the eyes of the statue. It was almost as if he could hear the president's voice, "Although I was directed by my beliefs, I could not have changed the world alone."

The young *seer* turned back to his foes. Adrian could hear the voice of Zepallo talking to the boys but he could not make out what the

Dark Lord was saying. He wondered whether they would come individually or as a group. His ring would only fire one blast at a time and he had no shield. He would have to fire and move in the same moment.

Deep in concentration, he was startled by a "whoosh" behind him. Spinning around, he found Alius…smiling. "How did you…?"

"You do remember the chocolate ice cream, don't you?"

"Yes."

"Well, I've been feeling you, hearing you since you left and now seemed the perfect moment to drop in to show that we love you."

"We…?"

"Of course…we!"

With that, Raffe, Simian, and Sky, appeared in a series of flashes. Master Chi arrived with a bit more finesse, a soft gentle glow expanding slowly, gracefully, to his normal form. "I believe that we are ready."

Adrian laughed, as Alius remembered, "Oh, I almost forgot to tell you that the Professor, Nanchez, and Dadeus are hard at work on tracking down their incubator."

Raffe interrupted, "Heck, we could just follow them home, after we have some fun with them!" He reached into his robes and pulled out the handle of a sword, Adrian's sword. "I thought you might be needing this! Besides, you're going to need some help, especially dressed like that!"

Adrian accepted the sword. He had not touched it since his last battle with the Dark Lord. Dadeus had done a marvelous job in repairing it. The balance was perfect. He pressed the handle and extended the blade in front of his nose, pointing at the sky. The young *seer* gazed around at his friends in utter wonder, "How did all of you know to be here…now?"

Master Chi laughed, "You know that we all feel the vibrations extending out into the universe from each of us. The *seer's* rhythms are stronger than those of normal human beings and some of us sense what is happening with our brothers and sisters. Alius was actually the one who informed the rest of us about this situation and Simian could see the four dark forms following you around the city. We're happy to help."

Sky pointed to Zepallo and his clones. Lightning erupted from the grand obelisk, rising like a white beacon against dark clouds rushing across the city, but the air at the surface was still and his laugh echoed across the plaza, "Let the games begin!"

Three ravens soared just above the surface of the reflecting pool, their wings spawning ripples that formed a graceful wake as they flew past. The clones lifted their swords and aimed at the group of *seers* who were still chattering. Three charges ripped through the air to scatter the swarm of *seers*, who turned to the battle.

Adrian rose straight up in the air, as the giant birds soared beneath him. He could see the determined smiles on the faces of their new enemies. They looked strong and well trained but he suspected they had no concept of defeat and, certainly, no idea that they were expendable. They were programmed for nothing less than victory.

Simian, Sky, and Raffe took the one on the right and Adrian guessed the gray aura might be Gamma, because he held back just a bit behind the other two. Alius and Master Chi tore after the cool blue aura on the left, which must have been Beta, while the third raven made a long slow turn and soared straight at the young *seer*. He could see the sizzling red glow of his aura and the purple tip of the extended sword and ducked to his right as a blast seared past him. *"This must be Alpha!"*

Twirling in a corkscrew, he flew directly at the boy *seer*, their swords clashing in a titanic shower of sparks that rained down in a fiery veil, hissing into the reflecting pool. Adrian flipped over and dropped feet first, away from Alpha. He aimed his sword and fired a single volley. The golden charge pulsed as it closed on the raven and the *dark seer* wrapped his arms around the giant bird, which squawked loudly, dipped to the left, and dove for the ground. The glowing sphere exploded, singeing the long black feathers on its tail.

Alpha released his grip and tore through the air, a black arrow homing on a target and Adrian flipped upside down, swinging his sword with all his might. The blade struck his rival's shield and slid across the purple glow of his sword, a cascade of molten embers exploded between them. The two *seers* tumbled through the sky, their blades probing and clashing over and over, searing glimmers flying in all directions, until they hovered, their sword tips sizzling and sparking. Adrian could see Zepallo's smile, in the distance behind Alpha, and he knew that this was the demonstration the Dark Lord had arranged by murdering his grandfather. The young *dark seer* was breathing hard but the look in his eyes betrayed his eagerness to please his Master and prove himself with a quick decisive victory, rather than worry with his own survival.

Adrian spun to his right, grasping the handle of his sword with both hands, aiming a slicing blow at Alpha's stomach, just as his enemy drove his own straight down at Adrian's head, with the practiced finesse of an executioner. The blow grazed the side of the young *seer's* skull, behind his ear, and he screamed in agony as his own sword tore into Alpha's side and they both plunged into the water of the reflecting pool.

~

Adrian awoke in his own bed. His head was bandaged and his mother was sitting in on old wicker bentwood rocking chair. She stared at her hands, her blue eyes sad and tired. "How did we get here?"

Sara smiled, "Oh, you're awake. It's nice to have you back. How's your head?"

Adrian closed his eyes for a moment, "It's throbbing."

"That doesn't surprise me. You're lucky you didn't break your neck, falling out of the sky like that."

"You were there?"

"Yes, we jumped into the limousines and followed you. We arrived just as the clones started their attack."

"Is everyone else alright?"

"Yes, they're fine. They've all gone to the observatory to see what the Keepers have found."

"What about Beta and Gamma, the other two clones?"

"They didn't fair quite as well as Zepallo might have hoped. All three were badly injured. When you and Alpha, is it…fell into the pool, they all disappeared. The *seers* brought the two of us back here and your father will be back as soon as he can. He had to stay on to finish with your grandfather's lawyer, Cokie...or Mr. Tierney. They were reading the will this morning."

"I'll bet that was...interesting."

Sara laughed, "I'm sure that, no matter how he wrote it, your aunt and uncles will be disappointed."

"I think they missed the point."

"And the point is...?"

"That people should show their love and respect for someone when they're alive, not after they've died."

"That's a rather sophisticated point of view."

Adrian paused, "I guess it's just something that I was made aware of, while I was taking my lessons from Orana. I can hear the sound of life but with each death, one voice in the chorus is silenced."

Sara leaned over and kissed her son. "I'm just glad that you're still alive."

"Are you mad at me for taking on the clones?"

His mother stared at him with a great sadness in her eyes, "I'll never get used to the idea that I could lose you in an instant. I understand that you feel obliged to confront the evil in our world but you could have picked a better time."

"As I said, I really didn't have a choice."

"Yes, you did. You could have climbed into the car and we could have left."

"They would have been waiting for us when we got back to the house. Zepallo set the whole thing up with one purpose in mind...to test out his clones against me. The reason I chose to follow them was that I felt confident about defending the area in front of the Lincoln Memorial, because it was open and they couldn't get behind me. They would have had too many advantages with all the trees around grandfather's house."

Sara just looked at him.

Adrian smirked, "Besides, I already know that I'll live to be three-hundred-years old."

"Oh, you rascal," screamed his mother, as she tickled him under his ribs. "I want to be mad at you for taking chances and scaring me to death."

"We both know that I have to stand up to Zepallo. We'd both be disappointed in me if I didn't."

"You're just a boy, how can you be so wise?"

He blushed, "I don't think it's wisdom. I'm not old enough to have earned that yet…but I do think that I'm learning to see things as they really are and maybe that's a start."

"Are you hungry?"

"Yes, as a matter of fact, I am…very!"

"Well, it's been two days since your last meal. I'll go and see what I can find in the kitchen," she said, as she rose from her chair, put her shawl and her book down on the nightstand, and walked to the door, which opened without comment. She turned and looked at her son, "I love you."

"I love you too."

~

Colburn Tierney stood behind the chair at Sir Jonathon's desk. He hesitated to sit, out of respect for his friend. "I understand why you chose to have our meeting here, in this room. It represents everything that he was and probably more. He was your brother, father, and grandfather but he was my friend and I will miss him, his wisdom, his insight, and his wicked humor, until the day I join him for an eternal game of chess."

He sat down in the chair and opened the file sitting on the desk, "I'll skip over the usual formalities and get to the…more personal parts. To Ralph, I leave the home that you were raised in, in hopes that it might inspire you to look beyond your more selfish and self-destructive pursuits. You've done well, you're a success as a businessman, but you are a total failure as a human being. There is no value in a life that is of no service to any other living creature. Open your eyes and you'll find people who need your intelligence and your strength, perhaps even your kindness, if you are willing to change. This is a house that should be filled with love, with children…it is a place in which fond memories should be born. I'm sorry that I didn't do more to make it that kind of home for all of you."

"To Margaret, I leave the contents of the house, with the exception of this room. You managed to capture financial security but you failed to find or to give happiness and meaning in your life. I must take some of the blame for the fact that you were indulged as a child and you never outgrew it. Now your children are spoiled and destined for the same misery that you suffer, unless you find it in your heart to actually become their mother."

"To John, I leave the contents of my office. It represents my best efforts, my successes, and my defeats. I have always been proud of you and, I think that I am more proud of what you are doing now than at any time in your life."

"My Sister Lucy is well cared for through a living trust that was set up several years ago. To you, my darling, my thanks for always being there to listen and to guide me to make the right choices at critical moments. I always admired you and felt privileged to have you as my sister."

"To my grandson, Adrian, I leave the rest of my estate, to be held in trust until he is of an age to handle his affairs responsibly. I am so very proud of you for standing up to evil, against impossible odds, for speaking the truth, and for doing it all for the right reasons. Our world will depend on you for its salvation."

Margaret and her children gasped, "I'll appeal this fraudulent will. I'll fight it with everything at my disposal."

Ralph gazed around the room absently, oblivious to his sister's ranting. Lucy looked calm and radiant, her skin glowed softly and her white hair shimmered in the dim light. A twinkle in her eyes hinted at her amusement over the exposure of raw character and the untruths that were finally being laid to rest. Jonathon was gone but she suffered agonizing apprehension through decades of dark adventures, knowing that he could have died a thousand deaths along the way, and every extra day that he was alive was a blessing for her.

Mr. Tierney, smiled calmly, "You may take this matter to court, if you wish, but you should know that there is a clause that states that anyone contesting this document for any reason will receive the sum of one dollar and will forfeit any claim to whatever your father left you."

"Well, I never…" hissed John's sister.

"There are several charities that are mentioned with specific sums which are to be paid for with his insurance benefits. According to the information that he left with me, there are seven accounts in seven countries, which at this point are still something of mystery. Whatever the final sum, young Adrian will become a very wealthy young man. At his grandfather's bequest, I will oversee these accounts, until such time as Adrian is prepared to take on those responsibilities for himself. In the meantime, he will receive an income from the interest on his investments."

John could not believe what he was hearing. He struggled to contain an astonished laugh, fearing that it might be an inopportune moment and certainly would not be taken well by his siblings. Adrian had neither interest or need for this inheritance but he was proud that his father understood the secrets he shared during their conversation in this room, just over a year ago. The old man grasped the reality and the threat of the parallel world of the Powers and acknowledged his grandson's abilities and praised his character.

Cokie stood, "Your father was my friend, a man who made a difference in the world, and all he wanted for each of you was happiness and fulfillment. If there are no objections, the necessary paperwork will be drawn up in the next few days and I'll have the final documents ready for your signatures by the first of next week. You may take possession of your inheritance when these steps have been completed."

The family members stood up and turned to leave. Tierney reached out and touched John's sleeve, indicating that he should wait. John followed his siblings to the door and closed it behind them. He returned to stand in front of the desk, dejected by his father's passing and dumbfounded by his bequest. Cokie walked around and guided John to the leather chair behind it. "It's your desk now."

John sat down, as the lawyer took a seat in one of the wing chairs opposite him, "I notice that you've started growing a moustache."

Cokie rubbed his upper lip, "I'm doing it in honor of my college roommate, who was somewhat less than enamored with his government or ours, let alone any form of authority. He always had long hair and at least a moustache, if not a beard. We were in the middle of protesting the Vietnam War and I'm afraid we both spent the better part of our semesters in the streets rioting rather than in being attentive in the classroom.

Those were exciting times, promising times. We could all see that the world was changing, that we were making a difference in the course of the war and the direction of our society. Our favorite music was mostly anthems of rebellion at full volume." He paused, "We often laughed with each other that we both turned out to be responsible citizens, supporting the governments that we fought with such spirit and conviction…and we often wondered what happened to all that courage, all the energy that drove a generation to get so passionately involved in trying to set things right. Where did they all go?" He paused again, then laughed, "They turned into attorneys and, worse, bankers!"

John smiled, "I remember him talking about those times…those truly were the good old days for him."

"There's something more that he wanted me to give to you and for you to share with Adrian," said the attorney, as he stood and walked over to a bookcase. He pulled a plump edition of Tolstoy's War and Peace from the line of books and reached into the open space to flip a lever. The entire wall swung out to reveal a smooth door.

Tierney wore an expensive dark suit, a banker's tie, and the air of authority, until he turned and grinned at Adrian's father with an impish smile that revealed the mischievous child that lives in every man. He must have been a hellion as a kid.

Cokey had been hanging around the house, since long before John was born, and he had always been a part of the family, the favorite almost-uncle who played with the kids, flirted with their mother, and had long, good natured arguments deep into the night over the chess table with his father.

John knew that he had been married to a college sweetheart, but that hadn't lasted, and he was fairly certain that he had married that gorgeous Cuban lady but, to be honest, he wasn't sure. He always suspected that he and Aunt Lucy might have been involved at some point but he had nothing tangible on which to base his assumption.

The attorney was extremely intelligent, worldly, and looked the part of his profession, yet he always seemed witty and smart, able to see the tumultuous world through some odd perspective that made it all seem ironic and funny. John smiled to himself, *"He's just so damned likable..."*

The smooth door slid into a pocket at the side of the frame and down-lights in the ceiling illuminated the contents of glass cases lining a long hallway. The attorney stepped back and gestured for John to enter, "This is also part of his study."

Adrian's father stepped across the threshold and found floor-to-ceiling cases filled with weapons of every description, a cabinet full of cameras and exotic lenses, another full of radios, recording devices, and communication gear, the complete uniform of a Soviet cosmonaut, a viewfinder from a submarine periscope, first edition leather-bound books, rare stamps and coins, volumes of documents and photographs. These were the mementos, the evidence of the significance of his life. The showcases continued down both sides of the hall, until it opened into a large round space lined with a row of red metal cabinets and large screens.

Cokie walked up behind him and said quietly, "If the study was the heart of his life, this was the soul."

"What is all of this?"

"With this equipment and his contacts, he could communicate with anyone in any government or secret service organization, anywhere on the planet. He was literally a one-man intelligence agency, dedicated to promoting freedom for every human being."

"That's incredible!"

"That was your old man and we were all the beneficiaries of his efforts."

"I never knew..."

"No one did, except those who needed to know and those who depended on him to accomplish what they couldn't or wouldn't do for themselves or their countries."

"Well, at least Adrian comes by it honestly."

"You son is an extraordinary young man. His battle over the reflecting pond was amazing. If anyone doubted the existence of the Powers, they understand now."

"What do you mean?"

"Well, that whole area was covered by security cameras...on the tops of buildings, in the memorial, on the peak of the Monument, several cameramen on the ground, and at least two helicopters that were shooting long range. No one will say who ordered the coverage but, considering how quickly they moved into place after the funeral, it could only have come from the White House. Those images weren't shown to the public but they were transmitted to the leaders of every nation. The president has been trying to make the rest of the world understand the threat that Palloze and his troops pose to civilization. If he succeeds, that will be his legacy."

"The people, who have been defending the Power of the Light, are a small but determined force. They've fought these battles for thousands of years, without revealing the secrets to the general population, because they believed that the common people weren't ready for the truth." He looked at his father's best friend, "Now Adrian is the one who must protect the real world against the Dark Forces."

"Maybe this will make it harder for the bad guys and provide the good guys with some support."

"I don't think it could come at a better time. The question is whether the next president will follow through?"

"I know that Bartlett has briefed both candidates and I use the term 'briefed' loosely. He can be very persuasive when he wants to be."

"I'm sure that a man in his position has to acquire certain...talents, when it comes to persuasion."

"I think whoever wins the election will understand the stakes. How they play the hand remains to be seen."

"What was it that you wanted to show me?"

"Oh, yes," replied Tierney, as he turned and hit a button on one of the consoles. The giant screens jumped to life and his father's face appeared in a video.

"Since you're watching this, I must assume that I am dead...and if the causes were somewhat less than natural, we might assume that I died at the hand of your enemy. There are things that I've learned over the past couple of years that might be of help to you and Adrian and the Forces of Light." The old man smiled and winked at the camera, "I'm sorry I couldn't reveal all that I'd learned but the conversation we had last fall supported my own investigations and these machines contain information that you will find useful.

I'm sure that no one else in the world, or at least no one outside of Zepallo's inner circles, has any concept of his vast financial holdings. He is a majority shareholder in countless, and I do mean countless, corporations in every country in the world. His representatives run the board of directors at many of those organizations. The stock pages from New York, London, South Africa, Japan, and China would only be a start.

Cokie has the codes to print out a partial list of his primary holdings," smiled the old man. "You'll find extra paper and ink cartridges in the cabinets beneath the printer. You'll need 'em.

I've also chronicled many of his political associations in various governments, religious organizations...and some of those are truly astonishing...banking, commerce, communications...he has his minions buried everywhere and they seem to be doing his bidding, without raising much suspicion from those who should know better.

Use this intelligence wisely and reveal it only to those who are willing to participate in the battle that will surely come." Sir Jonathon paused and waved his hand around the room behind him, "All of this equipment is modular. With the flip of a few latches, each module can be moved by two men or one *seer!* Set the equipment up somewhere safe, where your smartest people can use it. These machines automatically record reams of files on everyone of any importance in the entire world, on financial transactions, and there are contacts that will benefit your efforts. Your Keepers, as you call them, will find the software malleable and far ahead of anything that's commercially or governmentally available. I'm sure they'll find ways to use this equipment for things I never imagined."

He stared into the camera, "I'm proud of the things that I've accomplished along the way, although there are some that I might have done better, but where we fought against an enemy that we could see, I now understand that those governments, those people were just surrogates for a deeper evil. The one who hides in the background, the puppeteer who jiggles the strings and causes panic to ripple across the planet, that's the enemy you face and I'm sorry that I can't be with you to help. Just know that I'm proud of what you and Adrian are trying to do and I understand the danger.

Cokie has made arrangements for all of my personal and professional belongings to be removed from the residence by morning and they can be delivered wherever you choose. I trust that you will use them well." John's father looked sad, "Oh, and there is one more thing." He looked directly into the camera, "I love you…I love both of you and I should have said that more often, while I had the chance."

The screen faded to black.

Chapter 6

Adrian sat up, crossed his legs, and reached up to touch the white turban swaddling his head. A large pad protruded on the left side behind his ear. He touched the wound gently. It burned and throbbed in rhythm with the thump of his beating heart, driving a dull annoying jangle around the inside of his skull.

"If I'd dodged the other way, that blow would have hit me square in the face!" he thought with a grin. *"I have to believe the things that aged version of me said."*

Just knowing that he would survive provided a certain confidence and he tried very hard not to dwell on that expectation, when summoning his senses to be focused on the task at hand. But he could not ignore the question of whether his ancient self was just an illusion, a convenient fantasy masking his qualms and apprehensions?

Orana's words were clear and precise in his memory, "The object of your instruction is to multiply these things that you are sensing by an infinite scale, touching not only your immediate surroundings but the entire world, and then to teach you to synthesize them to produce something useful!"

He closed his eyes and tried to let his mind move into that calm place, where he could tune in to the vibrations of the world. The vision of the three clones racing towards him, the charges sizzling through the air trailing an acrid scent, the sound of his fellow *seers'* laughter, the cold determination in the eyes of his new adversary, and the sensation of Alpha's sword grazing the side of his head at the same moment he felt his own sword burning through his enemy's flesh, rushed through his mind and eclipsed his perception of everything else.

Concentrating, he could feel the hum in the background, slowly gaining strength and focus, as he pushed the battle to the back of his mind, but the tone was not smooth. Another hint that the peace of the last few months was beginning to give way to the most basic human instincts of primal domination and survival of the fittest. There were ripples in the sound of the dark vectors pulsing in counter rhythm and that faint grating, a texture he sensed before his grandfather's funeral, was getting stronger.

Adrian allowed his mind to close around the sounds, to follow them along the paths, and, slowly, dimly a vision appeared of three dark shapes, human shapes, against three white rectangles. Red smudges appeared, like daubs of paint on an abstract canvas, one on the left side of the first, another on the leg of the second, and yet another on the shoulder of the third. He could see his enemies!

Suddenly, a question exploded in his mind, *"If I can see them, can they see me or are they aware of this avenue between us?"*

His vision faded into a bright white light. Zepallo's face appeared with a menacing grimace.

Adrian's body convulsed violently, before his eyes popped open, with a start, to find his mother standing next to the bed with a tray in her hands. He could see the concern in her eyes. "What just happened?"

"I was listening to the vibrations and I heard the sound of the dark vectors and I followed it. I found the three clones. They're all wounded but, suddenly, Zepallo appeared inside my head!"

"Are you sure you're alright?"

"I'm not so sure," replied the young *seer*, sagging into his pillows with a sigh. His mother put the bed-tray across his lap and sat on the chair next to the bed to feed him slow spoonfuls of rich broth.

~

Over the next few days, Adrian drifted in and out of consciousness. He was aware of his friends and family passing through the room, each expressing their love and concern. He could feel their touches, gentle kisses, and hear their words, off in the distance, but he could not rouse himself to respond. Dr. Stevens cleaned and bandaged his wound, looked into his eyes, listened to his heart, and checked his blood pressure but there was nothing he could do except wait.

He knew his mother was sitting beside the bed by the faint whiff of her perfume, replaced for short periods by Elsie, who hummed a lilting lullaby when they were alone. He could hear them talking quietly and, occasionally, became aware that his mother was crying.

Memories flashed through his mind in some random, illogical sequence…yet there was something there, something he needed to understand. He saw Zepallo and the clones, the invasion of Morgan's Knot, the great cavernous command centers of the evil empire, the plane of the animals, the President's office, and the United Nations Assembly, and he flashed through the white world that had been his formal initiation, his introduction to the meaning of the Powers and his part in the future.

He saw Orana, bathed in a warm pool of light. Her eyes expressed so many emotional states at the same time…sadness, wisdom, exhaustion, determination, vitality, energy, hope, and love. It was as if she had seen all of history, all the joys and all the sorrows, all of the triumphs of those who believed in the Power of the Light through countless clashes with legions of Dark Forces rising to take power, only to be driven back, time and again, over the centuries.

The vision of his three-hundred-year old self appeared repeatedly, calling to him, *"This is not how it ends. You know that…we know that…so heal yourself and let's get on with this!"*

He pulled back his mane of white hair to reveal the scar on the side of his head, *"We pay dearly for the privilege of being who we are. This is only a scratch. You'll suffer far worse than this before we're finished…and we're not finished. You have too much to do!"*

Adrian woke in a panic. It was as if he had been jolted out of his unconscious state, as if someone dumped a bucket of cold water over his head, for he was fully conscious, annoyingly awake, and completely alert. His entire body felt pummeled and weak, drained of energy, but his spirit was anxious to begin.

He turned to his mother, holding a handkerchief in her hands to dab at the tears running down her cheeks.

"I'll survive this and I'll recover," said Adrian quietly, as he reached to take her hand.

"I know," replied Sara, "but every mother worries when their children are in danger, when they're sick or wounded, and when our enemies would see them dead."

"We've talked about this so many times and you know that I have to do these things. I have no choice but to defend the Power of the Light."

His mother looked into his eyes, "And you know that I'm very proud of the things that you've accomplished and the person that you've become. That doesn't change the fact that I suffer every time you go on one of your missions or they bring you home wounded, damaged, or near death. No mother should have to feel these things. It's as if someone's twisting a knife deep inside my heart and the only relief is believing that you'll live, that you'll be whole again."

Adrian smiled, "Perhaps one day, mothers won't have to worry about their children having to go into battle. Maybe that's what this is all about."

"I hope you're right." Sara stood and leaned over the bed to kiss her son on his bandaged forehead.

~

A week after the battle, John arrived in the tiny harbor on the trawler Jasmine with Travis at the helm. The hold was filled with large crates and Ponte, Nanchez, Dadeus, and Sammy met them at the pier. A line of trolleys waited along the quay and a small crane, mounted to one of the pilings, lifted the cargo from the belly of the old fishing boat onto the beds of the wagons. The four Keepers guided each crate with gentle, precise movements, treating the new equipment like fragile sculpture.

One by one, the trolleys moved off along the path to the observatory, where the computers would be assembled in a storage room next to the Professor's workshop. They considered installing them in the new dome but decided that they would prefer someplace quiet and more restricted…where they could master the software undisturbed.

John thanked Travis and rode with Ponte in the last trolley to leave the harbor. He opened a large metal briefcase to reveal a thick, leather-bound notebook. "Sir Jonathon left a manual of instructions for the software he developed. On the video, he said that you would be able to access the information that he'd gathered. It should contain all of his contacts, the trails that he was developing to expose the people that the Dark Forces have planted in governments, religious institutions…all of it. He also said that Zepallo has massive investments and controls giant international corporations."

"Why don't I find that unexpected?"

"Maybe because we, meaning the people who live on this island, don't really have any need or desire for wealth. This is probably one of the few places on the planet where money has no meaning." John laughed, "Did I tell you that he left his entire fortune to Adrian?"

"No!"

"Cokie's trying to come up with a final figure but he's having a hard time because there are multiple accounts in seven different countries. Whatever the final amount, it's huge."

Ponte laughed, "If ever there was a young person, who did not need an inheritance, it's your son!"

The Professor turned south to the House of the Four Seasons, when they reached the split in the track, "You'll be wanting to stop in to see the family. You can come by later and help us reassemble the equipment."

"I've missed them," said John, leaning back to gaze around fields full of growth in spite of the fact that winter was battering the island. They bumped through the gate and slid to a stop just outside the kitchen door. He looked over at the vegetable garden and noticed that it was overflowing with produce. He worried about his family, while he was gone, and, now, realized how much he had missed the magic of this place.

"I'll come by this evening to help," said Adrian's father, as climbed out of the trolley and grabbed his bag out of the back.

Elsie appeared at the back door, waved to Ponte, and gave her brother-in-law a big hug, "We've missed you."

"It's nice to be home," said John with a smile. "How's Adrian?"

"He's better but the Doctor has him confined to bed, until his wound heals. There's a good possibility that he suffered at least a minor concussion, so we're not taking any chances. He just needs time to heal."

"I must see him."

"Sara's with him. She hasn't left his side, since they got back."

John grabbed an *orb*, climbed the stairs, and turned to Adrian's room at the far end of the hall. The door swung open with a rousing but hushed, "Welcome home."

Sara rushed to her husband and wrapped her arms around his neck, "I was worried."

"It took longer than we expected to find the right freighter to carry our cargo." He kissed her and walked over to sit on the edge of Adrian's bed, "How are you feeling?"

"I'm better."

"Well, you might be better than the last time I saw you but you don't look quite yourself."

"Dr. Stevens has been by every day and, each day, he says that we'll see how I'm doing tomorrow. I'm getting kind of anxious to get out of this bed."

"I understand but you took quite a blow and you fell at least a hundred feet into the reflecting pool. Scared the life out of all of us!"

"I didn't get to see the end of the battle."

"Well, Zepallo gathered his clones and vanished. They were thoroughly defeated."

"I know. I saw them in their hospital."

John's jaw dropped, "How...?"

"I was listening to the vibrations and I could hear the grating sound of the dark vectors, so I allowed my mind to follow it and found the three of them and Zepallo."

"That's amazing. Do you have any idea where they were?"

"No. It wasn't distinct and I had no sense of direction."

"That's a shame." He paused, "I do have some other news."

"What's that?"

"Well, your grandfather left us a video which explained that he had been investigating Zepallo and the Dark Forces for some time. He found that Zepallo, in addition to his political and military interests, has huge investments in giant international corporations...everything from aircraft to toilet paper."

"That shouldn't surprise anyone. The Black Crystals produce black diamonds and he controls their flow to market, just as we use the products of the Golden Crystals here."

"That's true. He even owns a diamond distribution company that sells industrial diamonds around the world. It's just that I don't think that any of us ever considered the financial side of things. There's more. Your grandfather also developed leads to minions of the Dark Forces, who have been installed in governments, religious institutions, commerce...everywhere. The information's on some large computers I brought back with me. They'll be installed at the observatory."

"Wow! I wonder how he knew."

"I went to see him last fall, just after you connected all of the nodes, and told him the whole story. After seeing some of what he has on these computers, I think he started his investigation long before we had our conversation. I never understood why he retired when he did. Now it makes sense, he was looking into the Dark Forces and couldn't work under the constraints or the intrusive eyes of governments."

"Then he knew all along."

"I think you're correct."

Adrian smiled. His grandfather had known about the powers and about his talents.

"There's one thing more," said John with a small smile. "Evidently, he had a rather large fortune spread through accounts in different countries around the world and he left it all to you."

Adrian's jaw dropped, "But...why?"

"I think he felt that you would use it for the right purposes."

"I guess I'm going to have to learn about the world of finances."

"We don't know how much is really there but I would suggest that you meet with Mr. Tierney, when you're feeling better. He'll be looking after your investments, until you're old enough to accept that responsibility for yourself. Of course, you'll be paid out of the interest and dividends that your accounts produce."

Adrian looked dumbstruck. He mumbled, "I don't know what dividends are and I have only a vague notion of how interest works. Besides, I don't need any money, I have everything I could possibly want right here on Morgan's Knot."

His father took his hand, "Money isn't just for buying things. It can be used to fund educations, to help those in need, to build or buy businesses, or to purchase stocks. When you own enough stock in a corporation, for instance, you can control the direction or the policies of that company, just as Zepallo is doing."

The young *seer's* eyes brightened, "That opens up some interesting possibilities."

"I don't know enough to counsel you on this, you'll have to talk with Cokie. He's the expert."

"I'll be better soon. Do you think he could come here or should I go there?"

"It would probably be easier for you to go to him. On the other hand, perhaps it would be beneficial for him to visit Morgan's Knot just to understand what this is all about."

"I could go get him," snickered Adrian. "That would be a good introduction to The Powers."

"A flight along the vectors might be just the thing, although we still have to worry about Zepallo intercepting you."

"There are ways around that problem."

His father smiled and hugged his son. The other *seers* had surrounded Adrian and Sara and moved into the vectors, moments after Zepallo and the clones disappeared. There had been no choice and John stayed behind to tend to the family's business, worrying until this moment.

~

Zepallo strode into the infirmary, past the nurses' station, and straight into the isolated ward, sealed off for his clones. The three boys were sitting up in bed, although they were still bandaged and medicated.

Alpha's wounds were the most serious, although not fatal, while Beta had suffered a gash across his thigh, and Gamma a burn across his collarbone and shoulder. They had done well and Zepallo was not displeased with their effort. The outcome was somewhat disappointing but they would gain strength and maturity, now that they had tasted blood in the heat of battle. With some personal training, they would be ready for the next confrontation.

"How are we today?" he inquired.

The three young *seers* moaned, as the Doctor turned from his inspection of Gamma's bandage to greet their visitor. "They will survive. I'm amazed by how rapidly they're healing, it's superhuman."

The Dark Master smiled, "They come from good stock!"

The Doctor laughed, "Well, that's one explanation."

"How soon can they return to their training?"

"Well, Beta and Gamma can probably be released early next week. Alpha will need a little more time."

"Fine, I'll start with Beta and Gamma. Alpha can catch up with my lessons when he's mended."

Zepallo walked over to the first bed and bent over Alpha. "You fought well. I'm proud of you and I can assure you that you'll have your chance for revenge."

The boy managed a weak smile, as the Dark Lord turned to the next bed. "You held your own against their best. You should be proud."

He brushed around the end of the cot to the third and congratulated Gamma, "You have nothing to be ashamed of either. You stood your ground and used your skills to allow Alpha to test young Adrian. You'll all benefit from this experience and you'll all be stronger for it."

He spun around, his black cape flowing behind him, and marched out of the room.

~

John held Adrian's arm, as they walked slowly down the front steps of the old farmhouse under a bright sunny morning with a cold wind gusting in from the ocean. He was feeling better but his head still throbbed, when he moved too quickly, and his sense of balance was a bit wobbly.

Dr. Stevens stopped by earlier, cleaning the wound with his healing waters and applying a fresh bandage. Adrian knew that his physician understood his need to move, to participate in the campaign that was mounting at the observatory, and he made a convincing argument that he be allowed to begin to participate. The balance between the Light and the Dark might well depend on his talents and abilities.

The Doctor reluctantly agreed but demanded that these sessions be short, so he could get the rest he needed to recover fully.

Adrian stopped near the split-rail fences outside the kitchen and took a deep breath. The air smelled fresh and clean. The sun warmed his face and he could hear the caws of seagulls in the distance. He turned to his father, "I'll meet you there. I think I need to fly."

"Are you sure you're up to it?"

"I'm sure. I'll feel better when I get there." He hugged his father, closed his eyes, calmed himself, and rose into the air. He felt like Simian's feather. The wind lifted him into the sky and his pain and fever retreated for the first time in weeks, soaring across the fields to the pillar of rock in the northern plain. He spied Magnus flying along the bluffs. The beautiful eagle caught a thermal that carried him up into an apex in the deep blue sky, where he folded his wings and flew straight down at Adrian. At the last moment, he extended his feathers and settled in beside the young *seer*.

"I'm glad to see that you're better. We all worry about you."

"Thank you," said Adrian. Magnus taught him the ways of an eagle, before the invasion of the island by the Dark Forces, and those lessons probably saved his life. He felt a special bond with the magnificent bird and certainly privileged to fly with him.

"We've seen the *seers* and Keepers coming and going from the observatory and Brandy and Tic told us about the clones."

"The Dark Forces are moving again. We have to find out what they're planning and do what we can to stop them."

"If we can help, you know where to find us!"

As they approached the observatory, Magnus peeled off to follow a school of fish that might provide his breakfast, while Adrian landed gently on the path near the front door and found Alius waiting on the step.

"I felt you coming," she said, wrapping her arms around him. "You don't look well. How are you feeling?"

"I've been better but I needed to be here with you and Ponte and the rest."

"I understand how you feel."

"Aren't you supposed to be teaching our class today?"

"I've been playing hooky, just like you!" laughed the beautiful blond *seer*, holding his arm tightly. "They've postponed it until you're better and we have a chance to deal with some of the things that are going on inside."

"I can't wait to see what you've been doing."

Just then, the wagon rolled into the yard. John jumped out with a concerned scowl and hurried to Adrian and Alius, "I trust that you're alright?"

"I'm fine," replied Adrian. "Magnus escorted me."

"Your mother would have my head, if she knew that I allowed you to do this!"

"I won't tell if you won't!"

"Agreed."

"Then let's go inside and get on with this," said Alius, guiding Adrian up the steps and into the parlor.

He stopped just inside the door to take in his favorite room. The walls were lined with thousands of books, the solar system of tiny glowing *orbs* suspended in mid-air, the skeleton danced in the far corner, an incomplete game of three-dimensional chess on a table between two chairs, Ponte's gizmos and gadgets, half-finished and neglected beneath the tables and chairs, behind the couch, or any nook or cranny where there was a bit of open space…the fireplace with a small sputtering flame, threatening to die at any moment…it was everything a young *seer* might dream.

The far wall was lined with *messengers*, each displaying different information. Movements along the dark vectors, the international news, one tracked ocean currents and temperatures, and yet another showed the movement of power across the paths between the Crystals, Light and Dark.

Sammy was monitoring four *orbs* at once and turned to greet his friend, "I'm so glad to see you up and about. I heard about the battle. You must have taken quite a fall."

"I could have been more graceful," smiled Adrian, as the young Jamaican wrapped him in a hug.

"You survived, that's enough."

"What do we know?"

"Well, we're spread kind of thin, at the moment. The Professor and Nanchez are finishing the assembly of the new computers and testing the software with Sky, Simian, and Raffe. Dadeus is overseeing research into cloning with Mary and Master Chi…and Alius and I have been covering everything else."

"What have you got on the *messengers*?"

"Well, the most interesting thing is this one that shows the ocean currents and the temperatures of the water around the globe. We can look at any area and know the exact conditions at any given time."

"And this is important because…?"

Sammy laughed, "Dadeus and the other *seers* have established that the best medium for growing embryos is salt water. Purified, certainly, but ocean water would do nicely. It's what we're all made of, so now we're trying to establish where on the planet the water temperature stays near 98.6 degrees all the time. That would provide perfect conditions for harvesting pearls or growing humans."

"If I hadn't seen them clearly several times, I wouldn't have believed it possible… but they are, in every way, young teenage Zepallos. I could see it in Alpha's eyes, in his movements, his energy, and his determination to risk everything for victory. In some ways, the three clones are scarier than the Dark Lord. They're unpredictable...because..." his words trailed off.

Alius broke the silence, "I think the most terrifying part of this isn't the three clones but three hundred or three thousand clones. If they can create three, then they can create as many as they might need. According to Dadeus and the Professor, once they've cleaned up their process, they could produce an endless stream of embryos. That would qualify as a dark miracle."

"I'm afraid you're right. All the more reason I should be here to help."

John interrupted, "You can help for a while but you're under orders to get as much rest as possible. Doctor's orders...and your mother's."

"Then let's start with the computers," sighed Adrian, as he padded gingerly to the elevator at the back of the dining room. The ornately carved doors closed behind them and the little car raced at breakneck speed into the earth beneath the spire. It stopped with a gentle bump and the doors opened to reveal the white room ablaze in the radiance of the giant Golden Crystal, spinning at a moderate pace a foot above the floor.

They turned right, past the door to the workshop, to the next alcove, a storage room cleared of the Professor's failed or unfinished experiments. The room was now bare, save a circle of futuristic computer modules strung together around of a workstation that faced two giant plasma screens.

One monitor displayed a map of the world with pulsing lines running between the financial capitals, while the other flashed through hundreds or thousands of photographs of random faces. People of all ages, all ethnic backgrounds, from every corner of the globe. Their documentation was momentarily posted next to the pictures.

Ponte, Nanchez, Simian, and Sky all gathered around the young *seer* to give him a hug. Raffe stayed at the keyboard of the workstation but stood, waved, and let out a raucous cry. Sky kissed him on the cheek, "We're so glad you're with us. We've worried about you."

"I'm just thankful that all of you showed up at the exact moment I needed your help. That was amazing."

"I think we're just sorry that we couldn't have helped you with Alpha. They were all more agile and better trained than any of us. They'll be more frightening when they're a bit more mature."

Ponte added, "You'll have to talk with Dadeus, Mary, and Master Chi, they've set up shop in the observatory…something about us being too noisy. They've got the books and several *messengers* to assist with their research. I'm sure they're all experts by now!"

Everyone laughed. Adrian walked slowly to stand behind Raffe, facing the screens. The two *seers* hugged and Raffe sat down at the console. "I'm learning about computers!"

Nanchez laughed and cuffed him on the back, "He takes to it like a duck to water! And this one never had a formal education before Mary got a hold of him!"

Adrian asked, "What are you watching?"

Raffe smiled, "The screen on the left is organizing your grandfather's list of people that either are…or might be associated with the Dark Forces. They're all in positions of authority with governments, financial institutions, religious organizations…you name it. He developed an interesting bit of software to identify the most likely places that Zepallo would want to have influence and then he worked backwards, through the personnel of those institutions that seemed most promising."

"Wow," sighed Adrian. "That must have taken some time to work out. There are so many possibilities."

"Thousands and thousands," said Sky. "The computer is cross-referencing by type of organization, level of influence within that particular sphere, positions within companies that might be useful for collecting information or influencing policies, and then it looks at each individual in those areas. Only a well-informed spy could have found all of these possibilities. Your grandfather was incredibly intelligent and thorough."

He pointed, "The one on the right is looking at financial transactions, money being moved around the world, large scale diamond transactions, and those industries that we know Zepallo has an interest in. We want to know where he keeps his money, where it's going, and how it's getting there. We're just beginning to understand what Sir Jonathon uncovered and it will take weeks or, more likely, months to unravel all of it, let alone begin to use this system to find new information."

John put his arm around Adrian's shoulders, "He knew."

"That makes me proud," replied Adrian.

"Someone has to follow in his footsteps and I think that he was gratified that you chose to become the person that you are."

Ponte waved a chubby hand, "Come on, we'll go and check in on Dadeus, Master Chi, and Mary. They'll certainly have information that will interest you. We're really just getting started here."

He led John and the two *seers* to the elevator, where they crammed into the small cab and rose to the observatory within moments. The doors opened revealing an anxious Ester standing right in front of them, with a huge smile stretched across her too small teeth. She wrapped Adrian in a hug, "I'm so glad you're better!"

"Thank you, I'm really glad to be here!"

Dadeus, Master Chi, and Mary greeted their friends, "Come in, come in…we've much to show you." The group walked around the giant telescope to a line of *messengers* floating at eye level, on the far wall.

Master Chi pointed to the first, "You'll notice that we have several systems exploring the oceans for those places that offer the best environment for growing new life. We've discovered that pearls and humans require quite similar conditions during the embryonic phase."

Dadeus continued, "It's interesting that pearls were first harvested in the Persian Gulf, the Red Sea, along the coasts of India and Sri Lanka, and close to shore in Japan. Freshwater pearls were found in China and, as the Europeans discovered and exploited the new world, they found oyster beds along the coasts of Central and South America and in the Caribbean. They also found fresh water pearls in the river basins in Mississippi, Tennessee, and Ohio. Since then other places with the proper conditions have been found or developed. They ring the globe between the Tropic of Cancer and Capricorn."

Ponte added, "During Roman times, pearls were a most unique and valuable commodity. It was said that by selling just one of his mother's pearl earrings, the Roman general, Vitellius, bankrolled an entire military campaign. There was a legend that Cleopatra wanted to impress Marc Anthony of the wealth of her kingdom and wagered him that she could produce the most expensive meal in history. Her table was set with two empty plates, two goblets of wine, and a matched pair of large pearls. She crushed one of the pearls and added the dust to her wine, which she drank. The Roman declined his portion, admitting that she won the wager."

"When Spain pillaged the New World for gold, silver, gems, and pearls, they acquired so many that they began selling them across the continent to finance more exploration and exploitation. Their initial investment in Columbus' first voyage paid off handsomely!" exclaimed Ester.

"Yes, but it also drove our ancestors from their homeland," cautioned Mary. "Their greed had no boundaries."

"What does all of this have to do with the embryos?" asked Adrian.

"They need similar conditions!" cried Ponte. "We must assume that they don't have thousands of willing women of child-bearing age to carry these children, so they must be growing them synthetically and for that, they need certain conditions similar to those inside the womb."

The young *seer* pondered the information for a moment, "They'd also need a Black Crystal to power their facilities. Find the Black Crystals near the equator and you can narrow your search."

Mary smiled, "I knew there was a reason we missed your help so much!"

~

The Doctor found Zepallo standing in the control room with his hands behind his back gazing around the embryo incubator. The glow of a single black *orb* within a round worktable in the center bathed the pod in purple. The Dark Lord leaned over a set of plans for new nurseries that were nearing completion in the new wing.

"I thought I'd find you here."

Zepallo stood erect and gestured around the room to glowing green bubbles suspended in the purified seawater flowing through the test chamber, replenishing the nutrients and oxygen, and carrying away the waste. The forms inside the closest group of pulsing amoebas were nearing full term.

"We're within a few days of the birth of the next group," said the Dark Lord. "These new facilities must be finished before then and there are still details to be worked out."

"The construction crew is working around the clock."

"I know, I'm afraid that I'm becoming anxious and impatient. With so many advances being made in so many different areas, I'm stretched too thin and restless for the culmination of these many years of hope."

"I understand completely," replied The Doctor, quietly.

"Have you any estimate of the percentage of successes we might expect from this next batch of our…children?"

"We're hoping for fifty percent in the next group and, perhaps, seventy-five percent three months after them. The system isn't even close to perfect but we're learning more each day and that knowledge will be reflected in our rate of successes. In the meantime, we'll divide the next generation into groups as an experiment to see whether our team concept can be fulfilled."

"So, every three months, we'll have a new class, each larger than the last…each more deadly than their older brothers."

"The goal is within reach."

"What safeguards are in place to protect this technology and the future production of our clones?"

"Another facility is under construction in the southern Caribbean and samples of our stock of cells have been secretly distributed to every command center. If this facility were destroyed and I were to survive, we could be up and running again within a matter of days."

"Let's hope that eventuality never comes to pass."

"I am at your service, M'Lord."

"This peace that's swept across the planet will not last. The innocence of the children's campaign will wear thin in the harsh reality of mankind's inability to live without conflict or equitably share the wealth and, besides, our friends are far too eager to claim the spoils of the disruption that is to come."

Chapter 7

Colburn Tierney sat at his desk in a corner office, one floor below the penthouse, with a view that stretched across the Potomac into Virginia. He stroked the gray stubble sprouting beneath his nose. He shaved his last moustache off the day he graduated from law school, along with about a foot of hair that cascaded in waves down his back. He grinned to himself, "I wonder what the partners would think if I walked in here with my hair that long?" and then laughed out loud, "Stevens and Yasser would have heart attacks on the spot and the rest of them would probably lynch me from the crystal chandelier in the lobby with a rope woven from their French silk ties!"

He dispersed Sir Jonathon's estate as instructed. Ralph moved into the old mansion and seemed quite content, despite the fact that the house was sparsely furnished with the few things that he moved from his apartment. The attorney had been pleased when the youngest son arrived at his office completely sober and, seemingly, showing a bit more self-control than normal. Perhaps there was hope for him.

Margaret and her husband arrived in a limousine, signed the papers without so much as a "How are you?" or "Thank you." In fact, neither they nor their children uttered one word during the twenty minutes that they were in the office. From what Ralph told him, a truck arrived at the old mansion and the furniture disappeared that same day.

Aunt Lucy was well cared for through a trust set up several years before. There was little that she might want for, except the love and attention of her brother.

No, the hard part had been moving the contents of the study and the secret sanctuary in less than twenty-four hours, coordinating the transfer of those materials by truck to a waiting vessel, and making sure that no one, including the government of the United States, knew anything about their private business. He might be a corporate lawyer but a bit of the spymaster's ethic rubbed off on him and he rather enjoyed it.

Then there was the problem of finding and coordinating the bits and pieces that Sir Jonathon scattered around the globe in various accounts and investments. Coke's former roommate had little interest in finances or wealth, although his world provided ample opportunities and he had been smart enough to select extraordinary investment vehicles that moved him from being rich to being super rich.

They spent a long, rather drunken evening together over a chessboard, shortly after Sir Jonathon retired. He revealed his new project, as well as the instructions for his will. The old man never paid too much attention to the dangers he faced or the consequences of his own mortality. This was the first time he addressed the subject without prompting from his friend and attorney.

The old sailor sat back in his chair, a large cigar jammed in his craw, and a brandy snifter in hand. Long waves of silver hair covered his ears and his collar, framing a handsome face lined with the hard evidence of the extraordinary life he lived, "You know I've faced our enemies and looked death in the eye more times than I care to remember. In all these years, this is the first time that I'm sure I'll not see the end of my investigation. The stakes are too high and the enemy is more ruthless than any I've encountered through all these conflicts...and I've seen some bad guys. They can't let me live but, together, we'll see that they don't get what they're after. There's only one person in the world who will understand what I've been working on...and he is my grandson."

It was the lunch hour on a Friday...or maybe it should have been referred to as the lunch two-hours, as everyone seemed to need the extra time away from the office at the local watering hole and, on Friday, some never returned. He had given his secretary, Sandy, the afternoon off and closed his door. His calendar was clear and he was anxious to meet his only appointment.

A rustle of air roused him from his thoughts, as Adrian and Alius materialized on the burgundy carpet in front of his desk. They were wearing blue robes and long blue cloaks that brushed the floor. The young *seer* still wore a bandage around his head.

"I hope we didn't startle you," said Adrian. "I'd like you to meet my friend, Alius."

The beautiful blond *seer* curtsied and giggled, "I'm pleased to meet you."

Coke exploded with a hearty laugh, "You just materialized out of thin air! How do you do that?"

"I'm afraid it comes with being a *seer*. We'll try to explain some of that when there's time, but I must assume you have other business that you want to discuss and, if you're willing, we'd like to show you a bit of our world."

The attorney tried to calm himself but these youngsters could do things that every child dreamed about...and most adults never truly abandoned those fantasies. He found it hard to contain that inquisitive little boy, who still resided in the depths of his soul. He opened a file that was sitting flat on his desk, "Alright, do you want the legal version or the one I give in plain English?"

"We don't know anything about the world of finances, so small words would probably be easier to understand."

Tierney closed the file and smiled, "Okay, the long and short of it is that you are a very rich young man. Your grandfather had accounts scattered across the globe. He made good investments and those moneys have grown substantially over the past few years."

"How much money are you taking about?"

"Something in the range of a billion dollars."

Adrian was stunned, "How much?"

"You heard me, a billion dollars...or one with nine zeroes after it, if you want to look at it the other way."

"That's a lot of money," said Alius, quietly.

Adrian sat down in one of the deep chairs in front of the desk, "I don't think I can really fathom how much money that is...you'll have to understand, on Morgan's Knot, we have no need for money, so...this just doesn't really make much sense to me."

"Let's look at it another way. Do you know what interest is?"

"I think that it's when you put your money in a bank and they pay you a little bit for keeping it there."

"That's the basic idea...they get to use your money to make more money by, say, loaning it to a family that wants to buy a house. The family pays interest on the loan and you get part of it for having your money in the bank. It can get awfully complicated but that's the idea. So, if you were to just leave these investments where they are and we collected the interest, you would earn something in the neighborhood of one hundred million a year, give or take..."

"A hundred million? What would I do with hundred million dollars?"

Coke laughed, "Just about anything that you wanted to, I guess."

"I don't want it," said Adrian firmly. "At least I don't want the income."

"What do you want me to do with it then?"

"I want you to teach me...and my friends, how Zepallo has used his fortune to control different companies around the world. I want you to invest my money so it counters as many of his moves as possible. I don't care whether you make money or lose money, I just want it used for the right purposes."

"Well, that will involve investments, which will make you more money. Funny thing about having a lot of money, it starts growing of its own accord. We must assume that Zepallo has invested in solid companies, where he'd have representation on their boards of directors. You'll need people to stand in your place."

"What's a board of directors?" asked Alius.

"It's a group of people who determine the policies and direction of a company. They hire the President or CEO, who actually runs the company, and he hires other people to assume the responsibilities of making it all work."

"So, there would be people who would vote on my behalf. Could that be done without anyone knowing that I was behind it?"

"Yes, we could form a corporation or, perhaps, a foundation. I'll look into it for you."

"Thank you," replied Adrian.

"I take it that you've started going through the information on the computers your father took with him after the funeral?"

"I haven't but our friends, the Keepers, have and they'll have a list that we can start with, when we get back to Morgan's Knot."

The attorney sat back in his chair and smiled at the two *seers*, "It takes no time for people to understand that great wealth can be used for self-indulgence. Some of them never quite grasp the idea that it can be used to benefit others...or that it can be used as a weapon."

"I believe we understand each other," smiled Adrian. "As you'll see in a little while, there's no reason that I would want any of this for myself. I'd rather use them to help the poor or to protect wildlife across the planet, or to frustrate and confuse our adversaries."

"From what your grandfather told me, they represent the ultimate threat to all of us. I'll be happy to help in any way that I can."

Adrian stood up and reached across the desk to shake his hand, "Then we should be on our way."

Alius walked around the desk and took the attorney's hand, "We'll be traveling through the vectors and there's nothing to be afraid of. We'll be taking a rather unusual route to avoid any confrontations with Zepallo or his legions but I think you'll enjoy the journey."

Coke loosened his tie, "Will I need a coat?"

"Well, it is winter," laughed Alius, "even on Morgan's Knot!"

He pulled on his jacket and the two *seers* placed a hand on his shoulders, "Just relax and let yourself go."

The room disappeared and they zipped along a vector through the node beneath Lincoln's monument that would allow them to enter the plane of the animals. The low hum was smooth and the colors smeared past like a cosmic kaleidoscope in motion. The transit point happened to be forty feet off the floor of the entry lobby of the Smithsonian's Air and Space Museum. The tourists inside barely noticed a faint movement of air, as they passed from one plane to the next, but Coke was watching everything with a huge smile.

"What just happened?"

"We moved from the plane of your reality into the plane of the animals. This is a universe where almost every animal that's ever lived still exists in their natural form and habitat. It's as if man had never appeared on the planet."

"You're kidding?" laughed the attorney.

"No, we're not," smiled Alius. "In a little while, we'll be landing in a meadow, where you'll meet our friend, Unis, and her family. They're unicorns."

"Unicorns? I thought they only existed in fairy tales!"

"No, they're more amazing than fairy tales. They helped save our lives more than once," said Adrian.

The streaming colors gave way to the soft warm luminance filtering through the canopy of trees at the edge of the meadow. Unis was grazing at the far end of the field with Malan and looked up as they materialized. "Oh, I'm so glad to see you!" she whinnied and cantered over to them. "It's been too long since your last visit and I must say that I enjoy seeing you here rather than in the midst of a battle against that devil, Zepallo, and his fellows."

Alius and Adrian hugged the beautiful unicorn, "Unis, we'd like you to meet our friend, Coke."

The lawyer stared at Unis in total amazement. "Unicorns really do exist...and they talk..." he mumbled, as he reached out to brush her soft muzzle. "I'm very pleased to meet you."

"Welcome to the plane of the animals. I take it these young *seers* explained a little bit about our world?"

"They tried to tell me that this was a place where all of the animals that have ever existed live without humans."

"That's basically correct," replied Unis. "We've managed to rescue almost every species that has ever lived...and there are a few that we might have skipped over but we did our duty. They're all here."

"That's amazing!"

"No, it's the way life on this planet would have been if you humans had never become so prolific, so advanced...and so arrogant!"

Coke didn't know how to respond. He had never heard a joke told by any animal, let alone by a unicorn with a golden horn that stood several feet above her head. He was totally enchanted.

"I'm afraid we're just stopping through," said Adrian. "We're on our way to Morgan's Knot and used the plane to avoid any chance of running into Zepallo. If there's time, we'll stop on our way back for a visit but we have to get our friend back to Washington, before anyone realizes that he's gone."

"I understand," said Unis, with a bow of her golden horn. "Please come back when you can stay. The other animals would love to meet you."

"We'll do our best," said Alius.

The two *seers* each grabbed one of Coke's hands and vanished back into the vectors. A few minutes later, they landed on the ridge behind the House of the Four Seasons. "Welcome to Morgan's Knot," said Adrian, as he tramped down the path to the old farmhouse. A strong north wind whistled through the trees, twirling large snowflakes into white tornadoes that danced and swayed like graceful ballerinas on point in a winter festival.

They hurried around the barn, across the yard past the vegetable garden, heading for the front door, when Coke stopped and asked, "How can you have a garden full of vegetables in the middle of a blizzard?"

"That's why it's called the House of the Four Seasons. It's one of the magical places on the island, where we can grow crops twelve months a year. There are others, like Dr. Steven's, that's built on a spring that provides healing waters, or Samuel, the mechanic's, whose workshop is built over a vent that provides intense heat for metalworking and forming glass."

"That's amazing!"

"That's just the beginning," laughed Alius.

They led him up the steps and into the house. John and Sara met them in the front hall. "Welcome," said Sara, as she hugged the attorney, "I hope your journey wasn't too eventful!"

"Well, traveling through the vectors is...unbelievable...and we stopped in the plane of the animals."

"Ah, then you got to meet Unis. Isn't she wonderful?"

"I think the term miracle might be appropriate!"

"Well, come in. We've hot chocolate in the kitchen."

Elsie was busy at the stove and George rose from the oval table to shake Coke's hand. "I've heard so much about you and I'm pleased you've come for a visit."

"Coke, this is George and Elsie. The twins, Molly and Megan, will be home from school in a little while," said John. "Have a seat."

The family sat down around the table and Elsie and Sara brought mugs of hot coco for everyone. Coke asked, "Did you get everything delivered and set up?"

"Oh yes, Ponte…you'll meet him in a little while…and the rest of the Keepers are hard at work deciphering the first of the information. It seems it's almost endless," replied John.

"Your father dedicated the last part of his life to gathering that data and he told me that it was hardly complete. He also said that you were the only people on the planet who would know what to do with it."

"Well, we're learning," laughed John. "Did you and the children have a chance to talk about Adrian's inheritance?"

Coke looked over at Adrian and Alius, "Yes. Your son says that he has no interest in being wealthy and has instructed me to begin using his investments to counter the moves of Zepallo's clandestine financial empire. We'll be forming an entity to facilitate his wishes. We might call it 'Adrian's Gold'!"

"Good," said John seriously. "We'll have the initial list of target companies before you leave."

George sat up in his chair, "There'll be more to add to his inheritance."

The attorney glanced at him, "What do you mean?"

"As you'll see, the Crystals provide more than just energy. We have access to many of the Positive Crystals scattered about the world and their bounty will be channeled to you to add to the fund."

"I'm afraid I don't understand."

John laughed, "The Crystals have an odd extra benefit. They produce gold dust, diamonds, rubies, emeralds…depending on their color."

"Simian told us that he probably has several tons of emeralds that have been stockpiled over the years and that's just from one of the stones," added George.

"That makes this a more powerful tool. We'll have to work out a system to transfer these funds invisibly. We don't want to leave a trail for the Dark Forces to follow or any government for that matter."

"Right you are," replied John. "The power of Adrian's inheritance should benefit the world, not one nation."

"I hate to interrupt but we only have about four hours to show him everything we can, so we'd best get moving," said Adrian.

"Where are you going to start?" asked Elsie.

"Well, I think we should pay a visit to the dome first and then go on to the observatory. Knowing the Professor, once he gets started, we won't be able to get away!"

George laughed, "That's true. You might want to slip through the forest, if there's time…just to reinforce the idea of The Balance."

"Good idea," said Alius. "That is what this is all about!"

"I agree," added Adrian, as he stood up from his seat. "Shall we go?"

Sara and Elsie filled a wicker basket with hot drinks, cookies, and dried corn. Adrian and Alius led their guest out to the barn, where they climbed into the wagon. "You'll like this," smiled Alius, holding the door as the attorney slid onto the bench seat beside Adrian, and climbing in behind him. George had covered the open windows and Adrian was reminded of their ride on the stormy night when he became a *seer*.

"You're hardly old enough to drive."

"I'm hardly old enough to be a *seer*. Driving is nothing compared to flying through the vectors or fighting with Zepallo."

"I see your point," replied Coke, rather sheepishly for a lawyer. "I do have one question."

Adrian rolled the wagon out of the barn, past the garden, and onto the path heading south. A northeast gale buffeting the canvas roof, swirling clouds of snowflakes across the fields, "What's that?"

"This machine doesn't seem to have an engine."

"That's true," laughed the young *seer*, "you're very quick, aren't you?" He didn't wait for a response, "As it was explained to me, the power of the Crystal flows out on the vectors, which are like the petals of a flower or the spokes of a wheel. We can use that energy to push this truck along and, by reversing the energy, we can make it move the other way."

Alius chimed in, "You probably didn't notice that there were no lamps or lightbulbs in the House of the Four Seasons. We use what we call *orbs*, that need no wires or switches. That's part of the magic of this place. It all runs on the power of the Crystals."

The wagon bumped along past the interface to the new dome, through the fields along the coast to the edge of the forest. Adrian and Alius jumped out and grabbed the basket, leading Coke through a flurry into the trees, where they found protection from the wind. Within the first few steps, Harriet appeared above them, "I must say, it's been a while since your last visit!"

They stopped and looked up at the beautiful hawk, who was sitting on a branch of an ancient oak. "It's so nice to see you," exclaimed Alius. "We'd like you to meet our friend, Coke. He's only going to be here for a few hours and we wanted to introduce him to The Balance."

"Then you've come to the right place," squawked Harriet. "I'll go fetch some of our friends and we'll meet you at the brook."

Coke's mouth was hanging open as she flew off into the forest, "Did she really say what I think she said?"

The two *seers* laughed, "Of course she did! You'll find the animals and humans live and work together for the common good. There's no hunting and no animals are slaughtered for our food. They're our friends and none of this could exist without them. We call it The Balance."

"That's incredible!"

"Come on, you'll enjoy this," said Adrian, as he marched down the path into the darkness of the woods.

They found Daphne the deer and her mate, Beggar the bear with two cubs, several raccoons, some squirrels, a clutch of chipmunks, and a swarm of birds flitting around above the little stream. Alius sat down on a large rock and said, "Everyone, this is our friend, Coke. We can only stay for a little while because he has to get back to the real world, but we thought that this might be a good way to introduce him to The Balance."

The hawks, Harriet and Harry landed on the large boulder and Daphne stepped up to nuzzle the lawyer in the chest, "Welcome to Morgan's Knot. We don't get many visitors from the…real world and certainly none wearing clothes like those."

Coke reached up and stroked her muzzle, "I can't believe that I'm having a conversation with a deer."

Beggar wandered over and sat down next to him, "You'll be wanting to stay, if you're like everyone else!"

"And who might you be?"

"I'm Beggar," smiled the little bear, "and these are my cubs, Ashton and Ashford."

"Those are very proper names for young bears," commented Alius.

"Well, it only seems fitting," replied Beggar, "after all, they are my children!"

Adrian interrupted, "We said earlier that none of this could exist without our friends the animals but that was really only half the story. Without their help, we never would have defeated Zepallo and the Dark Forces, when they invaded the island."

Beggar chimed in, "Oh that was a lovely battle, they kept coming and we kept driving them back! The best part was the duel between Adrian and Zepallo, a hundred feet in the air over the ridge, amid thunder crashing and lightning bolts crackling across the sky. It was so spectacular that everyone on both sides stopped fighting just to watch!"

Coke turned to Adrian, "Is that true?"

Adrian nodded but Alius spoke, "Yes, it's true. No one else has ever defeated the Dark Lord. That's why he brought his clones to Washington to try them out on Adrian. He wanted to see whether three of him could overcome his enemy."

"Good thing you got there when you did," inserted Adrian.

"I saw that," said Coke. "I was in the car with your parents when you flew off over the Potomac. I couldn't believe what I was seeing, let alone the rest of your friends materializing out of thin air and then the fighting over the reflecting pool. If I hadn't known what was really going on, I would have thought that it was being filmed for some futuristic action movie! We all thought you were dead, when you fell out of the sky. Your mother was inconsolable."

"I know. She hates it when I have to go on one of my missions. She even asked me not to fight that day but I really had no other choice."

"Your parents love you very much and I know that they're proud of you, just as your grandfather was…and with good reason."

"Thank you," replied Adrian, "but this lesson is about the animals. I just wanted you to understand this part of the magic of this island. I wouldn't have believed it, if someone had told me about it…you just have to see it and experience it for yourself."

Coke looked around at the animals surrounding them, "I believe."

"Good, because we need to get going. How much time to do we have left?"

The attorney looked at his watch, "Oh, about two and a half hours, three if we stretch it."

Alius stood up and spilled the contents of the wicker basket on the rocks for the animals, but Coke and Beggar both grabbed a cookie. "Okay, let's get going."

The noisy menagerie escorted them along the path to the edge of the forest, where they stopped to say goodbye. Daphne brushed her muzzle against Coke's chest, "I hope that you can come again, when there's more time. There's so much magic here for you to see."

"I'd love to come back and I'd like to bring my wife. She'd love you."

They walked out of the shelter of the forest into the cold blustery afternoon. The sun was struggling to break through dense clouds, as they climbed into the wagon and headed north along the bluffs overlooking the ocean.

"Where are we going next?" asked Coke.

"To the dome," replied Alius. "There's another island, like this, in the Pacific and the people who live there inhabit domes they've built under the sea. In some ways, they're more advanced than we are and a group of them are here, helping us to build our first domes."

They rolled down a rocky road to the beach and pulled to a stop at the mouth of a large cave. Adrian and Alius led Coke into the cavern, down a winding tunnel, and into the first dome with the open view of the ocean surrounding them. Classrooms clustered in the curve of the land side of the sphere and the tunnel to the interface, opposite, dropped off beneath the sphere of glass.

Adrian waved at the classrooms, "This is one part of our school. The old school is up on the ridge, on the other side from where we landed earlier."

"This is amazing," said Coke, as he stared through the depths outside the enclosure. Swarms of fish glittered in the flickering sunshine filtering down through the water. They walked over to look through the window, just as a group of divers encased in silver bubbles flew past.

"Were those divers?"

"Yes, the people on the Island of the Children developed those diving suits. They allow you to move at high speeds and to work at almost any depth," replied Alius. "Come on, we'll introduce you."

The divers were emerging from the water, as they entered the chamber, and Coke stopped to gawk at the wall of water suspended at the other end of the interface, "How is that possible?"

"There are a lot of things that seem impossible until you begin to understand the science of the Powers."

Soule and Amy pulled off their helmets and hugged the two *seers*,

"When are we going to get you back to diving?"

"Well, I'm almost back to normal," said Adrian. "But we have a little situation going on."

"That's sounds normal," laughed Amy.

Alius introduced Coke to the diving instructors and found that Travis was one of the other divers. "Pleasure to meet you," said the trawler captain.

"Does everyone on the island dive?" inquired Coke.

Soule smiled, "Yes, almost everyone has been certified and fitted with their own suits. We can use all the help we can get, old, young, big, small, it doesn't matter. In neutral buoyancy, even little people can maneuver heavy objects. We were just laying out the markers for the next dome."

"This is fantastic," smiled Coke. "I'd love to learn."

"Well, Sara's little shop is still set up. She could fit you for a suit!" said Soule.

Adrian interrupted, "He's only here for the afternoon and we still have to go by the observatory. Hopefully, we'll get him to come for another visit soon."

"I'd like that," replied the attorney.

They walked back through the tunnel out onto the beach, and motored north, through fields still lush and green in spite of the cold weather and a dusting of snow, to the observatory.

～

Duties elsewhere demanded Zepallo's attention but he could not, would not leave in the final hours before the next generation was born. Standing bare-chested before the Black Crystal, his head thrown back in a primal howl, his arms extended as if he was about to embrace the giant whirling gem, while absorbing the power pouring through the chamber, energy that would roast a normal man from the inside out.

That dark, sinister laugh echoed through the rushing wind, "My seeds are sown and soon there will be thousands…perfect replicas growing, learning, and dedicated to the cause!" His dark eyes blazed and his thin lips twisted into a snarl, "Our time is coming, centuries of struggle are nearing fulfillment, and the goal of our ancestors is within my reach!"

Lowering his arms with a long sigh, he spun on his heel, swirled his black cloak around his body, and strode through the lock that sealed the grotto. His aide, Regis, was standing at attention outside and bowed, as the Dark Lord emerged. Having been within the inner circle of the *Dark Seers* for many years, he witnessed his Master consuming the energies of the Crystal countless times and learned not to look directly into his eyes after these sessions. The power was overwhelming, frightening, and Zepallo could control everything and everyone around him with just a thought...a look that could stop your heart, see into the depths of your soul, know your innermost secrets and your most primitive fears. There was no chance of hiding anything from him or denying his most outrageous command.

Since the Elders, who briefly held him check, died in the command submarine, during the invasion of Morgan's Knot, Zepallo was visiting the Crystals with increasing frequency and his personal powers were growing, his sense of destiny fanatical, and his dominance of the legions of Dark Forces had become absolute. No one dared speak against him, to do so was an invitation to a brutal and humiliating death. There had been several recent examples...hideous, disgusting, certainly too ghastly to describe.

"It's time to call the Whisperers together again. One week from today. Our annual conference is long overdue and there is much to be done. This time of peace is about to run its course. Young Adrian and his friends have disrupted our short-term plans over the past year and a half but, in each case, they didn't affect our long-term progress. We've built too many centers throughout the world and our technology is moving ahead at a stunning pace. What does Cadeau report?"

Still staring at the floor, Regis replied, "The filters seem to be working as predicted. We're drawing power from the vectors to each of our facilities throughout the world, without actually connecting the vectors into a traceable web. The Keepers of the Light Powers will never be able to detect the changes that are being made. The engineers are working on the second phase of the project, while the linkage continues to expand. We have the ability to transfer large masses of energy from one base to another and, over the next few weeks, our system will expand to allow those charges to be focused at any point on the Earth."

"It has always amazed me that *seers*, Light or Dark, can use the vectors to travel to any destination on the planet. We've used them to power our facilities, control the weather, facilitate untraceable communications, listen to the secret messages of the governments of the world, yet we could not master this power for its ultimate purpose! Our first demonstration of these powers drew international attention but never quite reached the target. Perhaps, this time, we should come up with something that will demand their immediate capitulation. Something monumental!"

Regis knew better than to venture a guess, "I'm sure you have the vision."

"Oh, I do and, when the time is right, we'll begin to prepare. In the meantime, we're within hours of our new beginning. Are the nurseries complete?"

"Yes, everything is ready."

"Are they staffed?"

"Seventy-five nurses are trained and standing by. Their accommodations surround the nurseries in the new pod. We have three-dozen physicians on call for the deliveries and examinations. Nothing has been left to chance. Everything that can be done to ensure the health of the infants is in order."

"Good. Anything less might result in…repercussions."

"Will there be anything else?"

"Yes, where are Beta and Gamma?"

"They're in hydrotherapy, Sire. Shall I summon them?"

"No, that will be all."

Regis backed away, his head still bowed, and hurried through a tunnel to the new pod to recheck the preparations. Zepallo walked to a window-wall and stared out into the blue-green ocean. The coral reef glowed in the sunlight, sea fans swayed in the gentle current, and schools of colorful fish flashed in and out of the shadows. *"The real world exists in the sunlight,"* thought the Dark Lord, *"but our shadow is growing longer and, soon, there will be no place to hide."*

He consciously avoided forging an invasive bond with the boys, instead, he allowed them limited access into his consciousness until they opened those secret sanctuaries to him. This was the prime moment to test the special connection with his offspring and empower their personal network. Certainly, he mastered the ability to use the power of his mind to dominate, dismantle, and overwhelm his adversaries but this was more subtle. If they were truly a part of him, then they ought to be able to sense his wishes, see his visions, and respond to his will without hesitation, even at a distance. Focusing on their images, their auras, he visualized the library. "Come…"

He followed the curved hallway around to the west, into a tunnel to the triplets' pod, passed through the gymnasium, and entered the library, with its stacks of books, large *messengers* floating above comfortable chairs equipped with the latest control devices…gloves, and monocles that could direct the information being displayed or the actions being taken.

No one was in the room, until Beta and Gamma entered behind him and Alpha appeared a moment later, hobbling on crutches.

"You called us?" inquired Gamma.

The Dark Lord's lips barely curled at the corners, "Yes, I did."

~

The old wagon rumbled to a stop beneath the crooked finger of rock pointing to the sky. Coke looked up and shaded his eyes, "Is that an observatory on top?"

"Yes. The Professor teaches our class on astronomy and we get to make observations," said Alius. The sun was beginning to fall into the ridge and the shadows were growing long, "If we're going to get you back in time, we'd best hurry!"

They scampered up the steps and into the parlor without

knocking. The attorney, like everyone else, stopped just inside the foyer to gaze in wonder around the room. The walls of books, the skeleton, the solar system, and all of the other bits and pieces brought out the wizard in everyone…or at least that secret wish to be a wizard…even in adults.

Ester walked through the dining room to greet them, "You must be Mr. Tierney, I'm Ester, Professor Ponte's wife, and I'm so pleased to meet you."

"It's nice to meet you," he replied, as her shook her hand. "This is a most extraordinary room. It's…enchanting."

"There's a bit of mischievous little boy in all of you isn't there?"

Coke smiled, "I believe that you are an observant woman."

"I have to be to stay two steps ahead of that genius," hookingher thumb over her shoulder. "I'd have no chance otherwise!"

She turned and led them through to the elevator and down to the white room. Coke stopped again, as he exited the little car and stared at the white walls curving into floor and ceiling surrounding the Golden Crystal, which was whirling at a moderate rate, certainly more slowly than the last time that Adrian entered it.

"Oh, my…?"

"This is our power source. There are many of these scattered around the planet," said Adrian. "For every positive, there is also a negative. The Black Crystal is inside the mountain and it's being used, in conjunction with this Crystal, in a positive way. The Dark Forces are using many of the other Black Crystals to power their operations, their communication, the weather, to monitor all information that's being passed from one point to another in the real world, and to allow their *seers* to move about the planet. Just as we passed through the plane of the animals, they have at least one and probably several they use for their purposes."

"This is the ultimate power in the world. As long as they're in balance, we have a chance," said Alius.

"I wouldn't have believed it…" murmured the attorney.

"No one could without being introduced to all of this. Sure, there have been myths and legends for centuries about the Light and the Dark, Black Crystals and Gold, or Green, or Red Crystals. The ancient stories of wars between man and the Gods, between one deity and another…they just neglected to include the fact that it wasn't fiction, it was fact."

"Now I understand what your grandfather was trying to tell me. I couldn't help but doubt his tales until he died as he predicted. I hope you understand that he was not murdered simply to draw you out into the open. He was killed because of the work he was doing and the information he had collected."

"No one else said that to me, but I guess I knew," said Adrian, sadly.

"He was so excited when your father arrived and confirmed his suspicions about you. That allowed him to hope that you would carry on his legacy, that there was someone within the family, who would understand and continue."

"But how did he know?"

"I have absolutely no idea. He just did."

"I'll wonder about that for a long time," sighed Adrian. "Come on then, we need to introduce you to the Professor and our friends."

Coke walked closer to the spinning gem and leaned down to touch the shallow dunes of gold dust on the floor, "It really does produce gold?"

"Between that and the black diamonds we collect from the Black Crystal, we have money to purchase anything we need for the island and to send the children to universities, when it's their time. The gold dust has been collected for hundreds of years. It seems to be a byproduct of the energy produced by the Crystal. Ponte's tried to explain it to me but even I don't understand what he's talking about and I have a PhD in chemistry!" laughed Ester.

They walked past the workshop and into the computer room. Ponte turned to shake the attorney's hand, "I am so glad to finally meet you. John's told us so much about you! And not all of it was good!"

Coke smiled, "I have to say that I've heard similar descriptions of you, sir."

Everyone laughed and Ponte clapped him on the shoulder, "Of course you know John, and this is Mary, a *seer* from the Island of the Children, and their Keeper, Dadeus. This is Simian, who's obviously from Jamaica, and his nephew, Sammy, who's in training to become a Keeper. He's already far ahead of me with computers, as is Raffe, another *seer* from the Island of the Children. And, of course, Sky and Master Chi, *seers*, both. They're here to guide us in our quest to understand cloning."

Coke shook everyone's hand and stopped at an arched keyboard in front of the giant screens, where Raffe and Sammy were controlling the searches. "I see that you managed to put it back together and make it work!"

John walked up behind them, "Well, I have to admit that I had very little to do with making it work, although I did take good notes on how we took it apart, so getting the right pieces in the right places was not particularly complicated. The rest of it leaves me in utter bewilderment."

"I understand what you mean," replied Coke, as he turned back to the screens. "What are you looking for?"

"At this point, we're running basic, low-level searches to see if we can begin to understand the flow of money and, at the same time, looking at the placement of their representatives and the positions they occupy," replied Dadeus. "We don't understand the entire system, so we're trying to learn it one piece, one function at a time."

"John told us about the inheritance and, I'm assuming that Adrian has convinced you to join us, which means that you'll need a list to begin building a financial empire that might frustrate our adversaries," said Ponte. "I believe that Raffe and Sammy have that information for you."

The young Jamaican elbowed Raffe in the ribs, "It's an interesting list, far from complete, but certainly broad enough to give you an overview of what they're trying to do. Obviously, neither of us understands anything about the world of finances but we keep finding interesting mixes of investments."

Raffe interrupted, "Yeah, like lots of armament manufacturing, defense contractors, aerospace, pharmaceuticals, petroleum and minerals…and diamonds in particular, agriculture and food processing, financial institutions, and the odd one…a toy company. We don't quite understand that one. The list goes on and on, country by country. It's endless and very incomplete…but it's a place to start."

Sammy walked over the printer station and withdrew a folder with several hundred pages of information, which he handed to the attorney, "We'll have more for you in a few days."

Coke leafed through the volume, "This will take some time to decipher."

"It's all collated and cross-referenced," said Raffe.

Mary grinned, struggling to conceal her pride and amazement at how far her young charge had come, since he descended from the surface of the Island of the Children, where he and the other children lived like animals. His formal education had only started a little over a year ago but he was racing through his lessons and their practical applications and already knew far more than she might ever learn about these computers.

"Give us a couple of weeks and we'll be able to provide far more useful information," said Dadeus.

"There is one thing that we came across that might interest you, Adrian," said Sammy, as he punched in a code.

"A photograph of Ambassador Anthony Robbins appeared on the screen with complete documentation on every facet of his life and his career as a diplomat for the Canadian Government. Next to the photograph appeared a series of poorly lit candid shots of Lord Robbins and Zepallo in deep conversation. In the final shot, Zepallo was holding up the stump of his right hand.

"Those were taken right after our battle, when Zepallo kidnapped my mother! Robbins was the one who asked me to talk to the president and set up the speech at the United Nations! I can't believe it! We even showed him the Golden Crystal in New York!"

Raffe replied, "Yeah, I thought he wasn't quite as awestruck as everyone else, when they first see a Crystal. It didn't feel right."

"Why didn't you say something at the time?" inquired Alius.

"Because, you all seemed so sure he was a good guy, so, I thought I was just being paranoid...until I found his file in the computer."

Adrian suddenly heard the words of his three-hundred-year old self, *"...as you will learn, the Dark Forces are layered like an onion, as deep as the sea, and more sinister and evil than you might ever imagine. Their tentacles reach into places that will truly astonish you."* He had certainly been right about that.

Master Chi said, "There's another part to this challenge, which we would like to share with you, if there's time?"

Adrian and Alius looked at each other, "We have about thirty minutes before we'll need to start back."

"Then come along," said Sky, as she led the group to the elevator.

They jammed into the little car and zoomed to the observatory and, once again, Coke stopped in his tracks to take in the giant telescope pointing up into the slot in the curved ceiling. "You weren't kidding about your astronomy lessons. I'd love to be in your class!"

Ponte laughed, "It's certainly an entertaining lesson and the children do seem to enjoy it!"

Sky led them to their worktables and the *messengers* that were lined up along the far wall. "While our friends, downstairs, are working on the files and information that Sir Jonathon collected, we're investigating the capacity of the Dark Forces to clone Zepallo."

"Obviously, they've succeeded with the three clones who attacked Adrian in Washington. After an initial look at the process of cloning, we began to dig deeper into the probabilities, the statistics of the operation," said Dadeus.

"And it is our conclusion that those three were probably the only survivors in their first batch," added Ester.

Coke interrupted, "You said 'first batch'...?"

"If they can get three out of however many on their initial try, they're certainly going to do better on their second trial."

"We believe that they'll soon have the ability to produce hundreds, if not thousands of clones in a regular cycle," said Sky. "The only major constraint will be housing and caring for infants, that takes trained personnel and facilities."

"Someplace on the planet, they're building a very large lair to house this operation but we haven't found it yet," inserted Ponte. "And we can be assured that the reconnaissance of the world powers will be blind to it, just as they can't see Morgan's Knot."

"There's one more interesting bit, that we've found over and over in the experiments that have been conducted in the real world, and it's that the growth rate of the clone is much faster than that of a normal mammal. There's a very good chance that the young men, we fought against, were only four or five years old!" said Sky.

Stunned, Adrian could not speak for a moment, "So you're saying that those clones will be fully grown men in another few years and the next batch that comes along will be ready for battle a few years after that?"

"That's exactly what we're saying," replied Sky.

Coke paused, "This is all far more frightening than I might have imagined, even with all my conversations with Sir Jonathon. There really is a war going on and the rest of the world is totally oblivious…and now they're producing dark princes!"

"That's what we've been trying to make you understand," replied Alius, impatiently, "It's the Light against the Dark…literally."

"You saw a glimpse of it during our confrontation over the reflecting pool. You were reminded again of the political and economic potential, when the New Coalition threatened the balance within your world."

"And your reply was the march of the children and the animals!"

"That's right…the Light and the Dark. That's why we need your help to represent us in the economic, political, and legal world that you live in."

"I'll be more than happy to help in any way I can," replied the attorney. "The old man knew what he was talking about, when he said that this was the most evil adversary he'd ever faced and that you are the only ones who stand a chance to defeat them. I understand the stakes."

~

Coke sat with his wife, Martina, in a dimly lit French restaurant not far from their home in Georgetown. They lived a comfortable life and dined out often but they only came to this establishment, with small booths, candles on linen covered tables, and a feeling of privacy, when there was something personal that needed to be discussed.

Martina could not help but notice the smirk on her husband's face, "What's going on? Why did you bring me here?"

"Because there's something that we need to talk about," replied Coke.

"What's that?"

"Well, I'm giving up all of my clients…except one."

"You're doing what? The partners will never put up with that! Besides, you're the manager of their farm team, you bring in all the young talent."

"Then I'll quit and open my own office. I've already submitted my letter, so we'll have their reaction on Monday."

"Obviously, there's a back story to this sudden…change of heart."

"You might say that," laughed Coke.

"Come on, you're driving me crazy with this! Tell me what happened."

"You remember Adrian, Jonathon's grandson?"

"Yeah, the kid flying across the Potomac, fighting dark figures in mid-air, and falling out of the sky into the reflecting pool. How could I not?"

"That's the one. Well, he and his friend, Alius, materialized in my office this afternoon to talk about his inheritance."

"How much is it?"

"A billion dollars…give or take…"

She whistled softly, "That's a lot of money for a boy of his age, even if he is rather extraordinary."

"He doesn't want it."

"What do you mean, he doesn't want it?"

"I spent the afternoon on Morgan's Knot, with a brief introduction to the magic of the Crystals and a challenge that threatens the entire world."

"Where is Morgan's Knot?"

"I don't know. It's in the northern Atlantic somewhere."

"How did you get there…and back in one afternoon?"

"They took me through the vectors."

"What vectors?"

"Do you remember, after Adrian was injured, how the other *seers* gathered around him and Sara…and they just disappeared?"

"Yes."

"Well, the other *seers* took them through the vectors back to Morgan's Knot, where he'd be safe."

"I don't understand. What are you saying?"

"I'm saying that there's another dimension that exists in the same time and space as this world. It's existed for thousands of years and no one, at least not normal people, ever suspected. They live a very simple life on an island in the middle of the ocean. The whole place is powered by a giant Crystal and the animals are an integral part of their existence. I met a unicorn in the plane of the animals. I sat in a forest and had a conversation with a bear and I visited an immense undersea dome that will soon be one of many. I watched divers race through the water with the speed and grace of some mythical aquatic creature. I'll tell you all about it but the point is that Adrian wants to use his money as a weapon against the Dark Forces and I've volunteered to help him. Nothing else is as important."

"You're serious about this, aren't you?"

"I am."

"What about retirement and your pension and all that you've tried to do for the firm?"

"It just doesn't matter anymore, I could quit tomorrow and we'd be alright. I've seen something that I can do to help in this war and, as Adrian says, I have no other choice."

"I guess your mind's made up."

"It is."

"Will this be dangerous?"

"Yes, I think it will and that's why I want you to understand what I'm trying to do and why we'll have to make some changes in the way we live."

"You want to move to Morgan's Knot."

"Well, someday maybe. but right now, there's too much work to be done here. I will say that, even though they don't have restaurants or fancy shops, you'd love it there. It's a model for the way things should be. I wish you could have been with me, you'd love Daphne."

"Who's Daphne?"

"She's a doe and she's sweet on me."

"Oh, you old charmer, you think all the girls are in love with you!"

"Just so you are."

Martina's beautiful eyes sparkled in the candlelight, "I am."

Chapter 8

Nanchez had been noticeably absent for the few days leading up to the attorney's visit. The Professor had spoken to him on the *messenger* several times, in their strange language of incomplete sentences and bits of thought and formula, but said nothing to anyone else in the observatory. Everyone was busy with the tasks at hand and they all assumed that he was attending to another piece of the puzzle they were trying to solve.

The bear of a man stood before the Black Crystal in the bowels of the mountain. A large black diamond, suspended from a golden chain that Ester provided, protected him from the intense energy streaming from the whirling rock. He eyed it like a matador facing a raging bull, as if he could will secrets from the cold stone, and paced back and forth, his heavy boots crunching through the diamond dust on the floor of the chamber, deep in thought, mumbling to himself.

He had not slept in days, instead confining himself to the workshop and his instruments. Since North and South had united, he and Ponte struggled and then succeeded in taming and merging the energies of the two Crystals, balancing the power requirements of the island, and creating a smooth network of vectors.

Several times recently, he noticed fluctuations in the power being drawn from the Black Crystal. The previous year, the Dark Forces attempted to connect all of the dark vectors to create the largest power supply on the planet and they would have succeeded, had not Adrian and his friends linked the nodes of the Positive Crystals and frustrated their efforts.

No, this change was far more subtle, energy being drawn from the vectors in small but continuous surges, and he found no way to trace it to a destination. It was almost as if the vectors were leaking, like a faucet slowly dripping one drop of water at a time into a bucket. At first, it seems inconsequential but, after a while, the bucket is full to overflowing.

The system was losing energy but he had no idea of where it was going…or how. The Black Crystal was not going to offer a solution to his problem but this enigma bore the fingerprints of the Dark Forces and, if they were siphoning energy from every Black Crystal on the planet, they were going to use it for something…monumental. The question of 'what' frightened him for, as a Keeper, he understood the potential.

He turned and walked to the giant metal doors, unlocked them, exited, and relocked them, before marching slowly down the hall. It was not as if they could stuff it in a bottle or charge up a giant battery to contain it, until they released it for whatever purpose. Intuitively, he knew that they had created a technology to harness the powers in a new way and the Balance depended on discovering their method.

~

Adrian sprawled on the floor of the girls' bedroom in front of the *messenger*. This had been his longest day since his injury and, after depositing Coke back in his office in Washington, he and Alius had returned to the island long after sundown, his mind and body exhausted.

The girls were required to watch the evening news for Mrs. Hammon's class and Adrian tried to join them every night to see what was happening in the world.

Tonight, the beautiful blond newscaster was not wearing her usual smile. "Today the children's campaign for peace came to an end. We have reports of terrorist bombings in Moscow, London, Tel Aviv, Bali, and New York. The calm in Central Africa gave way to a new wave of tribal conflicts and observers in the area report massive attacks, which have resulted in thousands of casualties. Iran, Algeria, and Argentina have stopped all shipments of oil and the stock markets around the world closed significantly lower."

"We will have reports on each of these stories in a moment, but, first, an unusually late hurricane has developed in the Gulf of Mexico and forecasters tell us that it is threatening to move onshore somewhere between New Orleans and the Texas coast. Residents have been put on high alert and should be preparing to evacuate. All of the offshore oil platforms are being shut down and evacuated. We'll return with a more thorough look at these stories in a moment."

"Does this mean that the children's campaign has failed?" asked Molly.

Adrian groaned, "No, it means that the grown-ups haven't grasped the message. It will take time to teach them that there really is another way, a path that benefits everyone. They don't want to give up their fear…and fear has always been an excuse to fight or kill to protect their homes or their families, their tribe or their country. The world took a giant leap forward, when the children marched and, now, we've taken a step backwards."

"Do you think the Dark Forces are responsible for any of this?" inquired Megan.

"Of course," replied the tired *seer*. "The battle never ends. It ebbs and flows from fearsome conflicts to something resembling peace…but it's never reached a point where either side wins and the other loses. At least, it hasn't in the past several thousand years. Perhaps it'll happen in our lifetime but I wouldn't count on it."

"That's not what I wanted to hear," replied Megan. "Why can't the elders of the world figure this out, when the children can see it so clearly?"

"Maybe if all wars were fought by old people, instead of youngsters, there'd be an end to it…but that's not going to happen either."

"What's happening at the observatory?"

"Well, the work's being done by teams. One group is researching cloning and trying to figure out where the Dark Forces have installed a gigantic incubator to grow the embryos. The other group is going through information that my grandfather accumulated on the computers my father brought back with him. Now that I think about it, no one's seen Nanchez in several days. I'll have to ask The Professor about that tomorrow."

"What about the attorney?" asked Molly. "We really wanted to meet him. I tried to talk Mom into getting us out of class in time but she wouldn't do it."

Adrian smiled, "You'll like him. He's very intelligent and offered to help manage the money that was left in the inheritance. He's also very funny."

"Funny, ha, ha?"

"Yeah, he was like a little kid around the animals and totally in awe of the dome, the observatory, and especially the Crystal. I think he'll become one of us, before he realizes what's happened."

Molly blushed, "I hate to ask but how much was your inheritance?"

Adrian started laughing and couldn't stop. It had been days since he last laughed and, although it made his head hurt, it warmed him, releasing the frustration that he had been carrying around like a heavy sack across his back. "A billion dollars."

"Say that again!"

"You heard me…a billion dollars…and Mr. Tierney says that it will earn somewhere around a hundred million a year!"

"What are you going to do with all that money?"

"I'm not. I told him that I don't want it."

"You what?" exclaimed the twins together.

"Yeah, I told him that I wanted him to use it to help fight the Dark Forces. The information my grandfather collected shows that Zepallo has massive holdings in corporations all over the world and even people who live in our world can understand what that means."

"It means that he has another way to dominate and control the world," whispered Molly.

~

Nanchez looked dreadful, as he stumbled through the front door of the observatory. His mane of white hair was matted and greasy, his dark bloodshot eyes surrounded with clouds of gray, and he stooped, unable to stand erect. He was a ghost of the huge powerful giant they all revered.

"What's happened to you?" exclaimed Ester, rushing to steady him. "You look terrible. Come and sit down by the fire."

"I'll be fine," sighed the Keeper as he crumpled into the sofa near the fireplace. "I'm just tired, that's all."

"You're more than tired. When's the last time that you slept?"

Nanchez ran his fingers through his hair, as he considered the question, "I'd say three or four days ago but I'm really not too sure…"

Ponte waddled through the dining room, "What's happened to you?"

Ester piped up, "He's not slept in three or four days and he won't tell me why!"

"I've been working on the vectors," said Nanchez slowly. "They're leaking."

"They're what?"

"They're leaking energy and I can't figure out where it's going."

Ponte hesitated, "Which vectors?"

"The black vectors."

"Is it like the last time?"

"No…they've learned a new trick. They're taking energy from all of the vectors individually, without connecting them together. It's subtle and smooth. If I hadn't been paying attention to the monitors, I might never have noticed."

"So, there's a third piece to the puzzle - the money, the clones, and the energy. The question becomes…what are they going to do with all of these…assets?"

The door opened and Adrian followed Alius in from the cold winter morning. "Have you seen the news? It's starting."

Ponte turned to the *messengers* that were lined up in the dining room and said, "News!" The monitors jumped to life.

The center *orb* carried the international news. A very good-looking man with dark hair was teamed with a tall blond woman with large hair and giant blue eyes. They traded lines and stories with smooth polish. "In the headlines this morning, tribal rivalries in Central Africa exploded into slaughter, as millions of innocent people fled their homelands and thousands have died in the conflict. Authorities are coordinating their investigations into bombings in London, New York, Moscow, Bali, and Tel Aviv and unnamed sources tell us that they believe the incidents are related."

"Hurricane Victoria has slowed but it's gaining strength over the heated waters of the Gulf of Mexico. It has developed into a category four storm with winds of one-hundred and thirty miles per hour near the eye. The cloud mass stretches from Florida to Mexico with bands of thunderstorms moving counter-clockwise along the western coast of Florida, across the panhandle, through the coastal lowlands of Alabama, Mississippi, Louisiana, and Texas. Again, she seems to be standing still, deciding which way she'll move next, and gaining strength in the meantime. Authorities have urged residents of the coastal areas to move inland and a mandatory evacuation will be put into effect as soon as the forecasters can predict where the storm will move next."

"Adding to the concerns raised by yesterday's announcement that Iran, Algeria, and Argentina have halted exports of oil, all of the oil rigs in the Gulf of Mexico have been shut down and evacuated, as well as the large refineries that are clustered along the coast. Prices for crude oil rose sharply with the opening of the market."

"With this sudden change in the climate of the world, we turn to Jenny Chin, our Washington correspondent, for more on the political ramifications," droned the man with the dark sparkling eyes.

The blond newscaster said, "Jenny, with the election only weeks away, how do these stories impact the candidates?"

"Well, Barbara, it seems that the voters are not blaming the government for these sudden changes but they will react to how President Bartlett's administration handles these crises over the next couple of weeks. Democratic candidate, Shannon, is still leading by a few percentage points but that lead could grow or shrink, depending on how events unfold. His opponent, Charles Atwood, has accused the administration of not stockpiling supplies in advance of Hurricane Victoria's landfall and of mishandling our foreign policies, with regard to the bombings, our war on terrorism, and our role as peacemaker in

Africa. He also called the move by Iran, Algeria, and Argentina a direct result of President Bartlett's complete disregard for sound economic strategy. I should note that the President has a doctorate in economics from Harvard University. If the election were held today, I don't think that any of us could call it. The race is dead even and what happens in the world around us will determine the outcome. I'm Jenny Chin in Washington. Back to you."

"Thank you, Jenny," replied the handsome announcer.

Ponte said, "Quiet!" and the sound from the *messengers* dimmed. The bobbing heads continued talking silently. He turned to the group, "We need to get everyone together and discuss these revelations and decide whether pursuing one avenue is more important than any of the others."

Ester walked over to the *messenger* closest to the living room, "Everyone, would you please join us in the parlor as soon as possible? Thank you."

Within a few moments, the elevator doors opened to unload Sky, Master Chi, and Mary. Then the little car reappeared with John, Simian, Dadeus, Raffe, and Sammy. The group assembled around Ponte and Nanchez.

Ponte spoke first, "Nanchez, tell them what you just told us."

Nanchez rubbed his beard and tried to focus his eyes, "Well, the long and short of it is that that black vectors are leaking energy and I…we think that the Dark Forces are behind it."

There were several gasps and a few murmurs as his observations were digested. The Professor looked from one concerned face to the next, "From a scientific point of view, massing this much energy can only mean that it must be discharged somewhere…either for useful purposes, although I can't think of any that might consume this much power, or for destructive intents."

He let the thought settle in for a moment before continuing, as he waved at the screen of the *messenger* with the silent news anchor yammering away, "We've just seen the headlines and two things seem obvious…the children's peace has come to an end and the winter hurricane that is threatening the Gulf coast of the United States is probably not natural. We'll conduct some tests to be certain, but we've seen this phenomenon before. Dadeus, you're far more advanced with these matters than we are."

"That's true," said Dadeus. "I'll look into it and we'll see how they're powering this storm. If they are behind it, they're far ahead of anything we ever attempted, but we never had access to that much power."

Alius interrupted, quietly, "All of these things are tied together, we just have to figure out what the sum equals."

"That's very astute of you," smiled Master Chi. "We've been researching the clones, while the rest of you have been investigating the information contained on the computers, which leads to individuals, companies, and a money trail. The peace, that blossomed across the planet these past months, has yielded to violence around the globe. Now we add the unusual behavior of the black vectors and this massive hurricane that has appeared out of season. These are like the tentacles of some evil creature and at the center, in the very heart of this monster, sits Zepallo."

~

A fleet of mini-submarines surfaced in the tiny port of Najin, along the coast of North Korea, on a brutally cold, moonless night. Diverse groups of passengers disembarked and boarded sleek black buses with covered windows for a four-hour journey into the mountains. At four-thirty in the morning, they pulled to a stop inside a large cave that had been carefully concealed in the side of a barren crag beneath an overhanging peak to avoid detection from above.

A crowd of one hundred men marched into the fissure to be ferried in sleek elevators, one thousand feet beneath the surface, to the giant cavern carved into bedrock. Each of the Whisperers stopped in awe of the sheer scale of the facility and then the technology that charged the enormous space. Clear bubbles floated from one enormous screen to another as technicians built a web of connections to harness the world's most awesome power.

Regis and Cadeau greeted their guests and guided them to a platform, suspended around the control pod hanging in mid-air at the center of the room. After they were seated and supplied with food and drink, Regis called their attention to the mammoth screen on the far wall.

Drums pounded and trumpets heralded an introduction, as an image of the Earth grew to fill the monitor. It was a night view taken from space and the glow of lights in the cities sparkled, amber gems heralding humanity. Gradually, the lights blinked out, one after another, beginning at the coasts of each continent and gradually moving inland, until only one beacon of glistening illumination remained. It was centered over a small island along the southern chain of islands of Indonesia.

While the Whisperers' attention was focused on the video, Zepallo materialized in front of the screen. "My friends, I welcome you to our destiny!"

He slowly descended to the elevated platform, raising gloved hands to greet his guests. "I'd like you to meet our future!"

Before he finished the sentence, Alpha, Beta, and Gamma materialized around him, each dressed in flowing black robes to match their Master's. They flipped back their cowls to reveal hauntingly pale faces surrounded by manes of long black hair, with icy blue eyes and thin red lips, to gasps from the audience.

"I'd like you to meet my progeny…the next generation!"

Scattered confused applause rose above a current of murmurs.

"Recently, at a newly completed facility constructed safely beneath the sea, seventy-five infants were born. Each of them will be exactly like these young men. Our next group will have a higher success rate and the one after that will provide us with even more. These young warriors, exact copies of your leader, are our future. They will lead the battles, the governments, the financial institutions, and they will move into the hierarchy of every religious institution."

The Whisperers, dumbfounded, stared in utter silence. Finally, someone started clapping, then another and another, until the group was on its feet with an ovation.

"My friends," said Zepallo, as he bowed and lifted his arms above his head, wallowing in the adulation, "great changes are coming to our world. Hurricane Victoria is a minor demonstration…an experiment to illustrate the powers that we have harnessed. The video that we showed you, at the beginning of tonight's entertainment, was not merely a graphic introduction but, rather, a prophesy of doom for our enemies."

Again, the cavern echoed with thunderous applause.

"Although our expedition into international politics has been highly successful, it remains incomplete. The allied nations stand ready to form a third power, as soon as the campaign of the children has run its course, which, I believe, happened several hours ago."

The audience quieted. "Unfortunately, that is not sufficient. Our forefathers fought the Forces of Light for centuries, sometimes moving forward, sometimes working from the shadows. In more recent ages, we created surrogate armies to fight our battles and move civilization in the directions they deemed most appropriate at the time…but never…NEVER have we attempted to control the entire planet through one great campaign!

Our allies in Argentina, Iran, and Algeria have started the sequence. Miss Victoria will inflict massive destruction, when she ravages the oil derricks in the Gulf of Mexico and the refining capabilities in the Southern United States. The fuel that drives the world's economy will become far more precious.

In a few weeks, Noah's flood will reappear. The coastal regions of the world will be submerged. New York and London will resemble Venice, their streets submerged, transportation at a standstill, millions fleeing inland…commerce will cease to exist and, my friends, the lights will go out!"

Again, the one hundred were on their feet.

"We will control the future, when the masses realize that only we can save them, we are the only force on the planet who can bring sanity and order back into their lives. They'll become the faithful, the true believers, because there will be nothing else...no one to show them the way, except you.

My young friends, here, are being trained to take command. Their younger brothers will be battle ready within five years. Because they're not only descended of me but are exact replicas in every sense, they also possess all of my powers, all of my abilities, and we will all be able to hear each other's thoughts, no matter where we are. Think of it, every position of power will be commanded by the same person. There will be no variables, no chance of mistakes, misunderstandings or miscommunication, no possibility of dissension. These young champions will inherit a world that we conquered and re-designed expressly for them, a world where everything is controlled by one mind, with one goal!"

The men leapt out of their seats.

"You'll be given instructions before you leave. When the institutions that you represent founder, you'll be prepared to pick up the pieces to direct the reformation as the leaders of the new world!"

The four dark *seers* bowed and disappeared, while the Whisperers began committing to memory the information and the instructions included on the scrolls that materialized before each of them. There were murmurs and gasps. Several of the men stood and wandered aimlessly, muttering to themselves as they read. No one spoke to or acknowledged any of their comrades.

When they finished, each rolled their scrolls and replaced the black ribbon binding. The parchments rose from of their hands and, when all were accounted for, burst into flames. Before the ashes floated down to the platform, the Whisperers were being moved to an exit. Each had a mission and there was no time to waste.

~

Shambala, Lala, and Maze arrived at the observatory several hours after the revelations had been shared with the group and the two teams split into four, each searching for answers to the questions raised.

Nanchez was prone on the couch, snoring softly, his whiskers fluttering with each breath. His right arm and leg dangled on the floor and his left foot was suspended over the dainty arm of the sofa, which sagged under his weight.

Adrian greeted his friends and ushered them through the dining room into the elevator to meet with the others, before stealing away to sit alone wrapped in a blanket before the sputtering fire. The rest of the group assumed he was still tired and recuperating from his injuries but he knew that, in the rush to find solutions, they were missing something vital and he needed time to think, time to be alone to feel the vibrations and revisit his lessons.

Each of the previous challenges had been one dimensional, while the current situation seemed to have many layers that overlapped like muddy bubbles around Zepallo. The financial maneuverings, the clones, the dark energies, the hurricane, the infiltration of governments, religions, and all the other institutions of power in every corner of the globe…it all added up to a master plan. It was complex but he knew that, at the very core, there was a strategic scheme for Zepallo's singular ambition of world domination. The Dark Lord would forge through minor disasters and incidental defeats, with unwavering focus, until Legio Obscurum ruled the entire planet. The body count would become irrelevant, when their cloning regime could conjure endless regiments of identical killing machines.

Adrian allowed himself to slip into a deep meditation. The smooth pulses, that flowed so easily over the past few months, were disrupted by the grating of the dark powers and the racket was getting louder. Flickering daggers of warm sunshine flashed through angry clouds tumbling across the sky with the fury of those that materialized during the battle over the reflecting pool. He sensed thunder in the distance, rumbling hooves of large animals charging through the heavens to deliver the next wave of darkness.

Animals? No one had considered the animals or all the other tools and weapons at their disposal. Everyone was trying to learn about the data on the computers, the science of cloning, and the energy required to create a monster hurricane. The facts were getting in the way of defining the real threat and mounting a defense.

One portion at a time…first, the hurricane. Zepallo created the hurricane that threatened Jamaica more than a year ago. The beautiful island was not his objective, rather a convenient target to demonstrate his power to the world. *This time he's using the power they're siphoning from the dark vectors but what's the point? What does he gain? What's along the southern coast of the United States? The news reports talked about the oil rigs and refineries!"*

"The question becomes, what does this destruction accomplish? It makes the price of gasoline go up, which makes money for oil companies. It also makes everything else more expensive because it costs more for energy to manufacture things and to move them around. Considering the amount of money in the accounts listed on the computers, Zepallo will make money on every piece of this…but that's not enough. He has a larger goal.

What would happen if there was no oil…none? Everything would stop. Cars, planes, trains, boats, everything! Factories would shut down, farmers couldn't harvest the produce that feeds the world, money would buy survival but not much else, and there'd be panic and fear."

The voice of his older self rushed through his mind, "Fear…with a capital 'F'!"

"When the entire population of the world is afraid, they'll seek protection from the strong. That's it, he'll use the clones as surrogates but, ultimately, he'll use them to run a world of beholden slaves, grateful for being rescued from certain starvation." An overwhelming vision of thousands of Zepallos working together seamlessly in every position of power in every corner of the globe flooded through his mind.

The group was pursuing information but they needed to go back to the source…The Books…the animals…and, if need be, the Crystal. He opened his eyes to find Tic, sitting on the arm of the chair, staring at him. The old cat inquired, "And what were we feeling on this cold afternoon?"

"I was feeling the vibrations. They're being disrupted by the dark energies. I thought about the hurricane and why it was headed for the Gulf Coast of the United States. It's about oil! If he can control the flow of oil, he controls everything! And the clones…maybe they're not for now, maybe all of these other parts of the puzzle are being created so they can be assembled in the future."

"I don't claim to understand even a portion of what you just said but it does occur to me that everyone is running around trying to collect information, instead of looking at all of this from a *seer's* perspective. You are still a *seer*, are you not?"

Adrian reached up and stroked the old cat's ear, "Part of the solution to every problem that we've faced was provided by the animals…and you in particular."

Tic inspected a paw and licked it, "That's true."

"No modesty in your part of the family!"

Tic stopped licking and stared at the young *seer*, "Just see who comes to your rescue the next time you're in trouble." He went back to licking his other paw.

Adrian leaned up and wrapped his friend in a hug. "It always comes back to you!"

~

Hurricane Victoria stretched from the Yucatan peninsula to Tampa, from Havana and Key West to Houston. Sweeping bands of vicious squalls steamed around her perimeter, ignited by a tight little eye hovering over the searing waters of the Gulf of Mexico. Hurricane hunters clocked the winds in the eye-wall at 134 miles per hour but, within the center, a warm column of moisture rose through the calm to feed the furnace driving the storm.

She idled in place for more than twelve hours, while her masters worked from the immense compound hidden beneath the mountain in North Korea, to ensure that the entire population of the planet recognized the significance of their demonstration, because anticipation is an elixir for panic.

Zepallo's face filled one of the giant screens floating against the wall of the huge chamber. The workforce was silent, unmoving, as they listened to their instructions.

"Let the storm fester for another twelve hours and then send her to Houston!"

The workers applauded enthusiastically and spheres flitted about the enormous dome, celestial moths drawn to the radiance of a light in the night.

"Our next demonstration will involve moving our focus to the Black Crystals that surround the Artic pole. The world's scientists are worried about global warming, let's turn up the heat!"

Cheers erupted from the technicians.

"Our facilities have all been prepared, troops moved to strategic locations, and our friends in the real world stand at the ready. When the moment is right, I'll deliver the focal point to the crystal palace and together, we'll create a new tomorrow for the citizens of the world…a future filled with darkness!"

The video panned back to reveal the Dark Lord standing in a sphere suspended above a circular nursery with doctors and nurses attending the seventy-five newest members of the Dark Forces. He held out his arms, "and these new warriors will lead our cause for centuries!"

~

The *seers* sat in a circle on the floor of the observatory with the gold and silver books between them. Alius and Raffe rounded up some blankets to ward off the cold of the evening and Sky brought hot tea and biscuits from the kitchen.

Adrian rubbed the bandage covering the wound on the side of his head, the throbbing a reminder of the threat. "We've all been trying to find answers to questions that relate to but don't really address the problem we must solve. As I see it, Zepallo wants to control the flow of oil and commerce around the world. Economic panic, enhanced by a series of seemingly catastrophic disasters, would allow the Dark Forces to take control."

Raffe grasped the idea first, "The oil production in the Gulf of Mexico must be a huge portion of the output and consumption of the United States."

"And the shipping in and out of the ports, the refineries, and the pipelines that lead to all parts of North America," injected Alius.

Simian continued, "Add to that, the timely announcements by Algeria, Argentina, and Iran that they've ceased all shipments of oil. That's enough to disrupt the markets."

Master Chi observed, "From the information in your grandfather's records, we know that Zepallo controls companies in a vast variety of industries. We must assume that he has major holdings in energy."

Adrian smiled, "You all see what I've been thinking about. By manipulating the movements of the financial markets and creating chaos, he'll gain more control of the message going out through the media and more influence over what people actually believe."

Mary asked, "What about the clones?"

"I think they're for the future," replied Adrian. "If the three we fought are four or five years old, then they'll be adults when they're seven or eight. We have to assume that there are generations of clones being bred to expand their ranks. I think they're the army Zepallo wants to have ready, when they've completed their campaign…thousands of Dark Lords in every seat of power on the planet."

"That's a frightening thought," whispered Alius.

"What do we attack first?" asked Shambala.

"Our own methods," laughed Maze.

"Here-here," giggled Master Chi. "Sometimes, we get so focused on the goal, we forget to pay attention to the path that we should follow."

Sky sighed, "There are many answers but there is only one solution. We must find the correct course."

"Let's go back to the books, to the animals, and to the Crystal, if we have to," replied Adrian. "We need to approach these problems as *seers* because, ultimately, this is about the Powers and survival of The Balance."

Master Chi rubbed the thin white whiskers under his chin, "And we are the only people on the planet, who have any chance of defending the Light."

~

Coke was awakened by the telephone on the bed-stand. He glanced at the clock. Who could be calling at 3:30 in the morning? He picked up the receiver and whispered, "Hello."

"Coke? It's Adrian. I'm sorry to wake you."

"That's okay, what can I do for you?"

"Well, I think we should move heavily into oil. Hurricane Victoria is being directed."

"I understand."

"We haven't figured it all out but we know that our...adversary is planning to manipulate the flow of oil, the markets, and, ultimately, through terror and turmoil, the population."

The attorney pondered the information for a moment, "I'll take care of things on this end. Have you informed your other friend?"

"No, I called you first."

"Do you want me to take care of that too?"

"If you would," replied Adrian quietly. It was strange talking to someone on the *messenger* without seeing their faces. Considering the hour in Washington, D.C., perhaps it was a blessing. He grinned at the thought, "You might call his secretary, Natalie. She could get you through."

"I know her well," whispered Coke. "Call me tomorrow and I'll have more information for you."

"Okay. Bye."

The phone went dead. Martina rolled over, "Who in the world is calling you at this hour? Or should I ask?"

"It's my favorite client. I have to make a couple of phone calls. I'll go down to the study."

His wife reached over to touch his arm, as he rolled out of bed, "You can make your calls from here. It sounds as if this is important and I want to know what's going on."

Coke rolled back into bed, pulled covers up, and leaned over to kiss her on the forehead, "The hurricane isn't natural. Zepallo's trying to turn off the oil in the Gulf to disrupt the markets."

"What do you mean it's not natural?"

"Just what I said. It's man...or *seer* made." He turned on the lamp, put on his glasses, and pulled a small address book from the drawer. Reaching for the phone, he punched in the numbers.

"Natalie? Sorry to bother you at this hour, it's Colburn Tierney. I just received a call from our young friend, who suggested that I should talk to your boss. Now."

"Oh, Coke...forgive me, I'm not quite awake. Did you say that you had a call from that lovely young man I spent a most interesting evening with a couple of weeks ago?"

"That's the one."

"I'll have him call you. At this number?"

"Yes, I'll be awake."

"Me too." She hung up the phone.

Martina was leaning on her elbow, "Did I understand that you just asked to have the President of the United States get out of bed and call you in the middle of the night?"

Coke's eyes twinkled and his face lit up with that cockeyed grin, "Yeah, I guess you did."

"And he's really going to do it?"

"We haven't had time to talk about this in depth but, yes, this is about the survival of the world as we know it. From what Adrian just told me, the hurricane is aimed at the oil production along the Gulf coast. If the bad guys can stop the flow of oil, there will be panic and that will provide them with a perfect excuse to seize power."

"This really is frightening," said the beautiful brunette, as she fluffed her pillows and settled in. "If everything you've told me is true, then I understand why you feel so committed."

"Thanks, I've been worrying about that."

"You'll have to admit that it's kind of hard to accept some of the things that you've been telling me...talking animals, giant crystals, the lot..."

"Have I ever lied to you?"

"Well, there was that one time when you tried to pull off a surprise party but you weren't a very good liar."

"All that money spent on law school and I couldn't even convince you that we were just going out to dinner..."

Martina grabbed a pillow and swung at his head. "I knew there was a reason I was attracted to you in the first place!"

The telephone rang and they both jumped. Coke reached over the lifted the receiver, "Hello."

The familiar voice said, "I understand that you've been talking to a friend of mine?"

"Yes, Mr. President. He asked me to call you."

"Why is it that children don't understand that adults need their rest?"

"I'm not sure whether that boy ever sleeps, Mr. President, but he was rather insistent."

"What did he have to say?"

"He said that hurricane Victoria is not natural...that it's being controlled by those... forces that you discussed and that the ultimate goal was to disrupt the flow of oil."

There was silence on the line, "I understand. I appreciate his...insight. I'll get back to you." There was a click on the line and then a dial-tone.

Martina stared inquisitively, "What did he say?"

"He said that he appreciated the information and he'd get back me."

"That's all he said?"

"Yes. It was almost as if he was being careful...as if someone might have been listening in..."

"I thought that he, of all people, would have secure lines."

"Me, too, but the children on Morgan's Knot told me that the Dark Forces can monitor any communications in the world and I'm guessing that the President is aware of that. I have one more call to make." He dialed the number. "Albert? It's Coke. I know, I know...it's almost four in the morning but I need a favor and I need it now. We have some funds that need to be moved before the opening bell."

Chapter 9

Nanchez slept, half sprawled on the couch, for twelve hours, before Dadeus could stand it no longer and roused him. The giant man sat up slowly and buried his head in his hands, coughed, hacked, and mumbled under his breath that he was seriously contemplating murder, if anyone spoke to him.

Ester brought some tea, which she poured into a dainty cup that was dwarfed in his hand. He devoured an omelet of a half-dozen eggs, a plate full of biscuits and gravy, and a basket of fruits before he raised his head, staring at Dadeus, "Alright, so maybe I won't kill you right now. I might let you live for another few hours, if you prove yourself useful!"

Dadeus wasn't quite sure whether the huge grumpy man was joking or not, "There's too much to do. I've investigated the power they're using for the hurricane and I can see where they're channeling it…but I can't find a single source."

"There isn't a single source, they're drawing power from all of the Dark Crystals through all of the vectors at once, so there isn't a trail! The energy is trickling through millions of tiny streams until they merge at the target"

"Then my next question is whether we could do the same, although opposite, with the rest of the Crystals?"

"Well, the children connected all the nodes last year, so in reality, the light vectors are already set up as a network…we'll have to get with Ponte to see whether we could jam their system. It would mean an awful lot of work to coordinate everything. It could take days…"

"We probably don't have days!" exclaimed Dadeus. "Are you up to going down to the workshop to talk with The Professor? He's been in there with Sammy, muttering to himself, for hours."

The sagging couch groaned as Nanchez stood to stretch like a bear rising from a long winter's hibernation. His white hair was tangled around his dirty face, his clothes were greasy and covered with black diamond dust, and Ester noticed that he was wearing two different boots but said nothing.

"Right then, let's get started."

Sammy sat on a stool at the far end of the workshop, focused on a *messenger* without blinking. It displayed the movements of energy on the dark vectors and, when the instruments were finely tuned, there was a noticeable charge, a thin halo around the filaments of the web. Where the vectors intersected, energy was being passed from one to the next and all of it was moving towards the Black Crystals near the Gulf of Mexico, focused on the eye of the hurricane. Ponte had found no way to trace the control point that was directing the surge.

Nanchez stormed into the workshop and clapped The Professor on the back. Ponte rose from a tangle of wires that connected instruments down the length of the bench pointing to two *messengers*, one, displaying the hurricane from a weather satellite, and the other, the golden vectors. Somewhere in the overlapping systems, there was a way to balance the two but the solution evaded him. Every once in a while, he called to Sammy for a report on the dark vectors but he already knew what was happening.

Although Ponte had theories, he turned an inquiring eye to Nanchez. Dadeus understood the workings of local power systems and the basics of the network of vectors that encased the planet like a shimmering spider web. He could produce storms over the ocean around the Island of the Children and understood far more about life under the sea than The Professor might ever learn...but he had yet to grasp the theory of the balance between the opposing vectors or the triggers that might release opposing energies against each other.

The giant Keeper patted Dadeus on the back, an act of sympathy for his frustration, "I've been through all the calculations, I've reviewed your notes, and I even went to your shop in the mountain to see what you'd found and, although I understand how you reached your conclusions, I still have no idea of how to counteract the flow of energy through their vectors!"

"Then we've reached the same point!"

"The question is how do we construct a circuit to counteract this rush of energy?"

"It's in the balance..." mumbled Nanchez, staring at the *messenger*.

"The way they've got their net organized, it's homogenous, so, no matter where you pour in more energy it all flows downhill to the Gulf..." said Dadeus.

Sammy was watching the *messenger* but listening to the conversation at the other end of the room. He said, very quietly, "Didn't you say that the vectors were leaking?"

Nanchez turned to stare at the young Jamaican, "Yes, that's what I said...it's as if they're leaking...but now we know where the energy is going..."

"But what if you could figure out a way to really make their vectors leak? What if you could draw off some of the energy...make it go someplace else just long enough to disrupt the flow...sort of like water...it wants to go downhill...and when it runs into a dam, it finds a way around it to continue the journey."

Ponte, Nanchez, Dadeus, and Ester all stared at each other, "I think he's on to something!"

"We could start by leaching energy back through our Black Crystal..."

"And I could get my friends on the Island of the Children to set up a similar circuit," added Dadeus.

"We could balance it with the excess energy from the Positive Crystals...but all that energy has got to go somewhere..."

"And we'd best be sure that we don't damage our Crystals in the process," said Nanchez. "We'll be needin' The Books and someone who can read 'em!"

Sammy followed the adults into the elevator, which shot up to the observatory. The *seers* were still gathered in a circle in the middle of the floor around a glowing *orb*, shaggy heads poking out of blankets gathered tight around their bodies against the cold.

"We have a theory about the energy on the dark vectors but we need to ask The Books whether shorting out their system might damage the Positive Crystals," said Sammy.

The *seers* all looked up, "and we think we've come up with some ideas for solving the other riddles too," replied Alius.

~

Alpha, Beta, and Gamma stood before the Black Crystal. Each wore a black diamond, suspended from silver chains around their necks. The capes of their black robes billowed in the whirlwind swirling through the chamber.

"This is the power!" screamed Zepallo, as he held out his arms to the spinning gem. "This is the source for everything we need!"

He spun around to the boys, "You've been schooled in the powers of the Crystals, the vectors, and our systems. Now it's time for you to see one of our other commands and to understand and control the power that drives everything around us. Want a hurricane? A tornado? A tsunami? Our technicians have built a network that allows us to direct this energy to any point on the planet...and that's just the beginning! After years of work, they're about to complete circuits that will allow us to control every power plant on the globe and every communications network and the content of every bit or byte of information that is passed from one point to another...and what will that mean?"

"We control the financial markets," said Gamma.

"And government communications," added Beta.

"And military channels...no one will know whether the messages they're receiving are real or not," laughed Alpha. "And they'll never know where it's coming from!"

"I think you've got it," smiled Zepallo, opening his arms to absorb one last charge from the Black Crystal.

He turned to the boys, "It's time for us to go."

"Where?"

"We'll be visiting North Korea tonight. Tomorrow morning, our hurricane will move ashore and the next phase of our program will begin!"

~

Hurricane Victoria churned through the night, her spiraling arms reaching out to rake the Gulf coast from Key West around to the Yucatan with heavy rains and eighty mile-per-hour winds. Tornadoes, spun up by the rotation of the storm, were dropping out of the heavens and destroying miles of beachfront properties. The eye was less than twenty miles wide and, like a skater pulling her arms to her body to increase the speed of her spin, the winds in the eye-wall were approaching one hundred and forty miles per hour. After rotating in place for more than a day, absorbing heat and moisture from the surface of the Gulf and gaining strength, she slowly started churning north, taking aim at Houston.

The counter-clockwise sweep of the storm pushes a tidal surge miles ahead of the eye, seas could reach thirty feet at low tide, forty or more during high tide. The devastation would stretch from the panhandle of Florida, across the coasts of Alabama, Mississippi, and Louisiana, and into Galveston Bay. The storm threatened hundreds of offshore oil rigs between the eye and the coast, a large number of refineries and harbor facilities that handled forty percent of the imports and exports for the entire country. If she followed her course, the eye would make landfall by sunrise.

~

Adrian and Sky posed questions for the Book of Wisdoms and Alius and Raffe fingered black diamond pendants to ward off the negative energies of the Book of Knowledge, lying open on the floor of the observatory. The *orbs* around the circumference of the room cast a warm glow on the faces of Shambala, Maze, Lala, Mary, and Master Chi, who sat in a circle around the young *seers*. The Keepers wandered back and forth between the *seers* and the *messengers* lined up along the curved wall of the dome, asking technical questions.

Simian sat cross-legged, hovering above a stool near the telescope, ignoring the proceedings. His eyes were closed and his breathing shallow, while he concentrated on the visions that streamed across the vectors. He opened his eyes and exhaled with a 'whoosh' of inhaled air, "They're moving!"

Adrian turned to his Jamaican mentor, "Who's moving?"

"The four dark *seers*...wherever they were, they're moving through the dark vectors to a new location."

"Something's happening! We're running out of time!"

Nanchez turned from a *messenger*, "The storm's moving again. It's heading north-north-west towards Houston!"

Adrian turned to Ponte, "The bottom line is that we're not going to get the answers we need from The Books in time to affect the storm. There's only one way to find the answers in a hurry."

"Are you sure that you're up to it? You still haven't recovered, perhaps one of the other *seers* should take a turn."

"No, I should do this!" snapped the young *seer*, standing to unwrap the bandage around his head and turn for the elevator.

The rest of the troupe followed and, in two groups, moved to the white room beneath the observatory. Alius clung to Adrian's arm, "Are you sure about this? I could go or any of the others. We're all ready to help."

"I know but this started as my battle with Zepallo and his clones. I have to finish it and this is the first step."

~

The Doctor gazed down at the nursery from the command pod that provided a view of all of the activities that were happening around the new generation. Doctors and nurses tended to the children's every need twenty-four hours a day. He watched as the attendants fed, bathed, and nurtured the infants, showing as much affection as any real mother might. They would have every advantage that could be provided, so they could grow to fulfill their duty and their destiny.

They succeeded in producing seventy-five healthy clones. By his latest calculations, the next group would easily double that number and their birthday was less than three months off. He looked out through the glass domes to the construction of additional facilities that were rising out of the sea bed, invisible from the surface and fortified against attack.

The Doctor met, each day, with the team of educators and trainers who were programming an academic, physical, and social course for these new souls. After working with Alpha, Beta, and Gamma, they realized that the personalities of each child were dependent upon external influences that forced the individuals to reach for their strength. Alpha assumed the role of forceful leader, Beta the strategist capable of seeing the broad view of each challenge and reacting with calm calculated assurance. Where Alpha might be a fierce warrior in one-on-one confrontations or lead a battalion of troops into battle, Beta would find a way to win the war.

Gamma controlled the other two through his masterful ability to organize, to put everything into a logical order in an efficient manner. His brothers argued with each other, constantly, but never sought a confrontation with the quiet one or questioned his demands or his insights. In some ways, he was the most frightening of the three, because no one, including his brothers, could decipher his thoughts or his mood. He maintained an internal shield fortified by a deep brooding intensity, ready to spark at any provocation, beneath a calm, efficient manner…a lethal threat and a cold dark promise.

Where Alpha and Beta would grow to guide and lead their forces into battle, Gamma would sit alone in a laboratory and devise a device that would devastate their enemies, a political scheme that would disarm and disgrace the leaders of the real world, or a trap to eliminate the only true obstacle in their path…the Forces of the Light.

The committee decided to expand the concept of team training to include ten groups of three and nine groups of five. They adapted the benefits that occurred as a result of the program to train the first group and wondered whether, by expanding the number in each set, they would find other strengths and personalities that might be useful to the cause.

The Doctor found in Zepallo a fascinating and frightening

persona. Certainly, he was a vital and commanding specimen for his age and his knowledge and powers expanded with each passing year. Before the elders had been lost in the submarine, he was viewed as a loose cannon, an angry egocentric buck, who possessed talents and abilities that amazed and intimidated dark *seers* with far more experience, reason enough to be chosen to provide the seeds for these children.

Within days of their defeat on Morgan's Knot, he consolidated undisputed control over the command in London and eliminated any who might challenge his right to preside over the future of Legio Obscurum. The Doctor witnessed many of the Dark Lord's sessions with the Black Crystals and marveled at his ability to absorb deadly energies, that seemed only to enhance his powers. His influence over the Council of Ollapez freed the scientists and technicians to race ahead with their programs, providing the means to fulfill his darkest wishes and a legacy of conquest passed down through hundreds of generations of his predecessors.

There was also the furious fire in the dark *seer's* eyes, a rage that could peer inside a soul and, with a mere whisper, snuff the life from their bodies. The physician was well aware that his own accomplishments, a scientific feat his colleges could only dream about, provided protection and respect. There would be no Nobel Prize for his genius but he was more than satisfied with the thought that his creations, these dark miracles, would rule the world for generations. His place in history was reserved and his position within the Dark Forces guaranteed, as long as they needed more copies. He had no doubt that the more clones the nurseries produced, trained, and readied, the higher the value of his expertise.

~

Adrian stepped through the hole in the side of the gigantic spinning Crystal and, once again, faced the test of his belief in The Balance and his dedication to preserving the future. The inner surface was whirling around, glowing with a blinding golden brilliance, and the figures, so familiar since his first encounter with The Books and The

Powers, marched in regimented formation. He always felt as if they were watching him or, perhaps, judging him, as if he was too young or not talented or wise enough to use the information The Crystal provided for its most worthy purpose…saving the magic, the hope for the future.

Their history existed since the molten Earth cooled, long before the first creatures crawled from the oceans and humans rose from the jungles of their ancestors, to set about conquering the world. The figures held the secrets of the planet, its history, and its future but they only responded to inquiry, as if demanding that the *seer* know the proper questions to ask to find the insight or solution. They rarely offered advice nor did they reveal their knowledge easily.

The globe appeared, the single continent broke into pieces moving to form the planet, as we know it today. The voice inquired, "It has been many months since our last conversation, how may we help you?"

"The Dark Forces have found a way to harness the powers of the Black Crystals. They've generated a hurricane that will devastate the southern coast of North America and I fear that's only the beginning…"

"You are correct. We sense the powers being harvested and transmitted from one vector to the next in a massive wave of energy far more powerful than anything they have attempted in the past."

"How can we stop them?"

There was silence for a long moment, "You will not stop them…but you might deflect their purpose. The only option is to counter the negative energy with a massive charge of positive energy, applied with meticulous accuracy."

"The Keepers believe that they can disrupt the flow and balance it with energy from the Positive Crystals by using the vectors as a web, connected through the nodes. They're worried that it might damage the Positive Crystals."

"That is entirely possible. They will need to be cautious."

Adrian was frustrated. "How do we stop them?"

"We have discussed these problems in the past and, in each of those cases, what was the most important part of our instructions?"

"To maintain The Balance."

"And so, it is with your current concerns."

The young *seer* pondered the response, "That doesn't tell me what I need to know."

"The Balance has existed for millennia and it will continue, as long as the Dark Forces are not allowed to disrupt the equilibrium. Your Keepers have balanced the Positive and Negative Crystals on this island with precision and care. This is one of the few places on the planet where these forces are being used in harmony. It is simply a matter of expanding those results to a grand scale."

"What about the storm?"

"The storm will continue until the wave of energy has been disrupted and refocused. We believe they will follow this destruction with something even more monumental. They will provide you with a target to receive the excess."

Adrian did not understand his instructions and he was beginning to feel weak. "What about their facilities? They must be directing the movement of the energies from a new lair and we think they're producing clones somewhere along the equator."

"They are fabricating new centers using the power of Black Crystals in many places around the globe. We sense that at least two of the chambers, that were destroyed by your efforts, are being rebuilt with technologies that far exceed their former potential. Use those technologies against them."

"But what about the clones?" asked Adrian. His knees were shaking and his vision blurred.

"You have gained many talents and a unique understanding of The Powers since our first conversation. Go back to the beginning. The tools you need to defend The Balance are the same as those you used during your first campaign. These most basic weapons have been available since the beginning of time. There is no need to reinvent them."

"Thank you," whispered the young *seer*, who listed to his right, the energy completely drained from his body.

"We sense that the time has come to end our conversation for the time being. We will talk again."

The last words seemed to echo from far away, as the hole opened beside him, the intense golden glow faded to darkness, and Adrian lunged through the breach into the arms of his fellow *seers*.

~

Four dark forms materialized at the entrance to the cave in the mountain in North Korea, buffeted by a fierce wind blowing large flakes of snow horizontally through the deep purple glow of the black *orbs* in the arch of the tunnel. It was the only light visible to the horizon as dusk withered beneath a blanket of dark clouds. Four guards snapped to attention and saluted as the Dark Lord led his young charges into the gap.

"Our last visit didn't offer you the opportunity to see or understand the wonders that our people are creating. You'll find that this facility has become the model for others under construction or being renovated. Within a few months, we'll have these technologies installed in more than a dozen fully functional centers around the globe. Within a year, we'll double that number and our powers will be linked together in a network that will dominate the information age."

Gamma spoke first, "That will be an advantage but nothing compared to having each sector managed by one of us. Our training is leading not only to unified systems but a centralized leadership that can be everywhere at once."

Zepallo patted him on the back, "I'm proud of the progress that each of you is making. Tell me, what am I thinking at the moment?"

All three boys smiled. "You're thinking that someday soon, we'll have another shot at the Light Forces, one in particular," said Beta.

"And that I deserve another duel with young Adrian," added Alpha. "I believe that I'll be the elder the next time we meet."

The Dark Lord led them into an elevator that would drop to the dome beneath the mountain, "Part of your training is to teach you to think as they think, a perspective that will allow you to prepare for any opposition they might mount against our efforts. We have to assume that they won't let this demonstration devastate the Gulf coast without putting up some sort of defense. I'm surprised that we haven't seen anything from them before now...but we should expect it! Whether from land or sea or air, they will come...they'll attempt to stop us!"

"There's no way that they could get into this command post!" said Gamma, as they stepped out of the car and stared up at glowing spheres darting around the giant chamber.

The four *seers* floated up to the platform suspended in midair at the center of graceful chaos. Regis and Cadeau, awaiting their arrival, bowed, "I'm glad that you're here to witness the first test of our new technologies!" said Regis to the boys.

"This is only the beginning," added Cadeau. "The technicians here, in New York, China, the Caucuses, and several other commands are preparing for the second phase of this chain of disasters."

"We'll get to that shortly!" commanded the Dark Lord. "Where do we stand at the moment?"

Regis smiled confidently, "As you can see on the monitor, the eye of the hurricane will move directly into Galveston Bay at sunrise local time. Wind speed in the eyewall is just over one hundred forty miles per hour. The storm surge will hit the coast from the Florida panhandle to Galveston at high tide, creating a wall of water approximately forty feet high that will roll inland for miles."

Cadeau added, "The storms in the outer bands have already spawned hundreds of tornadoes from Orlando to Dallas, torrential rains have caused flooding throughout the region. All shipments of goods into the affected ports have been diverted. All production of oil has ceased, the refineries are closed and will, undoubtedly, suffer severe damage, and the pipelines leading to the Midwest and the Northeast have been shut down. At the very least, it will take weeks for a recovery to begin and, perhaps, months before these facilities will be ready to resume normal production. Coupled with our allies' unwillingness to deliver their oil, we must assume that the financial markets will be...disrupted."

The Dark Lord's face twisted into a sinister sneer, "Well done!" He crossed his arms and stared at the spinning tempest climbing the colossal screen for a long moment, before musing, "As I said, I would have expected a bit more resistance than this. Surely the Forces of the Light are aware of what's happening?"

Alpha ventured, "Perhaps they have no defense?"

"Never underestimate the powers of their *seers* or the intelligence of their Keepers!" shouted Zepallo. More calmly he instructed, "It's better to over-estimate their threat and to be prepared. Rest assured, they will respond."

~

Adrian awoke, lying on the sofa in the parlor. His head was throbbing, his arms and legs limp, and his body completely drained. He stared around at the walls of books that reached to the high ceiling and wondered if there were any books worth reading that were not in this library.

Alius appeared above him with a damp washcloth to wipe his face, "How are you feeling?"

"As if a trolley ran over me...several times."

"You were in the Crystal for a long time. We were worried about you."

"I know," he said, taking the cloth press against his eyes. "It was strange. I kept asking questions and it was almost as if I couldn't get a straight answer...but I do know how The Keepers can control the powers."

He looked around the room, "Where is everyone?"

"They're all down in the workshop. The Professor, Nanchez, Dadeus, and Sammy decided that they couldn't wait for you to come around, so they've started putting together the circuits they think will work."

"That's what the Crystal said...that Ponte and Nanchez created one of the only places on the planet where the Black and Light Crystals are working together. The voice said they should just expand on what they already know."

"Great minds think alike!" smiled Alius, as she knelt down beside him. "Are you okay, for a minute, while I go tell The Keepers what you just told me?"

"Yeah, but there's one more thing," added Adrian. "The Crystal also said that the Dark Forces would provide a target for the excess energy."

"That means they're going to do something else. I'll be back!" said Alius, running through the dining room to the elevator.

She had barely disappeared, when there was a knock at the door and John and Sara, Elsie and George, the twins, Morgan, and Kelly walked in, trailing a cold blast. Adrian's mother rushed to her son, "What happened to you?"

"I had to have a chat with the Crystal again."

"I'm beginning to think that I'll never be able to let you out of my sight, without worrying that you'll be injured!"

"I'll be fine in a little while. I have to be, there's too much to do!"

Everyone else crowded around the prone *seer*, who looked from face to face, "What are you all doing here anyway?"

"Well, all of you are hiding away up here and you never come home, so, we had no other choice but to come to you. We've brought baskets of food and we'll help in any way we can!" said Elsie.

"What's happening here?" asked Morgan, with warm concern.

"Well, the hurricane, that's about to hit Houston, is being controlled by the Dark Forces. They've found a way to harness the powers of the dark vectors and they've channeled them to form the storm. The Keepers and everyone else are downstairs working on a circuit to deflect the energy. We've established that they built a new facility to produce the clones, somewhere along the equator, and we suspect that the three that we fought in Washington are sort of the prototypes for many more to come."

Little Kelly's face lit up with her incredible smile, "Why don't you ask the whales to find the clone-house?"

Adrian looked up at her, his mouth hanging open, "Why didn't I think of that? You're brilliant!" He sat up to hug her, felt the blood rush from his head, and took a deep breath to steady himself, "We'll have to talk with Master Chi and Sky and Mary...they're working on the clones and they could tell us where to look first."

Ponte appeared at the elevator and strode into the parlor, "Well, I see we have some new volunteers!"

Elsie gave him a hug, "Well, volunteers bearing hot food and good intentions!"

"We can use both," laughed The Professor, who looked down his nose through his little glasses at Adrian. "Tell me what you learned."

"The Crystal told me that you and Nanchez have created one of the only places on the planet, where the powers of the Dark and Light Crystals are working in harmony, and that you did this with precision and care. It said that the way to balance the powers is just to do the same thing on a grand scale. It also said that the Dark Forces would give us a target for the excess energy."

The Professor pressed a chubby knuckle to his lips, as he pondered Adrian's words, "Alius said that there would be another phase to this and I couldn't doubt her perception. I think we're on the right track."

He turned to leave, already lost in his thoughts, as Kelly said, "What about the clones?"

"Oh, yes," said Adrian. "Kelly suggested that we ask the sea creatures to find the incubator."

Ponte turned back to the group, "What a splendid idea! Very good Kelly! Why don't you come down to the workshop and talk with Master Chi and Sky...and Mary too...they can help with that!"

Everyone moved to the elevator and John leaned over and picked up Adrian.

The son protested, "I can walk!"

"No you can't," said his father, as he carried him to the waiting car.

The Keepers were huddled in the storage room. Raffe was

frantically punching codes into the keypad, opening a pathway to the *messengers*, "I think we've got that program running for you, Professor."

Everyone looked up at the two giant *orbs*, one displayed a satellite view of the hurricane swirling towards Houston and the other the flow of energy across the dark vectors, a faint blue haze rolling through overlapping green curves that resembled daisy petals.

Sky was entranced, "It's almost like a series of waves moving across the surface of a still pond. There's a rhythm to it, a pattern..."

"The filter works! We can see the progression of the powers across their network," commented The Professor. "Now we need to find a drain to pull the plug!"

He rushed out of the room to the workshop, bellowing before he got to the door. A few minutes later, all of the *orbs* got very bright and then dimmed, the back-up systems clicked on with a whir and a hum, and a cheer erupted from behind the closed door of the workshop.

~

Zepallo focused on the progress of Hurricane Victoria on the giant screen suspended on the wall of the enormous chamber, while the clones leaned together, talking in quiet tones as they watched from just behind their mentor.

A hissing crackle preceded the screens blazing brighter and the video fading to fuzz. The Dark Lord turned to his offspring and his grimace transformed into a knowing smile. In a very calm voice he commented, "As I suggested earlier, never underestimate the opposition's propensity to show up at the critical moment!"

Regis cowered and Cadeau spat instructions into a small *messenger* on his wrist. He turned to his master, "It seems that a pulse has disrupted the flow of energy across the web. Our technicians are working on it."

"And what effect will it have on the storm?"

"The hurricane has enough stored energy to complete its task without any additional input from us. It will deteriorate rapidly, once it makes landfall at dawn."

"What of our predictions of damage?"

Regis was still bowed, staring at Zepallo's shoes, "If left to its own powers, it will still inflict, at least, fifty percent of our objective and probably more."

The Dark Lord stared at his assistants, "Then let us begin the second phase of the program. And make sure the technicians find the hole in the network and plug it up! We don't want this to happen again, now do we?"

Regis bowed, "No, master."

Cadeau whispered into his *messenger* and the spheres began to zoom around the dome, with the ferocity of disturbed bees defending a hive. The giant screens flashed with data and graphics, as the technicians began to set up connections for the next assault on the environment.

~

The Keepers rushed out of the workshop, clapping each other on the back, and greeted the rest of the group in the computer room. "We've done it!" laughed Ponte.

Nanchez looked concerned, "Yeah, but we've got a problem with all the excess energy. It's channeling into that cavern in the Southern Atlantic, where that island used to be, but we can't keep that up forever."

Dadeus replied, "They'll find the gap and they'll fill it, but, at least, the storm will weaken. There will be less damage."

"Maybe it will set them back," mused Sammy.

Alius said solemnly, "No, they'll move on to the next target and I'd bet that happens sooner rather than later."

Raffe interrupted, "It looks like they've found your hole."

Everyone turned to watch the messenger displaying the vectors. The blue haze stopped moving towards the dumping site in the South Atlantic and the petals at the center of each cluster twirled like parasols in a strong breeze.

Nanchez walked over and patted Adrian on the back, "How're you feeling? I think we've both spent too much time on that couch!"

Adrian smiled, "I'm better thanks. How about you?"

"Oh, I'm fine...better now that we've got this problem solved for the moment. Did the Crystal give you any idea about what we might expect?"

"No, other than there will be another target. I have a feeling that this was only a test run, to make sure their systems are working properly."

"You're right about that, if we know the Dark Forces, they'll be wantin' to use this to wreak panic across the globe so they can take over."

Morgan and the twins walked over to stand behind Raffe's chair, "Is this the equipment that Sir Jonathon sent?"

Raffe turned and grinned, "Yeah, it's incredible!"

"What does it do?" asked Molly.

"Well, so far we've figured out that it's got a database of people suspected of being involved with the Dark Forces. People in governments, banking, religions, you name it...any place where there is a seat of power or financial center, they've got representatives. It also has a program that watches where money is moving around the world, particularly accounts that he thought were tied to Zepallo. The Keepers managed to wire the machine into the vector system, so we can use it both ways."

"That's amazing," commented Morgan. "How did Adrian's grandfather collect all of this information?"

"Well, from what we can gather, he was the spy's spy. He knew all the secret channels, all the people who made decisions, and all the alliances that only exist behind the scenes," added Sammy. "We're learning about this system but we're just beginning to understand his logic. Eventually, we'll be able to put it to good use."

"It seems like everything is changing in the magical world. The Dark Forces seem darker, even more sinister in what they're trying to do. Now we've got giant computers and lawyers and financial holdings...it isn't just the wonders of The Balance anymore," said Megan.

"That's why we've got to find a way to stop all of this, to put an end to it...at least for the time being," said Adrian quietly. "They're getting stronger, expanding their technologies beyond anything we have, and they're digging deeper into the system."

Elsie almost whispered, "It's all about The Balance, it always has been and it always will."

Everyone turned to look at her. "It seems that it's time to begin an offensive campaign," said Master Chi.

Sky took the twins to find the dolphins, Spot and Dusty. She stood between them, holding hands and levitated them up and across the fields. They landed on the beach, slipped off their shoes, and waded into the shallow surf. Small frosty waves lapped at the sand as the sun peeked over the eastern horizon and splattered the heavens with reds and golds.

Molly and Megan, shivering violently, clapped their hands and smacked the water. Within a few minutes, the two dolphins surfaced and swam into the shallows, "Oh, thank you for coming!" squealed Molly.

"We've got a job for you," said Megan quietly, rubbing Dusty's snout. "Someplace along the equator, the Dark Forces have built a new facility. We need to know where it is and how it's constructed. Could you help us find it?"

Spot and Dusty both clicked rapidly, "Certainly, we'll send a message along the whalemail and let you know as soon as we learn anything. We'll find Travis in the harbor, when there's news."

"Oh, thank you," replied the girls as the dolphins slipped beneath the surface.

Sky stood ankle deep in the frigid water, watching the twins and staring out across a placid ocean. She was reminded of the lessons of her youth, when her teacher, Mantis, taught her to walk across the moat around the temple. It seemed an impossible task but he had convinced her that the only restraint was born of her own fears. All of the *seers* and Keepers were mining their vast knowledge to stop this new aggression and she sensed a bit of anxiety in each of them...not fear necessarily, but doubt about their ability to use ancient weapons to fend off the threat of new technologies.

The Balance existed through thousands of years, with two ancient opposing forces vying for control. Perhaps there was a balance in the equilibrium of the two sides, as long as they followed the path laid down by their ancestors, but now the battle was spilling over to include the financial world, the scientific world, and the real world, where people always found it easier to ignore the possibility that there was more to reality than they could see.

Adrian told the world twice and Zepallo muscled his way into the headlines during his campaigns to disrupt the political world. The children listened and shamed their elders into a time of peace but that could not last. The Dark Forces were pushing for a major conquest against which the real world had no defense, other than the Forces of Light.

Their last battle was merely a skirmish, a test for Zepallo's new clones. They fought well and they would quickly become far more powerful…and soon there would be many more. The future depended on the outcome of the next encounter, she was sure of it. "Come on girls, let's go tell Travis to keep an eye out!"

Chapter 10

The meteorologist, peered out from a flapping yellow rain slicker and struggled to remain upright in the squall lashing Houston, "We've had reports of serious, although not catastrophic, damage along the entire coast. We're clocking winds at more than one-hundred miles per hour, rain is falling at almost a foot an hour, and the eyewall has yet to strike land with a tidal surge of twenty feet or more.

Our experts predict that Hurricane Victoria will lose strength as she makes landfall, dropping to a category two storm. We should all be thankful that she is not the category five hurricane she was last night."

Ponte turned from the *messenger*, "Silence!"

The group was milling about the dining room and parlor. Elsie and Sara set up a buffet line and everyone settled in for a hot meal, wherever they could find a seat. John sat on the floor by the sputtering fire, his plate resting on his legs, "It looks as if you've spared a great many people a disaster."

The Professor pushed his glasses up his nose with his index finger, "I don't know that we've completely avoided the disaster. That storm's going to produce a real mess for those people."

"But it could have been much worse," said Mary.

"It's the next one that I'm worried about," commented Nanchez, between spoonfuls of the rich soup that filled his bowl for the second time.

Sammy added, "At least we'll be able to monitor the movement of the energy. We should be able to see the next one coming."

"If we're lucky…and we were lucky this last time," said Dadeus. "I've been trying to imagine the technicians and the facilities, they must have to control such a massive structure as this web of dark vectors. We use the Powers but they're controlling them, playing them like the finest musical instrument. I believe it might be time to contact the other Keepers across the planet. We'll need their expertise, their observations, and their help."

"I agree," said Ponte. "We've learned how to deflect the movement but we certainly have no idea how to stop them."

"I don't think we should send a message through the normal channels," pondered Nanchez, "I think we should send personal emissaries. It would be safer that way for everyone."

"I agree," replied Master Chi. "The *seers* could fan out in different directions. Even if the Dark Forces are monitoring the positive vectors, four or five people traveling individually shouldn't arouse too much suspicion. Besides, they're probably busy with the preparations for whatever they're planning for their next entertainment."

"I think you're right," said Shambala quietly. "I'll take Africa, Sky you go to Europe and the Middle East, Master Chi will meet with our friends throughout Asia, Maze and Lala can move from north to south through the Americas."

Alius protested, "What about the rest of us?"

"You're running the things that are happening here. Mary understands the cloning, Raffe is helping with the computers, and you and Adrian have to keep everything on track. This is the best solution. If there is an immediate emergency, send out a call and we'll return."

"Then, so be it," said Ponte, as he sat down at the dining room table and wrote out five copies of technical notes that each of the *seers* could carry to the other Keepers. Each of them could contact their circle of wizards and the information would flow to everyone who needed to know.

"Here, each of you take these notes and deliver them to every Keeper you can find."

Sky hesitated before asking, "What if one of us gets caught?"

Nanchez' dour frown melted, as he burst out laughing, "Eat the notes!"

Dadeus was more serious, "That information must not fall into the wrong hands! Please be careful."

Maze scanned the sheet, "I can't understand a word of this!"

"Nor can I," laughed Master Chi. "It's a language of symbols."

"All languages are merely a series of symbols that everyone in that particular society has agreed on. This is mathematical language. Any good engineer, who understands the powers, could figure this out," said Nanchez. "It's just numbers and formulas, theories and equations."

Adrian, listening to the conversation from his seat on the couch, added, "I think you should consider moving through the plane of the animals, at least for the first part of your journeys. If they pick up five of you leaving the island at the same time, in different directions, they're going to know that something's up. At least they couldn't see you in the other plane."

"I agree," said Lala, her aura reaching to touch the other *seers* and Keepers from the dining room. "We have a lot of people to see and it would be tragic, if we were to lead the dark forces to our friends. We must remain as invisible as we possibly can."

"Agreed," said Sky. "We can enter the plane of the animals on the ridge, behind the House of the Four Seasons. Let's go."

Everyone stood and hugged the *seers*, who, one by one, closed their eyes and moved into the vectors and then to the plane of the animals.

After they disappeared, Alius asked, "What was in those notes you sent?"

The Professor put an arm around her shoulders, "They were instructions for each of the Keepers to synchronize their Crystals, so they would all be ready, at the moment when we'll need their power, to deflect the energy moving through the dark vectors. The hurricane was a test of their system. The next effort will be far more massive and we don't possess the means to defend against it, without all of the other Crystals working together in perfect harmony."

"I thought that connecting the nodes would allow all of the Light vectors to work together," said Adrian.

"Well, they do but, just as we use the power from our Crystals to power the island, many of the other Crystals are being used in the similar fashion. To obtain the massive power that we'll need requires taking energy from all of the other systems and channeling it into the vectors in a precise sequence."

Sammy injected, "Think of it as giant electro magnets, the more power you put in, the more pull the magnet can produce. The more energy they put into the system, the more energy it takes to equalize it."

"I guess I understand," said Adrian, although he was not quite sure of how they were going to control that much power.

One of the *messengers* in the dining room beeped and the Keepers rushed to check their monitors. They all stared at the image of the dark vectors. The blue wave of energy was beginning to move, a subtle swell rippling from south to north.

"Where's it going?" wondered Dadeus.

"It's not like the last time, when it was all pooling to one point on the globe," said Sammy.

"Look at these Black Crystals, up here around the Artic Circle," observed Nanchez. "They're beginning to glow."

"It's almost like they're charging up their batteries," added The Professor. "Like giant capacitors…and when they're full, the dark forces could discharge that energy all at once on a single target or a focused wave."

The four Keepers rushed to the elevator and disappeared into the workshop.

~

Zepallo led the clones out of the giant chamber through a tunnel to a smaller assembly room, to inspect an enormous black crystal that had been sculpted into a long spear, broad and hexagonal at one end and razor sharp at the other, etched with the smooth supple scales of snakeskin. Dark *orbs* scattered around the ceiling glimmered in the facets, the purple reflections skittering around the room, as the three young *seers* slowly walked around the diamond in awe.

"It's beautiful," mused Gamma, as he reached up to run his hand across the serpentine spike.

Alpha whispered, "It's got to be the largest gemstone in the world…"

Beta stood back, inspecting the needlepoint at the top, "What's it for?"

"Ah, now that is the question, isn't it?" replied Zepallo.

The three clones turned to stare inquisitively. "The hurricane was a test...a demonstration of the system. Our next campaign has already commenced and this lovely sculpture will make it possible."

"You haven't answered my question," said Beta.

"You are persistent, aren't you?" replied the Dark Lord. "Alright, the Powers are being focused through a ring of Black Crystals surrounding the North Pole. You've studied global warming and, now, we're about to test the hypothesis. What would happen if the Artic ice were to suddenly melt?"

"The coastal areas of the world would be flooded," replied Alpha, without hesitation.

"Correct! Now, what would follow?"

"Major capitals would be submerged, shipping would cease, production and commerce would come to a halt, resulting in global panic," said Gamma.

"Correct, but not far enough!" He turned to Beta.

"All of the systems of control in the world would fail. Governments would be powerless, instantaneous universal coverage by mass media would induce collapse of the social order, and religious institutions would be unable to deny that this disaster was not heralded in their sacred books. The masses would have no food, no transportation, no security...nothing to believe in, unless something else...or someone appeared at the perfect moment to offer them hope."

"Ah, that's wonderful!" screamed the Master. "We must give them...HOPE!"

"But you still haven't answered my question," demanded Beta.

Zepallo smiled, patiently, "This is the target for all the power that's being generated and transmitted through the dark vectors. We're going to install this lovely gem in an ice palace that has been constructed precisely above the North Pole. It will conduct the energy out through the ice and, slowly, it will begin to melt!"

The three young *seers* smiled, "When?"

"Tonight!"

~

Sky knocked at the door of a small cottage nestled into a dense forest in the English countryside, not far from Stonehenge. A heavy latch clanked and the solid wooden plank on cast iron hinges that creaked swung open a crack, as a single bloodshot eye peered out to scan the young woman from head to toe, "You're Ms. Sky. I remember you from the meeting on Morgan's Knot."

A hand reached out and pulled the young *seer* inside, before the door was slammed shut and locked with two large bolts. The old man's bright green robes glistened and his white beard glowed like liquid silver in the candle light. He tipped a bowler hat, that sat slightly askew atop his balding head, as he bowed.

"And you're Sir Isaac, if I remember correctly?"

"To what do I owe the honor of this visit?" inquired the ancient Keeper, taking her by the arm through a tiny hallway into a snug library, its walls covered with rare books and strange instruments. "Please come in and warm yourself by the fire. Might I offer you some tea?"

"That would be lovely," said Sky, as she sat in a tiny wingback chair beside the fireplace and noticed that the flames flickered in all the colors of a rainbow. The table in front of the sofa turned inside out and a silver tea service appeared.

She accepted an ornate china cup from her host, "I'm afraid that I've come from Professor Ponte and the other Keepers on the island. Hurricane Victoria was created by the Dark Forces and they're about to try something far more frightening."

"I noticed the change in the pulse of the vectors a couple of hours ago. It seems that a lot of energy is being dumped into the submerged remains of a small island in the South Atlantic."

The beautiful *seer's* dark eyes shimmered in the firelight, "I have something for you. I'm afraid that I must ask you to read these notes and return them to me, so I can deliver this message to your fellow Keepers across the continent."

Sir Isaac took the single sheet of paper and unfolded it. Donning spectacles on a slender hooked nose, he hummed a strange tune absently, as he read through the symbols and equations, coughed into a rag he pulled from the pocket of his robes, and then read them again. Finally, he looked up at his beautiful guest, "I understand what they're proposing and I'll begin making preparations immediately. There will be a few of our friends, who depend on the Powers, who might be a bit frustrated by the sudden unexplained loss of energy but, hopefully, it will only be a brief inconvenience." He paused, brushed a hand to whiskered chin and smiled mischievously at his guest, "One might presume that, if the inconvenience is extended, it won't matter anymore."

"It would be better, if no one else knew what they're planning."

"I understand," nodded the old Keeper, waving the paper up and down several times, "I'll just make a copy." Numbers and formulas flew off the page like fireflies gathering into cloud of glowing symbols at the center of the room. Suddenly, they swarmed into a murmuration, spinning around and around until, finally, arranging themselves into a cylinder from floor to ceiling etched with a long series of equations. Sir Isaac took off his glasses and knelt down on the floor, staring at the bottom line of the message, and slowly worked his way up, until he was standing on his tiptoes.

"Right then, I think I've got it all." He folded the paper and returned it to Sky, as she moved to the door, "I'm sure that you must be on your way to visit the other Keepers, there's little time to waste."

Her host did not see her out. He was transfixed with the information that he had just conjured in the middle of his parlor.

~

Dawn was fast approaching, as Shambala materialized on a flat, grassy plain surrounded by large majestic mountains. In spite of the warmth of an African summer, there was snow at the summits. The first embers of sunlight were creeping through a crevice between peaks to the east and she sensed a pride of lions moving along a stream meandering through the savannah to the south. She turned her back to the sun and started loping silently through the tall grass, with the grace of a gazelle, to a cluster of huts sheltered beneath a sparse thicket of umbrella trees near a crook in the river.

An old woman tending a small fire alone in the twilight, did not look up, as Shambala approached out of the glare. The tiny woman poked at the fire with a stick and the coals exploded into fireworks that lit up the sky, "It's about time you got here!"

The tall *seer* leaned over and hugged her friend, Danali. "I couldn't send a message to you, for fear of it being intercepted by the Dark Forces."

"I knew that you were coming, I could feel it in the chill of the morning," laughed the little woman, tugging at a dark red shawl draped across her shoulders, over a tattered black blouse and jeans. Her feet were bare, her hands calloused from grueling work, and there was nothing about her appearance that might indicate her position as a Keeper. "We've been pleased with the efforts of the children, even if it only lasted for a little while. It proves that people can live together in peace and, after this global experience, perhaps a few more will understand."

"The Dark Forces couldn't let that last for long, the hurricane in the Gulf was a test run and they're getting ready for something else," said Shambala quietly, pulling the twice-folded paper from the pocket of her robes. "The Professor sent along this message for you."

Danali poked the fire, which erupted in a pillar of flames four feet tall and held the sheet up for inspection. "Oh, that's too much trouble," hissed the Keeper, as she shook the information from the page. Glowing symbols and numbers bounced off the thatched walls of the nearest hut, aligned themselves into a long slender chain, and then twirled into a corkscrew around the blaze. "That's more like it!"

"What does it tell you?" asked Shambala, accepting the paper from the outstretched hand of the tiny woman, who was preoccupied with interpreting the information.

"That I'd best get busy. You'll be wanting to get this message to all the Keepers. Come back for a visit after we resolve this riddle…"

mumbled Danali, her right hand planted under her jaw, as she stared at the spiraling sequence glowing brilliantly in dawn's shadow.

~

Maze moved across the northern continent, while Lala started in the Yucatan and moved south. Each of the Keepers reacted in the same fashion and none would reveal the contents of the message to the messengers.

Master Chi spoke with six individuals and made his final stop at a tiny shrine in a slender, impenetrable valley in the northern foothills of the Himalayan Mountains. A fierce wind piled snow on outcroppings of vertical rock walls rising into a dusky sky, yet the grasses grew green next to the warm stream trickling down through a tangle of boulders lodged temporarily in this ever-changing landscape. A small curved bridge spanned the brook and a twisting path ceased at a moat surrounding the graceful monastery.

He smiled and stepped off the bank to walk across the surface of the water and up the worn steps to the heavy beamed doors but, before he placed his foot on the landing, a slender shaft of warm light flashed across the threshold and a whisper of a voice said, "My Master is waiting for you, please come in."

A tiny waif of a girl stepped aside to allow Master Chi to enter and closed the door silently behind him. She smiled and floated along a narrow hallway to a large room illuminated by hundreds of candles. Master Jung wore deep red robes that shimmered, as he turned to greet his friend, "My hope is that you come bearing good news but, from the expression on your face, my sense is that you have not…"

"I'm afraid your premonition is, unfortunately, accurate," said Master Chi, as he bowed. "Professor Ponte sent along a sheet of equations for you."

He handed the now worn paper to the old Keeper, who flipped it open, spilling equations across the floor. They gathered together, spinning into a glowing ball of embers and lined up in mid-air. Master Jung sighed, as he inspected the information. "This is madness!" he cried, "but it is brilliant too!"

"What does it say?"

"You know that I can't tell you that and, besides, it would take days to instruct you on the physics of The Balance. I hate to be rude to the finest *seer* in the world and, certainly, my best friend, but you must not keep me from my work. There is much to be done!"

Master Chi bowed and, bewildered, backed to the door, which opened silently behind him. The tiny girl bowed and escorted him back to the entrance.

~

Two-dozen technicians and a legion of troops escorted the floating spire through a series of tunnels to a hanger carved into the shadows beneath a cliff in the mountain. A strange saucer shaped craft hovered above a smooth polished floor. Its gleaming metallic surface pulsed with rippling static and a magenta glow swirled beneath the perimeter.

The clones stopped to stare at the sleek machine. "Is that a flying saucer?" inquired, Gamma.

"Yes, it is, although I find that term rather quaint. Do you honestly believe that all those normal people, who reported sighting strange objects in the sky, were completely unbalanced? Our propaganda led them to believe that the flying machines were from some alien world, which is far easier to grasp than the real explanation. We try to fly only in the vectors but, occasionally, necessity has forced our pilots out into the open. We have several newer versions in testing."

"So, they've been ours..." pondered Beta. "I read reports about them in our studies but I never imagined..."

"I'll bet it really moves!" laughed Alpha.

"That it does, stealthily," smiled the Dark Lord, as he turned to oversee the technicians loading the harpoon into the cargo hold. The four *dark seers* marched across the hanger, past columns of uniformed troops standing at attention, and up a ramp into the belly of the saucer.

The boys stopped at the head of the gangway in awe of the

gleaming interior. Pilots and navigators manned stations clustered in front of a central podium beneath glowing ribbons of dark *orbs* that snaked across the domed ceiling. Their hands touched screens that curved up around them, information projected into clear visors on their helmets allowed them to monitor every function on the craft and scan for hundreds of miles in every direction.

Zepallo led his charges to a bank of formfitting, pressure resistant seats on an elevated platform just behind the commander. Troops and technicians filed into several open cabins that lined the circumference of the interior.

The ramp closed with a hiss and the whisper of the engines roared into a growl, as the saucer lifted off the pavement and darted out into the night sky, followed by a pair of similar, though smaller, versions flying protection for the mothership and transporting additional personnel.

~

Adrian found Simian floating a foot above the floor in the observatory. He had been in a trance for almost a full day and the young *seer* was worried about him. Tiptoeing from the elevator, he was startled by the old Jamaican's deep voice, "You've come at an opportune time."

"I didn't mean to disturb you, I was just worried."

"I appreciate your concern but you should know, by now, that we can maintain this state of concentration for long periods of time, without feeling tired or hungry or even thirsty."

"I do know but…"

"We're in a holding pattern…there's nothing to do but wait for their next move."

"You are so perceptive."

"I see…just as you hear…"

"And what do you see?"

"They're moving something very large and heading north into the Artic. I see the four dark forms surrounded by many warriors. They're prepared to defend the very precious object they're carrying in a strange flying machine. It's not like a normal airplane. Whatever it is, it's round and it moves at a rather astonishing speed."

Adrian remembered the words of The Crystal, "They will provide a target." He sat down opposite his mentor, crossed his legs, and closed his eyes. Slowly, he rose off the planked floor of the observatory and hovered. Still and unmoving, his breathing slowed, he allowed his mind to take in the sounds of the world. The most obvious was the usual hum, the sound of life, but not too far in the background he could hear the wail of destruction, the sounds of devastation emanating from the remains of Hurricane Victoria and confrontations erupting across the globe. Farther back, he heard the grating sound of evil…the movement of an energy wave across the dark vectors and, for a moment, he almost believed that he could hear the sinister laugh of Zepallo fading away in the distance.

A vision flashed through his mind of four dark *seers*, seated in form-fitting black seats moving at great speed inside a vehicle, instead of flying through the vectors.

He opened his eyes. Simian was staring at him, "What have you found?"

"Whatever they're carrying in that craft, it's the target for the next phase of their plan. We have to discover where they're going and we have to stop them."

"That might be easier said than done. I sense many people around the object and I would guess that they're the elite troops of the Dark Forces, protection for their precious cargo."

"Then, we'll need help," said Adrian quietly. "Send out the call, while I go tell the others."

~

Professor Ponte strode back and forth in front of smoldering embers in the fireplace, gnawing on his knuckle and muttering to himself. "Alright, we've tracked the Dark Forces to the magnetic North Pole and we can see the waves of energy surging towards the Black Crystals that surround the Artic Circle. Our calculations suggest that they're installing a target, a focal point for that power to pour into...the question is why?"

"What happens when you add heat to ice?" inquired Kelly.

"Water...lots of water..." replied Sammy.

"And what happens when lots of fresh water is added to the ocean?"

"Flooding!" cried Alius

"A disruption of the balance of the ocean currents, massive changes in the weather all across the planet," added Raffe.

"An end to commerce and production," said John.

"Panic..." whispered Adrian. "Control the oil, control the weather, make it seem that the end of the world is at hand...and the people will follow whoever offers them hope."

"And we all know who that would be," smiled Master Chi.

Nanchez' booming voice filled the room, "The only way to stop this is to destroy that target. We can work with the vectors and deflect some of the energy but it won't be enough to avoid this catastrophe, until that is accomplished."

"Then we'll have to face the Dark Forces!" exclaimed Alius.

"And take away their toy!" laughed Raffe.

"It won't be that easy," added Sky. "We all know their capacity and we'll be fighting against trained troops in the harshest environment on the planet. They'll control the situation."

"That's true," said Simian quietly, "but we'll have help."

Just then, Molly, Megan, and Morgan stormed through the door, panting, "They found it!"

"Found what?" asked Elsie.

"The lair where they're growing the clones. It's in the ocean south of Indonesia. The whalemail said that there was some sort of energy shield around it and they couldn't get inside," replied Morgan.

Molly hooked a thumb over her shoulder to the open door and a cold wind blowing into the parlor, "There's something else you need to see..."

Everyone trooped outside, into a chilling gale, to find three massive boats floating above the yard. They were, certainly, not normal sailing ships but grand ancient vessels, each with three stout masts supporting three tiers of sails that seemed to be made of clear crystal, for they shimmered beneath the light of a waning moon and, otherwise, would have been invisible.

Adrian looked up to find Orana leaning over the rail of the largest of the ships, "How did you? Where did…?"

Orana smiled. "I must assume that this might be my last opportunity to contribute to the cause and I've brought some friends to help," she said, as she waved her hand to several hundred warriors manning the three ships.

"Where did they come from?" asked Alius.

"There are many more of us, than you might have realized, and there hasn't been reason enough to endanger any of you by revealing the rest. Now there's no choice but to combine all of the *seers* and the networks of Keepers to defeat the Dark Forces!"

A great cheer went up and everyone scurried around to prepare for the departure of the *seers*. Ester produced a box of black crystals, paired with golden gems, for protection against the dark powers. Raffe distributed weapons, shields, flashpans, and crystal grenades, Sara had extra cloaks and gloves, and Ponte handed out three pairs of the glasses that the children had worn while connecting the nodes. "I don't have enough for everyone, but, at least, we'll be able to communicate and pass along information."

Dadeus opened a metal box to reveal a dozen crystalline patches. They were, perhaps, the width of a grown man's fist and reflected vivid rainbows rippling across their smooth curved surfaces. "Since our last encounter with the Dark Forces, I've been working on something new. These are the prototypes and I call them refractors."

"What do they do?" inquired Alius.

"When a charge is fired at you, these will reflect the charge back to its source or in any direction you might choose. I call them refractors because they gather and focus the energy that's been captured. The return volley is far more powerful than the original. They're designed to be worn on the wrist of the hand that wields the sword."

Adrian stared at his reflection in the refractor on his arm. He could see his face glowing in every color in the spectrum. John and Sara hugged their son. "I know that I shouldn't say be careful...but...I'll worry about you, until you're safe at home," said his mother.

"I know you worry but I also know that you understand what's at stake. I have no other choice."

"I know," said Sara sadly, pulling him to her. "Just come back to me."

Adrian turned to his father, who said, "I hope you already know how proud I am of you."

"I know."

"Be careful, son. I love you."

Adrian hugged his father and walked out the door to climb the gangplank to Orana's crystal ship. Morgan caught up with him as he stepped onto the porch. Her green eyes welled with tears, "You keep doing this and we all worry. Just be careful, we don't want to lose you." She wrapped her long arms around him and held on for a moment too long.

The *seers* lined the rails, to wave good-bye, and the three ships lifted into the night, turned north, and disappeared in a glittering rush.

Adrian walked over and hugged Orana, "I guess I shouldn't be surprised but I am."

"If I'd been allowed to keep you longer, I might have been able to prepare you for specific challenges that you'll face...like this one."

"I'd like to continue, when there's time."

"I'd like that too," whispered the ancient *seer*, staring off into the distance. The cold wind lifted her mane of white hair into a halo of glowing wings behind her. Her eyes were strong and sad, with no hint of the humor or levity he felt during his lessons. This was Orana the warrior and he knew that this mission would be a practical extension of his studies.

Sky, Shambala, and the group of Africans waved from the rail of one of the other ships, while Master Chi joined Lala and Maze in a bow of the third crystalline wonder.

"Tell me about these ships," said Adrian, as the other *seers* gathered around.

"These vessels have seen more than their share of duty in the many battles fought over the centuries. They were constructed in the second millennia before the modern calendar began. The hulls were cast from molten crystals and are impervious to a cannon charge." She gestured to the sails, which were taught and firm, driving the craft through the sky. "The sails are woven from threads pulled from those liquid crystals. As you can see along each side of the main deck, we have a dozen cannon and the hull is filled with weapons and ammunition. The Keepers have installed the latest *orbs* and *messengers* and our three captains have several hundred years of experience between them. This one is named 'Destiny'. The others are 'Hope' and 'Grace'."

"We're traveling at an incredible speed, what's driving us?" asked Raffe.

Orana laughed, "The power of the vectors. They produce a cosmic wind that moves very much as the winds blow across the oceans."

Alius mused, "...straight on 'til morning! I almost feel like one of the children on that pirate ship with Peter Pan flying over Neverland!"

Orana turned and patted her arm, "We'll be there long before that!"

One of the crew, a slender Australian, by his accent, stepped up, "Message from the captain, Ma'am. He says they're detecting a force field around the perimeter of our destination and he's not sure that we can penetrate it."

"I don't care how he does it, over, under, around, or through, just get us to the North Pole."

"Yes, Ma'am!" said the crewman, scurrying back to Captain Maniford Ruhl, who stood beside the helmsman piloting a large wheel at the stern of the ship. The sailor yelled Orana's instructions above the din and the captain turned to look at the *Master Seer*. With a slight smile, he bowed his head slightly and touched the brim of his hat.

She looked from one *seer* to the next, "Prepare yourselves, this is going to be a rough voyage."

~

Tiny ice crystals billowed into a shimmering blue fog above the Pole, as the three saucers landed on an open terrace beneath a vast crystal palace surrounded by immense walls and looming turrets, fortified with batteries of cannon, and sculpted from massive blocks of frozen water. A tower, glowing with the deep magenta of dark *orbs*, rose into a gleaming spire in a black sky, a beacon to initiate an eruption of dark miracles.

The four *dark seers* directed the unloading of the spire and escorted it through an entry in the base of the palace. Workstations lined the perimeter of a vast sheet of smooth ice beneath the conical tower. The black diamond was levitated into an upright position and the dark energies lifted it twenty feet off the floor.

Zepallo turned to the boys, "The process is starting, we must evacuate this level."

They climbed a circular staircase that wrapped around the outside wall of the chamber, allowing access to an observation deck that offered a protected perch to monitor the tip of the diamond lance and the icy floor below.

A loud pulsing hiss filled the chamber and a deep purple flash fired down the length of the shaft, vaporizing a hole in the ice that grew wider and deeper by the moment. Gamma turned to his master, "Should we be worried about the growth of that cavern?"

"This facility was designed to support this system and the well won't grow any larger than it is at the moment. What you can't see is the energy expanding out from a point deep beneath our castle to melt the ice at the perimeter of the snowfield hundreds of miles away. It will become an ocean of fire!"

Gamma grinned, "There's always more to learn."

Zepallo patted him on the back, "Remember what I said during the hurricane? Never underestimate the powers or the determination of our enemies. I suspect that they'll do their best to disrupt our fun." Suddenly, serious, he whispered, "Be prepared!"

~

Vast power surged through the vectors from the Dark Crystals rimming the northern continents, in perpetual waves contracting around the black spire, condensing in the ice tower, and radiating out through the ice sheet across the top of the world.

Along the shorelines, beneath a glacial cap of snow and ice, the ocean waters began to boil. The temperature differential heaved the ice sheet and deep cracks split off in all directions, resonating with the ferocity of a thousand thunderclaps. Great chunks of glacier fell into the roiling sea, firing steam-jets of glittering purple sparkles into the sky, until they melted into cold fresh water that sank to the bottom of the ocean.

The movements of the weather and the volatility of temperatures across the entire world are governed by currents that carry warm salty water from the tropics near the surface, heating coastlines along the way, until they cool down in the artic, then return as cold fresh water in a deep flow to be reheated by the energy of the sun. This conveyor provides nutrients for the sea life in the northern waters of the Atlantic, as well as the Pacific, in latitudes that would otherwise be uninhabitable.

As the polar ice melted, the sea level would begin to rise dramatically, flooding would spread slowly, relentlessly gaining momentum as it rolled south. The change would also slow the loop carrying warmth from the tropics, encasing the north in terminal winter and the equator in stagnant heat.

The primary current in the Atlantic, the Gulf Stream, was first noted by Benjamin Franklin in 1726 and the fast-moving flow peaked his interest to take sequential temperature readings each time he crossed the ocean in an effort to understand and map its course. Whalers worked the boundaries of the stream for centuries, knowing that plankton lived along the margins, where cold and warm water caressed. Krill and shrimp consume the tiny creatures, at the base of the food chain, and whales found plenty of nourishment to supply their yearly journeys from the Tropics to the Artic and back.

Keepers all over the globe worked frantically to construct their portions of the system that The Professor had proposed. Each saw the logic and feared the process, knowing that any failure, any misstep would lead to the destruction of the Positive Crystals and all life on the planet. They would have one chance to succeed and Ponte, alone, held the controls.

~

The great ships flew low above great swells in the northern ocean, crossing a raging line of fire bubbling up in the boundary where liquid water rages against a continent of ice. They raced across a white plane that stretched to the horizon in every direction. Adrian turned to Orana, "This seems familiar!"

The old *seer* pulled her cloak tight, "At least your previous lessons were temperate."

Alius pointed to the north, "There's a purple glow on the horizon!" Her glove followed a series of vibrant magenta arcs, an umbrella of power streaming into the target.

The captain brought the bow around, as the other two ships veered off east and west to scout the fortifications, and called out "Man your stations, lads and lassies!"

~

A loud alarm sounded in the control room buried deep inside the ice palace. Troops moved out in transports, flying inches above the surface of the ice, to man their stations, while technicians scrambled to secure a perimeter.

Zepallo seemed calm and, almost, amused, "As I said, expect them to show up fashionably late, just when the party's beginning to get interesting."

Alpha was primed, "Where should we go to help with the defense?"

"Relax, you'll have your chance," laughed Beta.

"Our master has plans for us," added Gamma.

"How right you are!" laughed the Dark Lord. "Our place is here with the diamond. Our defenses are formidable, our troops well trained. Let them deal with this disruption for the moment. We'll ensure there's no interference in the process.

Always focus on the goal, no matter the obstacles that stand in your way. See your path and follow it, until you succeed or you die. That is the way of the *seer* and the reason that we're here!"

The clones returned to their stations to assist the technicians channeling the system through their *messengers* and monitoring the threat. Three faint blips broke formation to circle the fortification. Red dots appeared in concentric circles surrounding the ice palace, each representing a firing point.

Zepallo spoke softly, "Tell them to hold their fire, until I give the command. Let's see what happens as they approach the barrier."

Chapter 11

Orana handed out earplugs to each of the *seers*. Raffe asked, "What are these for?"

The old woman laughed, "They've set up a force shield that's designed to defend against our entry. They thought about humans, *seers*, and battleships like these but they didn't consider the natural world, if I know our enemy."

Simian smiled, "Whalemail!"

"Correct, you are!"

Adrian was confused, "I don't understand…"

The old Jamaican wrapped an arm around the boy's shoulders, "Have you ever seen the trick where someone with a very strong, high voice can shatter a crystal goblet just by singing a single quavering note?"

"Yes, I remember something about that from television when I was…before I became a *seer*."

"Well, then think of the sound that a whale makes, it's very deep and produces incredibly strong vibrations. The tones carry for hundreds, if not thousands, of miles. What would happen to a very large glass dome, if lots of whales started singing the perfect note at the same time?"

"The force field would shatter!" smiled the young *seer*, as he stuffed the plug into his ear.

Alius clutched Adrian's arm. The look in her eyes was not, so much, fear, as anticipation. A deep rumbling shuddered through the hull of the crystal ship, as thousands of whales, calling in unison, surrounded the ice cap, transforming it into a continent-sized loudspeaker shuddering with violent tremors.

The ancient ships forged ahead at speed, sweeping across the night sky and aiming for a hazy magenta glow on the horizon. Shimmering with flashes of energy flickered across its glistening dome, the smooth sheen of the bubble flexed and rippled as a long trembling tone pulsed the air inside.

Everyone on the ship muffled their ears against the intensity of the chorale, and, eyes wide in awe and terror, cringed as the tiny ship hurtled towards terminal impact with the massive quivering shield looming over the ice cap. Gradually, a staccato crackling tinkled over the thundering chorus and tiny fissures skittered across the dome, refracting the magenta light into delicate fingers of lightning sizzling across the surface. Small flakes began to fall away, then great quavering shards, until a large gap opened, just as Destiny and her sisters breached the perimeter and sailed through a slender gap in a glittering cascade of shattered shield.

Purple charges roared from a tight circle of cannons in defense of the palace and the towering spire. The captain yelled, "Man the lifeboats!"

Orana turned to Adrian and Alius, "Quickly now, take to the boats. We'll drop you off and then attend to their defenses. You must get into the palace and destroy the target. The world is depending on you!"

Adrian and Alius jumped into the long, narrow crystalline boat hanging on the port side, while Raffe and Simian took the other. Orana leaned to yell, "You'll find this craft moves right along, just steer with that handle in front of you and control the speed with the lever under your left hand! Good luck!"

The huge ship bounced off the surface of the ice with a mighty thud and released the slender craft in that precise moment of contact. The lifeboats vaulted into a long skid and Adrian struggled to grasp the handle protruding from the hull beneath the seat. He pushed the lever full forward and pulled the handle to the left. Alius screamed, as the long boat swerved to port and took off like an arrow skipping across the ice.

Adrian spied the other boat following close behind and a line of cannon straight ahead. He turned around to Alius, "We've got to get beyond those cannons! Hang on!"

The young *seer* pulled hard to the right, as the first charges flew past, then back to the left, dodging each successive volley. He pulled back hard on the stick and the sleek craft jumped a few feet off the ice and settled back down as he pushed forward. The charges were coming faster and he searched for a path to breach the barricade.

Alius yelled in his ear, "Look up!"

Adrian ducked as the massive keel of the crystal ship surged overhead and tacked hard to starboard, her cannons blazing. One of the fortifications on the ice exploded, the munitions erupting in a green iridescent halo, and the young *seer* aimed directly at the wound in the defensive line.

Another blast of golden charges traced across the sky and leveled a pair of guns. Adrian glanced to his right to spot Raffe dodging and weaving through volleys of mortars tracing purple ghosts on the ice. He pointed to the glasses that Ponte handed out.

Adrian ruffled around in his robes, found the glasses, and fumbled to put them on. "Can you hear me?"

Raffe's voice crackled, "Yeah! Isn't this fun?"

"Are you nuts?" screamed Adrian. "There are a couple of cannon stations that Destiny knocked out. You take the one on the right and I'll take the other. Good luck!"

Raffe yelled back, "See you on the other side!" The other boat peeled off, heading for the gap.

A brilliant barrage from the magnificent old ship eliminated another emplacement and Adrian noticed that the angle between the fire from the Dark Forces and that from the ship was narrowing around their course. "We'll be lucky if we're not blown up by friendly fire!"

He turned hard to starboard, avoiding the line of charges, and at the last possible moment pulled back hard on the handle. The little boat jumped into the air and vaulted the defenses, as tracers flew in all directions around them.

Adrian glanced to his right to see Raffe and Simian sail over the barrier beneath a trail of fire exploding across the ice behind them. In the distance, a giant sculpted crystal mountain rose into the night. Flashes of deep purple lightning radiated from the tip of its spire down into a walled base. Artillery ringed the perimeter and he sensed they were preparing to fire, so he pulled hard to the starboard and then back to the left, weaving into range.

The moon's shadow of Destiny's hull crept over them and the crystal ship heaved to port, loosing a broadside. Several of the cannon emplacements erupted into brilliant infernos, while others returned dazzling mortar shells that skittered through the air and across the ice. Adrian sensed a repeating lull between the explosions. It was almost as if the forces firing the cannon were working to a rhythm or beat, their movements mechanical and, perhaps, predictable.

Off to the right and left, behind the giant crystalline castle, they could see Hope and Grace firing in the distance. The three ships were circling the fortress in a coordinated attack, slowly closing the noose. Adrian tried to connect with the energies of their friends but, in the hail of fire above their heads, he was afraid of losing his concentration. He could only hope that they were rushing across the ice from the opposite direction.

Alius pointed over his shoulder to a break in the line of fire and the little skiff pulled hard to port, taking aim on belching smoke and small explosions. Suddenly, the cannon emplacements just ahead stopped firing, pausing to allow four black attack craft to blast through the barrier, firing jets of blazing missiles that seared through the darkness with a venomous hiss.

Raffe's voice sputtered through the earpieces, "I've got four of them headed right for us, how about you?"

"We've got the same," yelled Adrian. "Let's see if I can jump over them!"

He could distinguish the torsos of the dark troops leaning out of the sides of the speeding iceboats, firing splashes of molten purple streaks zipping past. Alius shook his right shoulder, pointing at a handle that was nestled on the floor next to his seat. He pulled up a mounted cannon and she grabbed the trigger, twisting the lever to aim at the first of the enemy's craft.

A red flash bristled from the right side of the skimmer, with a deep whistle, and the lead ship exploded. Adrian yelled into his headset,

"We've got our own guns. It's on your right!"

Red charges erupted from the other boat and two crippled enemy vessels tumbled across the ice. "Why didn't they tell us about this before we started?" crackled Raffe's voice.

Alius fired again, clearing out the other boat on the starboard side, before turning to the next two. Adrian turned hard to port, taking a direct line between the two black daggers rushing across the ice. Alius bit her lip, aimed and fired two volleys. The pair of attack craft flew into the air and burst into skating fireballs. Adrian twisted the handle hard to starboard and raced beneath the exploding debris, before it crashed and shattered into flaming fragments.

The tiny skiff ducked under Destiny's furious volleys of blistering shells and between the emplacements at the base of the ice castle, as two black saucers lifted out of an open courtyard behind the wall, returning persistent volleys of charges. The two ships separated and heaved to the attack at an astonishing speed, one fore and the other aft of the old vessel. The crystal ship veered hard to starboard, which afforded a twenty-four gun salvo between the two attackers.

The cannon fired in rapid succession, golden charges illuminating the ice beneath them as they closed on the two strange saucers, which rose out of the line of fire and responded with blazing salvos of their own.

Alius looked up as the foremast splintered and three shimmering sails sagged to the deck. She shouted into Adrian's ear, "They're in trouble! Don't look back! We've got to keep going!"

Orana's voice crackled in his headset, "We'll keep them busy! Don't stop!"

Adrian peeked to his right and saw Raffe and Simian heading for the ice castle at top speed. The sentinels in the fortifications around the base of the wall opened up and another set of ice runners flew out of the castle. He pulled and pushed the lever, weaving back and forth across a line of deadly purple sparkles towards the nook where the black craft appeared.

Alius manned the cannon and fired between the four defenders.

Again, they dodged into two pairs streaking down each side of the little skiff, except this time, the two inner pilots turned to cross in front at the last moment. Alius hesitated, then pressed the trigger. Four charges zipped through the darkness and caught the two, just as they lined up, erupting with a brilliant phosphorescent flash.

Adrian pulled back hard on the yoke and the little boat jumped the flaming hulks and darted towards the opening in the castle. Alius pulled on Adrian's sleeve, "One of those saucer things is coming up behind us and the Destiny seems to be going down!"

The young *seer* spun around in his seat. The saucer was fast approaching and, behind it, the old ship looked as if she was slowly sinking into the ice field, her foremast dangling over the port side in a tangle of rigging, but beneath her, he could see troops sliding down ropes and another squadron of iceboats being lowered. The saucer fired two short bursts at the skiff, just as the old crystal ship opened up with a blast that caught the strange craft on the starboard side, spinning it into a steep angle, catching an edge, out of control and spiraling across the ice, trailing a tumble of brilliant sparks and fiery fragments.

Adrian pulled hard to port to avoid the flaming wreckage, coursing across the endless white plain into the base of the castle wall, to explode just in front of the gap. The tiny craft slid backwards for several hundred feet before the young *seer* could gain control. He looked up to see the second saucer spin through the sky, taking aim on the ancient vessel. Orana was silhouetted on the bow, her arms outstretched, her white hair trailing behind like a glistening cape, as she rose into the night, pointed and twisted both hands around each other. The saucer twirled one side over the other, firing a meandering stream of charges that fell short of the old ship. At the last moment, the tumbling craft crashed into the ice and bounced over the rigging, catching Orana as it passed. Her aura exploded into thousands of gleaming golden glimmers streaming into an enormous halo, the glare transforming frigid night into day.

Adrian screamed and gunned the little boat back towards the ship. Alius wrapped her arms around his shoulders, "You can't go back!

We have to get into the ice palace!"

He continued until she yelled, "Orana didn't die to help you fail! She died so we might win!"

The young *seer* hesitated for a moment, then pulled the stick to port and zipped across the ice sheet to the castle. Alius squeezed him with all her might, absorbing the sobs ravaging his body.

Hovering, Destiny fired into the emplacements along the base of the ice castle and her troops stormed the outer defenses. Adrian slowed the slender skiff and pulled up in the shadows behind the gate where the ice runners had appeared. The guards were busy attending to survivors of the crashed saucer and failed to notice a second craft join the first.

Simian and Raffe climbed the icy bank to find Alius consoling a weeping Adrian,. "What's wrong with him?" asked Raffe.

"We just watched Orana die," said Alius quietly.

The other two *seers* joined the hug, "We all know what she meant to you," said Simian, gently, "but she gave her life so that we might have a chance to succeed. We have to go forward!"

"I know," whispered Adrian, standing slowly, wiping frozen tears with the sleeves of his cloak. "She knew before we left Morgan's Knot. I could see it in her eyes."

Raffe hugged his friend, "I'm so sorry."

"We've got to be quick," whispered Simian.

"Our target is at the base of that spire," said Adrian.

A huge wall of ice bricks towered above the four *seers* and behind it an enormous shard jutted into the night sky, bristling with waves of deep purple energy gushing down from the needle point. The four *seers* ducked into a crevice, evading a squad of troops rushing out through the gate to confront the rush of invaders from Destiny, who were storming across the ice to the base of the castle.

"Their troops are worried about our forces, maybe we can just sneak through," wished Alius.

"I don't think it'll be that easy," laughed Raffe. "Let's split up. You two go to the left and we'll try to find a passage through on the right."

Adrian peered around the ice block, "Let's go!"

Slinking close to the wall, they moved inside the fortress and crept to a corner that opened onto a large courtyard. Adrian yelled, "Down!" as two packs of ice runners zipped past. He leaned forward and spied a squad of dark troopers running in the opposite direction. Two guards stood on either side of a doorway to the left and another pair before an entry at the far end of the courtyard.

Adrian pointed at Raffe and Simian and held up two fingers and pointed to the right. He looked at Alius and pointed to the left.

The four *seers* stood up and marched out onto the frozen plaza, Raffe and Simian walking casually to their right, as Adrian and Alius approached the two guards on their left. The sentries lifted their chargers and inquired, "Who goes there?"

In one swift movement, the two *seers* levitated to either side of the black caped militia, striking them down, with short blasts from their rings, as they swept past.

"That was too easy," said Alius.

"You're the optimist tonight, aren't you?" said Adrian, stepping through the door to press himself against the inner wall. Through the ice blocks, the light of purple *orbs* ringed the center of the structure. In silhouette, they could see two more guards at a station across a hallway.

"Okay, time for a little deception," said Adrian.

"I don't like the sound of that!" whispered Alius.

"You just walk up to them and I'll be right behind you."

"Yeah, right!"

"No really! If you can distract them, I can take them out."

"A little blond girl in a blue cloak?"

"Have you got a better idea?"

"I think I should be crying…"

"Nice touch! Now go!"

Alius stepped into the hallway and buried her face in her hands, her white hair concealing the handle of her sword. She let out a wail and the two guards raised their weapons. "Please help me!" cried the beautiful blond *seer*, turning to point, "They're right behind me!"

Before the guards could ask "Who?" Adrian attacked, striking blows as he flew through the hall. Alius rose up and crowned the nearest foe with an overhand sweep. "C'mon, let's go!"

They slipped into a tunnel that pointed to the center of the castle. In the distance, they could hear a rasping noise and the scratching of something heavy sliding across the ice. A purple flame billowed across the intersection of passageways and a giant white serpent slid out of a crevice on the right, another appeared behind it, slithering slowly down the long hallway, towards the *seers*. The huge creature lifted its snout, opened its mouth, and belched out a blazing flare that melted the inner surface of the ice, transforming it into iridescent liquid crystal.

Adrian tapped the arm of his glasses, "Are you seeing this?"

"That can't be good," laughed Raffe. "We've got some nightmares of our own!"

A jumpy image appeared in the lens in front of his right eye. He could barely make out jiggling images of a giant lizard lumbering through a similar tunnel over Raffe's shoulder, as he ran for safety. "Good luck with that!"

Alius grabbed his robes and pulled him into an alcove that led to a stairway. They levitated up through the spiral, landing on a terrace that spanned the exterior circumference of the castle. Beyond the wall, they could hear fierce fighting illuminated by flashes of exploding charges blazing in the night.

At least three layers of ice blocks separated them from the center and, in the refracted glow of the dark *orbs*, large creatures patrolled inside the circles they had to navigate. Adrian suddenly realized that the palace had been constructed like a three-dimensional circular maze...the snow snakes and the stairway led them back outside. They were farther away than when they started.

Orana's voice sounded calm in his mind, "Feel your way to the center."

Adrian looked up and noticed a blinking purple *orb* on top of the ice blocks. Touching his glasses, he said, "Raffe! It's a maze and they're watching us through blinking *orbs*, just like on the Island of the

Children!"

He pointed his sword at the *orb* and fired.

~

Zepallo paced behind his apprentices, who were monitoring three stations in the hub of the palace. The *messengers* displayed the movements of the Light Forces and the ships around the exterior, as well as video feeds that followed the *seers'* efforts to penetrate the gauntlet so carefully prepared for them. The outer layers of the palace had been stocked with a fearsome herd of deadly creatures, hallways and staircases leading nowhere, and traps at every turn.

"There are only two ways to enter this chamber and you seem to have them covered. We're being invaded on three sides. Eliminate the other two groups, so we can concentrate on young Adrian and his friends. They pose the greatest threat and I know that you children have been looking forward to this opportunity."

Alpha laughed, "I'd like another shot at him."

"Deservedly so," cried the Dark Lord.

"I'll move all the creatures to the far side, that should slow them down," replied Gamma, as he turned to Beta, "and you set the traps at the entrances. Let's see how many we can take out with one blast!"

Beta punched in a series of codes, as he watched the two groups probe the doorways on the opposite entry to the castle. "Come on, not that one! Try the next one! I have a surprise for you!"

Two small people with pointed hats appeared on his screen and he tapped a key. A bright flash blinded the camera for a moment before their bodies appeared sliding across the ice beyond the doorway. "Gotcha!"

Alpha spoke into a microphone on his headset and a dozen black caped troops, astride giant ravens, swooped down out of the frigid night to attack Sky, Shambala, and the third group of *seers*, who rose up to meet them. Gold and purple golden charges flashed through the starry heavens, the clash of swords rained fountains of sparks sizzling onto the ice, and the haunting caws of enormous birds echoed through the palace.

Gamma watched a split screen of Raffe and Simian sneaking through a tunnel on the second level with anticipation. They were about to come face to face with one of his favorite creatures, the poison-tongued ice frog which weighs in at six-hundred pounds and whose bulk easily filled the passageway from side to side. It could leap twenty-five feet in a single bound and deliver a lethal dose of serum from twice that distance.

Adrian destroyed the primary camera over the entrance but a second was watching from a tower on the wall. They were about to enter a doorway into a stairway descending to the lower level and access to another passage that might bring them one level closer to the central control room. Unfortunately, a very large ice lizard was waiting impatiently for his evening meal.

~

Ponte, Dadeus, Nanchez, and Sammy huddled around the *messengers* in the parlor and the rest of the family and friends were busying themselves preparing a meal in the kitchen and setting the table in the dining room.

John walked over and asked, "What's happening?"

Ponte pointed, "Well, this one's monitoring the Artic ice sheet. As you can see, an orange ring has formed around the edges, indicated increasing temperatures. Basically, it's melting from the outside in. The energy is flowing through the vectors from the Dark Crystals to a point just above the North Pole and radiating out to the perimeter of the ice sheet."

The second screen displayed the power rolling through the dark vectors. The overlay of the light vectors showed no movement. "This shows the dispersion of that energy and, until that focal point is destroyed, we have no way to neutralize the effect."

"On this third screen, we're watching the rising tides in the northern Atlantic. You can see by the color change from blue towards red where the tides are moving ashore along the coast of Canada, the northern United States…Boston, New York, and rising in the Delaware Bay and the Chesapeake. Norway, Sweden, Great Britain, and fast approaching the Netherlands, and it won't be long before Japan begins to feel the effects. If this continues, all of the oceans in the northern hemisphere will overflow."

The final *messenger* showed a view of the ice palace from an *orb* on the Destiny's mast. The sky was flickering with enormous explosions flaring through billowing clouds of smoke and the image vibrated violently, as the ship's twelve cannon let loose a volley and the enemy returned fire from bunkers along the wall. Long slender launches were ferrying the troops of the Light Forces across the ice to join in the battle raging around the fortified entries to the glimmering castle.

"Do we know where the *seers* are?"

"Unfortunately, we've lost the direct link to the glasses that Adrian and Raffe are wearing in the rush of energy that's flowing around that spire. I wish I had a better answer to your question but the only information we have is that they're trying to gain entry into the castle from three directions. From what I learned from Captain Ruhl of the Destiny a little while ago, the whole place is built like a three-dimensional circular maze and defended not only by troops and fortifications but fearsome creatures."

Sara was listening from the dining room, "Do they have a chance?"

"They're the best we've got," replied The Professor, with a gentle hug. "They've faced stiff challenges before and I have every faith in them. I just hope they find a way to get to the core soon. Millions of people are depending on them."

He walked into the kitchen and found Molly, Megan, Morgan, and Kelly, "Girls, I want you to find Spot and Dusty and ask them to send a message to their friends who found the incubator."

~

Adrian and Alius pressed against the wall on either side of the entrance. A faint blinking on the battlement across the terrace caught

Alius' attention. She raised her sword and fired. The blinking stopped.

Adrian waved his sword in front of the doorway. Nothing happened. He leaned around the edge and spied a stairway leading down into darkness. Reaching into his robes, he withdrew a flashpan, pulled the string, and tossed it down the stairs. A loud bang followed a blinding white burst and something hissed, slithering across the ice to spew a fearsome magenta flame that melted the steps into a slushy skid.

Adrian led Alius across the terrace to the parapet, where they turned around to look at the fortifications. The young *seer* turned to his friend, "We could poke and probe for hours and not find our way in and, even if we did, we'd just have to face those monsters they've got roaming about in every tunnel. There's got to be a better way."

He closed his eyes and calmed his breathing. He felt the arcs of dark energies charging the spike at the top of the spire, merging into a roiling furnace warming the ice shield beneath them, sensed the clash of forces beyond the walls, his friends struggling to gain entry into the bowels of the ice palace, and the power of Zepallo rolled up his spine like a fizzling fuse to detonate in his brain. He forced his aura to explore the structure of the castle, the very essence of the physical forces that held it in place, and slowly roamed its surfaces, until he came to the ice sword plunging into the black sky. He opened his eyes and pointed, "What holds that tower up? With all that energy flowing through it, all the ice around it should be melting. I wonder whether it's connected to the rest of the structure?"

Alius' face crinkled into her mischievous grin and she grasped his hand, lifted into the air, over the peaks of the palace, circling as close to the column as they dared. The whole surface shuddered with streams of sizzling static frothing from the gleaming tip into the bowels of the castle. Huge blocks of ice were cantilevered over an enormous space beneath and they framed but did not touch the spire.

"I think I know how we can do this," said Adrian quietly. He closed his eyes again and pictured his friends, one by one. Simian and Raffe, Sky and Master Chi, Shambala, Maze, and Lala. "Bring your friends, join us on top of the steeple. We're stronger together."

Within moments, they began to appear. First, Raffe and Simian, followed by Sky, Shambala, and several dozen African warriors, and, finally, Maze, Lala, and Master Chi and hordes of very small people.

Waves of troopers riding ravens circled the spire firing charges as they slowly closed on each successive pass. The *seers* returned fire and backed into a defensive ring. Blasts exploded all around them, on the surface of the castle and on the sleeve of ice that encased the spire. Suddenly, the dark forces stopped firing, for fear of damaging the black crystal, and swooped in for an attack.

Adrian hovered before his friends and yelled, "There seems to be a weak spot between the blocks of the ice castle and the tower. I think that, if we all fire our weapons at the same time around the base, we have a chance to melt the supports and break into their control room."

The group turned their backs to the ravens diving on the rooftop, aimed at the space between the blocks and the spire, and fired repeatedly. Huge cracks rippled across the ice and the scaffolds around the tower began to crumble and fall away. A hole opened up at Adrian's feet.

He turned to Simian and yelled, "You hold these guys off and we'll see what we can do down below!"

The old Jamaican cackled, "Don't worry about us!"

Adrian grabbed Alius, Raffe, Sky, and Master Chi and leapt through the chasm into a vast ice cavern pulsing with cascading waves of purple light.

Zepallo whirled around, with blasts exploding above the domed ceiling and meltwater gushing down the spire. The few troops, who remained in the command, drew their blasters, aiming at the intruders spiraling down through the chamber. "Stop, you fools! You'll damage the crystal spear!"

Technicians ducked for cover and scrambled to the rear exit but the Dark Lord screamed, "Return to your stations at once!"

He pointed the index finger of his right hand at the cowering servants, who were too scared to stay and even more afraid to run. One by one, they filed back to their control panels and resumed operations.

The *seers* did not hesitate to fire on the Dark Forces, who had taken up positions to cover the perimeter of the gaping hole in the ceiling. Spiraling down, their backs to a trembling column bristling with crackling purple static, they eliminated the resistance with a hail of charges.

The three clones soared past their Master, out into the open to meet the invaders. Alpha spotted Adrian, extended his sword, and tore through the quaking chamber. Beta and Gamma flew in opposite directions, spinning around the interior of the ice cave, sizing up the other four *seers,* as they levitated into the battle. Zepallo took up a defensive position near the control center and followed the clones' attack with rabid anticipation.

Raffe and Alius split off to the left, Sky and Master Chi to the right. Adrian presented his sword, ready for combat, as Alpha fired a charge that whizzed past the blond *seer's* head, singeing waves of blond hair over his ear. He twisted his wrist, raising the shield to deflect a second round.

Cold gray sparks ricocheted off the refractor, the dark energy fusing into a tight gleaming bundle that roared back at Alpha. The dark *seer* screamed as the blast seared over his shield in a blinding flash. In that moment of confusion, Adrian soared past his foe, raking his sword along his enemy's body. The wounded warrior fired an errant stream of charges, as he tumbled through the cavern into the raging inferno churning in the abyss beneath the black crystal spike.

The young *seer* could feel the desperation of his friends' struggles with Beta and Gamma, but he tuned out the chaos to focus on the frenzy in Zepallo's eyes. The Dark Lord was blocking the entrance to the control room, his arms extended to trace the furious clashes rushing around the spire, firing streams of cold gray glimmers spreading like splattered globules of mercury to tear at flesh without destroying the shimmering spike.

Adrian reached into his robes and grabbed two crystal grenades, clicked the timers, and dropped them into the well beneath the spire.

Extending his sword, he swooped down on his nemesis.

Zepallo laughed and pointed his right hand at the young *seer*, discharging a series of pulses that ripped around their target. Adrian flew straight on, spinning into a corkscrew, diving through the dome. He twisted his right arm to position the shield to return the next barrage, just as the Dark Lord loosed another round. The electric cobalt flashes fused into a fizzing specter refracting back to their source like packets of menacing moonlight fired from a crystal cannon.

The Dark Master stepped into the alcove, as the charges seared through mammoth ice blocks. A moment later, he soared into the open, leading his rival away from the controls.

Adrian heard Sky scream and saw Raffe begin to fall, as Zepallo spun to face him with a sinister smirk and a wink, before splitting into two identical forms, that split again. "I'm far more powerful than I've ever been before. I can be reproduced thousands of times through my clones," said the four images, waving their hands towards the battle raging around the ice cavern, "or I can simply duplicate myself!"

The forms split again and again until they ringed the perimeter of the gigantic vault, each pointing the index finger of their right hands at the young *seer*.

"I am all powerful and you will not stop me!" roared the black robed demons in unison. "I'll be everywhere and I'll control everything. Our time has come!"

Adrian heard Orana's voice, "The point of your lessons was to allow you to feel everything around you and to react with calm deliberation."

Sixty-four blue charges sizzled through frozen chaos, targeted to strike Adrian's heart and avoid the spire. In that moment, Adrian's grenades exploded in the molten pit beneath the floor and he sensed Raffe's limp body dropping through the madness in slow motion. He twirled to his right, his refractor deflecting a barrage of blasts to strike the ice collar surrounding the spire.

A surging cascade of dark energies sparked and flashed, as the ice shattered and pealed away from the gleaming black diamond, releasing a wave of iridescent purple energy that rolled out to lap at the walls of the great chamber, erasing the black smudges that had been Zepallo. Beta and Gamma vanished in gray glimmers, when fractures rippled through the diamond spear and the whole chamber began to rumble and groan.

Adrian swooped through a vicious purple geyser to snag Raffe's smoldering robes, just as he plummeted off the precipice into the magenta caldron. The young *seer* summoned all his powers to haul his limp friend up to the peak of the dome and out through a ferocious fracture crackling across the crumbling ceiling.

Alius and Master Chi lifted Sky out into the cold night air, just as walls of ice blocks began to collapse into the chamber. Adrian reached up to touch the arm of his glasses, "We're out!"

~

The Professor picked up Adrian's faint and scratchy cry through crackling static from the transmitter and punched two buttons on the panel in his workshop. Nanchez, Dadeus, and Sammy stared impatiently at the *messengers* lining the workbench. Golden vectors started to glow near the South Pole and the surge slowly swept north, as if the Earth was dropping out of eclipse into sunshine, the intensity increasing as the power from each successive group of Crystals joined the circuit. On the monitors, it resembled a golden wave ringing the planet, expanding at the equator and constricting as it closed on the North Pole. Keepers in every corner of the globe waited for the precise moment to add the energies from their Crystals to the swell rushing across the planet, rising to stem the tide threatening the coastal areas of the northern hemisphere. The golden curtain rippled and shimmered with the grace of the aurora borealis, a wisp of luminescent silk draping across the ice sheet, the energies closing to snuff the dark energies emanating from the ice palace.

~

Adrian and Simian bore Raffe's unconscious body between

them, as they flew over the walls to follow hordes of troops retreating across the ice to the Destiny. Master Chi and Alius followed close behind, pressing close to support Sky, who suffered a wound to her shoulder.

The troops of the Dark Forces vanished in the same instant Zepallo disappeared. The *seers* and Forces of Light rushed to the ships, knowing that the Keepers would be sending a massive wave of energy to halt the threat to the oceans of the world. They expected something cataclysmic, a reaction of horrific proportions that would surely vaporize the ice sheet and anything foolish enough to remain on its surface, when the most powerful energies in the world collided.

Word spread through the crews that even the Keepers were unsure of the outcome and many feared it would be the end of the Powers altogether. Everyone was clambering aboard so they could move the ships as far south as fast as possible.

Deckhands labored to cut her foremast free, while Destiny hovered a few feet above the ice, ready to depart, as soon as the last of her troops scrambled aboard. Adrian and Alius landed amidships and laid Raffe on the deck. Master Chi knelt over the injured *seer*, whose robes were seared, exposing a deep wound on the thigh of his right leg visible through the tear. The old *seer* searched through his pockets to retrieve a deep blue bottle. He pulled the cork with his teeth, pouring half the contents over the lesion, which hissed and smoked.

Simian and Alius brought Sky to the Master *seer* and he poured most of the remaining liquid into the gash on her shoulder. Finally, he dripped the last few drops onto his hands and allowed the liquid to trickle into Raffe's closed eyes.

Within moments, the injured *seer* gasped and exhaled very slowly, as his eyes squeezed tightly, then blinked open to gaze around at his friends, who were anxiously standing and kneeling over him. "Did we win?"

"Yes, we won!" said Adrian, hugging his friend. He leaned back, as giant snowflakes dropped out of a cloudless sky, piling up in small drifts on the deck of the crystal ship. Everyone turned to a cataclysmic crash from the palace, as the spire toppled to the ice and the shattered spear plunged into the sea. Within minutes, the castle melted to slush that poured into the hole, leaving no trace on the smooth surface of the glacier.

Chapter 12

Two long black limousines pulled to the curb in front of the headquarters of World Oil, the largest and most powerful production company in the industry. The contracts and agreements, that allowed its tentacles to reach into every major oilfield play, also provided the necessity for close contact with the governments of every producing and consuming country. Revenue generated by the corporation and its countless subsidiaries rivaled the economies of many of the developed nations and bought influence with kickbacks and bribes.

Sir Jonathon's computers provided information that Zepallo controlled the conglomerate through his representatives on the board of directors. He could preside over the majority with just enough seats and leverage to sway the course of the decisions being made. Nothing could impede his domination, unless another investor controlled enough shares to demand more seats on the board or possessed the voting support of those already seated.

Shares in a portfolio of companies, purchased with Adrian's inheritance, had almost doubled the value of his original fortune. With the addition of considerable sums from the Keepers around the world, as well as a group of major shareholders, who had been coerced into joining the cause, a new and rather mysterious financial entity moved into the markets. The Crystal Foundation was now in a position to demand nine of the twenty-four seats on the board, one more than the Dark Forces.

Colburn Tierney led a small army of associates through the entrance, past the gilded reception desk, into golden elevators, and up to the penthouse. The doors opened into the executives' private lobby, classically ostentatious with heavy wood paneling and miles of marble. The parade turned right, past the offices of vice-presidents, the president, and the chief executive officer, to a large conference room, that commanded an atrium atop the far corner of the building.

The Directors and their staffs surrounded an enormous round

table, sitting directly beneath a domed skylight, surrounded with tropical plants standing tall, in spite of the dreary gray haze. At the far end of the room, a tall man, dressed entirely in black, was droning through a series of financial documents reflecting scandalous profits, that resulted from the disruption of production and the interruption of shipments from Iran, Algeria, and Argentina.

"As directed by the board, we have also completed the purchase of Artic Petroleum, the Central States Pipeline Company, and Meridian Shipping, which provides transportation for almost ten percent of world production. The bottom line is that we now control more than thirty percent of the market."

The applause from the directors faded, as Coke and his associates barged into the room. "I'm sorry to interrupt your meeting but there are several things that need to be addressed and, considering The Crystal Foundation now controls enough shares to demand nine seats in this room, I suggest we begin our discussions immediately."

The president of the company stood, "This is most unusual!"

"I'm glad we agree," smiled the attorney, "and that's only the beginning!"

~

It was a bright blustery spring day on the coast of Cape Cod. A gale force wind blew cold from the northeast and President Bartlett could see whitecaps rolling in from the horizon on choppy seas through brass binoculars mounted on a tripod near the broad windows of his study. In the distance, he spied a two-master, flying a storm jib and a small cleated mainsail, plowing to refuge in the harbor to the south. "Only a master or a fool would dare brave these conditions," thought the President.

He had been busy since his last day in office, more than two months before, but he would only admit to himself that he missed it...being at the very center of every major event in the world and having the power to influence the outcome, to make a difference in the lives of the people and the course of history. Nothing could replace that sacred and precious burden.

He sighed and turned back to the folders on his desk. The Secret Service contingent that is assigned to protect every ex-President is smaller than the force that surrounds the current Chief Executive but no less professional or deadly. Bartlett complained that, in spite of their concerns and good intentions, they inhibited his movements around the house, so they had withdrawn to the perimeter of the residence, leaving only two agents inside and they were confined to the kitchen.

For the first time, since leaving office, he had blocked out an afternoon on his calendar with no meetings, telephone calls, or interruptions. His daughters were pursuing their own lives, shielded from the spotlight, and his wife was attending a foundation meeting in New York for some new philanthropic group that was determined to clean up the oil industry. He was convinced that she believed she was sent to this Earth to make things right and he never dared to impede her determination, capitulating when her convictions proved resolute.

He pulled off his glasses, as something stirred in the room and Adrian and Alius materializing in the center of the blue carpet before his desk. Bartlett shook his head, "I wish I could do that!"

"I'm sorry but you either have to be a *seer*, and we can be fairly certain that you're not, or you have to be with a *seer*," laughed Alius.

"I'd like to thank you, on behalf of…I don't know, how about everyone in the world, for all that you've done to stop our favorite madman."

"I doubt we defeated him, he'll be back," said Adrian. "This war will never end but it will continue to ebb and flow back and forth, as it has through centuries, until enough people join together to change things forever."

"In spite of my eight years in office, which provided plenty of opportunities to become a pessimist, I honestly still believe in the goodness of man," said the President, "but I would suggest that we not hold our breath in expectation that others will come to see things as I do. Tell me, what happened to the clones?"

Adrian smiled, "Well, I'm fairly certain that Alpha's dead and the other two were severely wounded. From the reports, we got back through the whalemail…we'll explain that later…the incubator for the clones was installed in a large facility burrowed into a reef beneath the ocean off one of the islands along the Indonesian arpeggio. When the wave of positive energy swept across the globe, their defensive shield went down and several pods of whales inflicted considerable damage. Although it was not entirely destroyed, it will be years before production can begin again."

The two *seers* walked up to the desk. "Are you sure you want to do this?" inquired Alius.

"Of course, I want to do this, are you kidding? I've been wondering about your world, since Adrian's grandfather first told me of his suspicions about the Powers, and that was several years before I met you children. They've promised me another four hours of solitude. Can we get there and back before then?"

"It will be a fast tour but one that you'll find inspiring," said Adrian.

Alius asked, "Do you have a jacket?"

"Yes, yes, I do," said Bartlett as he stood and pulled a weathered wool parka from the back of his chair.

The two *seers* took his hands, "Now, there's nothing to be afraid of, just relax and let go. We'll be taking you through the plane of the animals, so we won't have to worry about the Dark Forces," instructed Alius.

The President squeezed their hands and his lips curled into the impish smile of a schoolboy playing hooky, as they disappeared.

The Cast of Characters

Adrian – son of John and Sara – long and lanky, blond hair and intense blue eyes

John – Adrian's father – a large man with dark hair and dark eyes, sailor and ship designer

Sara – Adrian's mother – blond, blue eyes, housewife, grew up on Morgan's Knot, daughter of the former *seer*, Paul

George – Adrian's uncle – tall, strong, rough hands, salt and pepper hair

Elsie – Adrian's aunt and Sara's sister – small, round, impish, mother to everyone

Molly and Megan – George & Elsie's twin daughters – curly blond hair blue eyes, a year younger than Adrian

Morgan Keelty – sister of Josh – tall, long curly brown hair, green eyes

Joshua Keelty – Morgan's brother – dark eyes, jet-black hair

Ian Sheridan – Kelly's brother and Adrian's second cousin – tall, slender

Kelly Sheridan – Ian's younger sister – incredible smile, brown eyes, blond curls

Spot and Dusty – dolphins

Professor Ponte – Keeper of the Powers on Morgan's Knot, astronomer, teacher, and Adrian's mentor

Ester – Ponte's wife - highly intelligent and Ponte's equal, slender, big glasses, thin lips, small teeth

Tic – talking black and white tomcat, Adrian's guide in the animal world

Brandy – Keelty's Irish setter and Adrian's companion and protector

Travis – harbormaster

Jasmine – Travis' fishing trawler

Dr. Stevens – doctor on the island

Dr. Carringsworth - Headmaster of the upper school

Mrs. Hammon - political science teacher

Daphne & Dante – deer

Damien – their foal

Beggar – small bear

Ashton and Ashford – Beggar's cubs

Magnus – golden eagle

Harriet & Harry – hawks

The Book of Wisdoms – The Golden Book on Morgan's Knot

The Book of Knowledge – The Silver Book used by the *Others* to master the Dark Powers

Jamaica

Simian – wise old Jamaican *seer*, Sammy's uncle

Sammy – Simian's nephew – young Keeper in training

Lorraine – Simian's wife

The *Others*

Alius – daughter of Jofre – the *Other's seer* - petite, blond, blue eyes, tough, independent, and beautiful

Jofre – father of Alius and Master of the *Others* – a huge domineering man with white eyes

Mandor – Supervisor of Production and Security – dark eyes, long straight white hair

Nanchez – Keeper of the Dark Powers – a grumpy giant of a man with white hair, dark eyes

The Island of the Children

Raffe – young, athletic, and naïve *seer*

Gabrielle – leader of the Underworld – Mary's husband, long white hair and beard

Dadeus – Keeper of the Powers for the underworld

Mary – Gabrielle's wife, *seer*

Book of Natural Balance – The Golden Book on the Island of the Children

Soule and Amy – diving instructors

Additional Characters

Sky – tiny Thai *seer* – from the Temple of Spiritual Harmony, Thailand

Master Chi – M*aster seer* - Temple of Ancient Truths – Himilayas

Master Jung – slender old Keeper – Temple of Ancient Truths

Mantis – Sky's mentor

Sir Isaacs – English Keeper

Shambala – African *seer*

Mambazi – little girl in Shambala's village

Danali – Keeper in Shambala's village on Lake Victoria

Lala & Maze – *seers* from the southern tip of South America

President Bartlett – United States

Natalie – Bartlett's secretary

Lord Robbins – Canadian ambassador to the United Nations

Prime Minister Langdon – British Prime Minister

Donald Sloan – Director of the CIA

Sir Jonathon – John's Scottish father – submariner and spymaster

Ralph – John's alcoholic brother – corporate attorney

Margaret – John's sister

Michael – Margaret's husband

Sam and Julie – Margaret's spoiled children

Aunt Lucy – Jonathon's sister

Colburn Tierney – Sir Jonathon's attorney

Martina Tierney – Coke's wife

Richard Morrissey - funeral director

Sir Robert Montague – British Gov't representative - organizes Sir Jonathon's funeral

Lorraine - Sir Jonathon's cook

Angela – Lorraine's daughter

Audrey – Lorraine's niece

The Reverend Malcolm Cousins – minister at Bethlehem Chapel for Sir Jonathon's funeral

Captain Maniford Ruhl – captain of the Destiny

Addicus Bellsley - captain of the Hope

The Plane of the Animals

Orana – the oldest *seer* on the planet

Unis – female unicorn

Malan – Unis' mate

Legio Obscurum

Zepallo – The Dark Lord – A Minister of Cultural Relations of the Council of Ollapez

Cadeau - Senior Security Technician – Korean complex

Regis – Senior Regent for Command and Control – Korean complex

The Doctor - a brilliant and determined renegade scientist with a shock of white hair over a pallid complexion, dark deep-set eyes, German accent

Alpha, Beta, and Gamma – Zepallo's clones

Whisperers – surrogate moles buried in positions of power in the seats of government, the pinnacles of military commands, corporations and industries, and every major religion.

The adventure continues in
Islands of Wisdoms
Morgan's Knot - A Serial Fantasy
Episode VIII

Seers and Keepers from around the world converge on Morgan's Knot to found The School of Seers and Keepers, under the guidance of Chancellor Bartlett, to thwart frenzied expansion of Zepallo and Legio Obscurum's fortifications around the planet.

Visit: www.morgansknot.com

Eric T. Stiller is an award-winning commercial photographer, an educator and advocate, and a Master Gardener.

His novels

The Morgan's Knot Serial Fantasy
Morgan's Knot
Island of the Children
Ice Island
Islands of Concrete and Steel
Islands of the Mind
Islands of the Sky
Islands of Dark Miracles

(for mature audiences)
Dealer
Nellis Gray

Visit: www.rickstiller.com for more of his books, photographs, and music and www.morgansknot.com for the latest on the Morgan's Knot series.

If you enjoyed this story, please give it a five-star review on my Amazon sales page and like my 'Eric T. Stiller - Author page on Facebook.

Islands of Wisdom

Morgan's Knot – A Serial Fantasy
Episode VIII

By

Eric T. Stiller, Jr.

Former President Bartlett accepted his new role without hesitation, although convincing the Secret Service of the need for a change in their security procedures involved far more thumb-twisting than persuading the Israelis and the Palestinians to sit down at the same table or convincing both Houses of Congress and the members of two opposing political parties to agree to pass any measure that might benefit all mankind.

With all the other commitments and requirements of an ex-president, he could only dedicate three days a week to his new position but the rewards far outweighed the imposition and he cherished the time he spent in this endeavor. Spinning his chair, he turned to bask in a wash of sunlight cascading down through the blue waters of the northern Atlantic. An endless school of silver tuna, shimmering daggers, glinted close to the glass and, beyond the third dome, he could see divers moving massive curved beams into place for the newest bubble being constructed for this city beneath the sea.

Although most of the world would never know of his new title, he was as proud of it as he had been when he took the oath of office as President of the United States, Chancellor of the International School for *Seers* and Keepers. Given his druthers, the title might have included wizardry or magic, for he still viewed the Powers of the Crystals and the things these people could do as magical, but he was pleased and honored that he had been asked to help organize the institution.

His years in the economics department at Harvard provided a model for the structure of the school but offered nothing to define the scope of concepts and information that were required to reach the level of Master *Seer* or a first-class Keeper of the Powers. Those who achieved that lofty status had invested their lives in the quest and, now, they were trying to break it down into actual courses that followed a definitive path, compressing decades of experience into a five-year program.

After the battle over the North Pole, *seers* and Keepers from all corners of the globe descended on Morgan's Knot, taking up every spare bed on the island, congregating around the observatory, arguing over the obvious and ominous technical advances of the Dark Forces and the lack of a unified effort by the Forces of the Light to merge their collective knowledge to counter the next confrontation that was sure to come.

There were too many ideas and opinions to reach a consensus or to develop a plan of action. After two weeks without progress, Adrian and Alius brought the former president to mediate, under the guise of providing a short tour of Morgan's Knot and the wonders of the Powers. Bartlett was still unsure about how they managed to transform time, so no one at the house on the Cape knew that he was missing, something to do with that little blond girl, Kelly, who repeatedly asked to sit on his lap and kept fiddling with an old pocket watch.

While everyone else crowded into Ponte's parlor, kitchen, and hallways, spilling out onto the lawn and the path beyond, five *seers* and five Keepers sat at the dining room table for three days, before an accord was reached. Bartlett grasped the concepts in short order and pushed the negotiations forward with absolute focus on the question, "What is the best course of action to give us the greatest opportunity to impede or defeat the Dark Forces and develop the wonders of the Powers to benefit all mankind?"

He never wavered, listening patiently, as endless opinions were proposed, discussed, and noted. In the end, they decided on a foundation of coordination and education. Sky, Master Chi, Mary, and Simian accepted the task of building a curriculum to teach young apprentices and expand the knowledge and powers of every *seer*, while Dadeus, Sir Isaacs, and Master Jung assumed a similar challenge to develop laboratories to facilitate the education of aspiring Keepers. Ponte and Nanchez chose to act as coordinators in gathering the technologies and techniques from every Keeper on the planet. The ancestry of every *seer* would be traced back through centuries to see whether there might be other *seers* who, like Adrian, had yet to discover the purpose or reason for their special talents. Jofre, George, and John volunteered to oversee the construction of a cluster of new domes that would become the center of knowledge. In addition, they agreed to expand Adrian's campaign to educate those who lived in the real world, especially the children, for, in the end, the responsibility for the future would become their burden to bear.

Systems were being constructed to connect every Keeper on the planet with instantaneous communications and the sum knowledge would be brought together in an atmosphere modeled after the ancient library of Alexandria, where the world's recorded wisdom, from Greece, Rome, Persia, Egypt, and empires across the globe, was collected, translated into all the major languages, and made available to the finest minds of their time.

It was a bold concept that demanded a unified effort and absolute commitment from everyone involved but it was the only path that offered a chance to defend the Powers and life, as we know it, against incessant assaults by the Dark Forces.

The former president faced down countless enemies and sent young men and women into battle to preserve freedom and democracy but, as Sir Jonathon informed him almost five years before, this adversary was the real force behind the puppets, who carried out those barbaric campaigns.

The old spy's husky Scottish accent still lingered in Bartlett's memory of that late-night conversation, "These are the people who live in the darkness, who'll not be satisfied to control one country or even a major empire. These forces want to control the entire world and rebuild it on a model shaped by the Devil himself. We have no defense against their powers or their weapons and there is only one group on the planet that has any chance of stopping them."

"And who might they be?" inquired the president, who might have been even more skeptical had the authority not been Sir Jonathon.

"The Forces of the Light." He paused, "I don't know enough yet, because they exist in a shadow world that we don't see. I know that's confusing but, it's my understanding, that they've always moved within society without anyone really noticing that they were any different than the rest of us. Just as the Dark Forces live in an invisible place, I'm convinced that there are places on the Earth, where societies of these people live and work to defend everything that you and I believe in. I just have no idea of where to look. There certainly isn't any evidence in the archives of the intelligence world."

He sipped his Scotch, "There have been myths and legends for thousands of years about these two forces facing off against one another in gargantuan battles that were recorded as fable, because the realities were far beyond our capacity to accept them as truth. From what I've deduced, there are moments in history where man made giant leaps in technology, architecture, social organization, and belief systems, transforming, seemingly insignificant, clans into empires. I would offer Egypt, the tribes of Central and South America, China, Greece, Rome, and, Atlantis, if you care to indulge in myth as history, as a few examples. On the other side are those dark chapters, where humanity seemed bent on consuming itself...Germany, Cambodia, Kosovo, Africa, more than a few episodes in Central and South America...for that matter, our ancestors who administered the Dark Ages and the white settlers who pillaged the New World."

"So, you're saying that those periods that reached either extreme were somehow the result of the struggle between these two phantom forces?"

"That's exactly what I'm saying!" thundered his aging roommate. "It's there for the finding in the history books and it continues to this day."

The president sat back in his chair and took a sip of his drink, "You know that I've always been a student of history but…what you're saying is outside the boundaries and constraints that our version of academia has created for itself. I'm not sure that I want to believe you but it solves so many mysteries…"

"The point is that we need to learn much more about these conflicting forces and find a way to do what we can to support the Forces of Light."

"I agree," said Bartlett quietly, musing on the insight. "The future of mankind might well depend on it. If you're willing, I'd like you to undertake this investigation. Personally."

The old spy's eyes crinkled into a sly grin, a shrewd smile that brought them to the brink of being expelled from the university more than once, back in the day, and sipped his whiskey before he replied, "I've been thinking about retirement anyway. Give me what I need and you've bought yourself a new secret government agency. The opposition would have a field day with this one!"

The two men shook hands, Sir Jonathon stood almost a head taller than the president but they shared equal admiration and respect.

~

Zepallo was suspended inside a gray bubble in the incubator beneath a coral reef in the Caribbean Sea. Special circuits had been set up to balance his internal energies in a process that would take weeks, if not months to complete.

The wave of power that rolled off the spire in the ice castle caught the Dark Lord, in that instant before he moved into the safety of the vectors. His habit of exposing himself to the enormous intensity of the Black Crystals was legendary. Unfortunately, the wave born of the energies of all of the Black Gems overloaded the fragile tangle of nerves within his body. The Doctor could not be sure whether there would be permanent damage, should he be lucky enough, strong enough to survive.

Beta and Gamma were both in critical condition, although with the advances that the medical team was making, it was entirely possible they would recover. The clones were being cared for in the infirmary and he would check on them shortly.

Outside the sphere, in the purified ocean water of the incubator and alongside the gray bubble containing his Master's body, floated smaller, iridescent green balloons nurturing the surviving embryos, in various stages of development, from the damaged center in the Savu Sea, south of Indonesia. The new lab was not fully functional but he was pushing the technicians to finish preparations as quickly as possible, so they could begin production with the DNA samples that had been replicated and delivered to thirteen of their installations around the world for safekeeping. Of the seventy-five infants, he had only been able to save thirty-three but they were healthy and thriving in their new home.

Memories of that day still made him queasy. His escape depended on quick thinking and good fortune. He was not a man of action, not one to lead the troops, rather he prided himself on using his mind to overcome impossible tasks and untangle the riddles and mysteries of life.

The Forces of Light generated a positive wave that crippled their defenses and, almost simultaneously, pods of whales crashed through the facility, smashing into the domes, one after another, until cracks appeared and the ocean rushed in. Their effort had been synchronized with a pulse of positive energy that surged through the circuits, coupled with the coordination of the attack, indicating planning and execution worthy of the finest military minds.

The Doctor gathered as many of the embryos as he could manage, moved several other physicians, nurses, and the babies into a mini-sub that was docked in an interface near the nursery and slipped into the safety of open water.

The facility in the Savu Sea was the only one damaged, although it was not destroyed, and construction teams were already beginning restoration and repairs. Renovations were nearing completion in New York and the Caucuses, three new compounds were under construction, and this new incubation center was already in use.

The campaign had failed and, in the days since the battle, several distinct groups were maneuvering for political position. Each maintaining a diplomatic cloak of invisibility, should Zepallo survive and reclaim his throne. They had witnessed his retribution and none relished the idea of provoking his wrath.

One thing was assured, the Doctor's expertise was needed now more than ever. His knowledge provided security and, in this time of flux, he found that comforting. No matter who assumed power, the technology of the clones would be an integral part of the future.

~

Alius found Adrian meditating, floating a foot above the floor in the observatory. Sunlight slipped through a slim crack in the curved doors housing the telescope, slicing through the dust hanging in the still air, tracing a silhouette of the young *seer* in a slender arc of golden light on the worn planking of the floor. With his arms outstretched and his legs crossed beneath him, the shadow resembled a cross within a crescent. It was a symbol known through thousands of years as the emblem of the Forces of Light.

Adrian opened his eyes and slowly descended to sit on the floor, "I sensed you coming…"

"I was worried about you," whispered Alius quietly.

"I was thinking about Orana and trying to find her energy…" his voice trailed off, distracted, as if some new thought had crept into his mind.

"And what did you find?"

"I feel her in exactly the same way I felt her before she died. It's as if she's in her cave in the plane of the animals."

"Maybe we should go and find out," sighed Alius. "We haven't had a day off, since long before the battle and, I don't know about you, but I was scared that we wouldn't succeed...that, maybe we wouldn't survive..."

Adrian stood and wrapped his arms around the little blond *seer*, "As long as we're together..."

"That's what worries me. Raffe and Sky were injured. We lost a number of others, including Orana, and she might be the greatest loss of all. When you and I fought on the mountain, the Powers seemed huge and the world that we were fighting over was confined to this island. Now it's become something else...there's no innocence about it, no sense of wonder. It's about survival and we're in the middle of an arms race between opposing sides, each using science, technology, and wealth to claw ahead of the other. Isn't this exactly the same thing that happened between the United States and the Soviet Union or the nations of Europe?"

"Yes, it is," smiled Adrian, "but it's also been repeated many times throughout history. With each new discovery, each new weapon, one side or the other gained leverage and battles were won or lost. I understand the Keepers point of view but I want to be very sure that the *seers* learn to use the Powers, not just the technology. They need to learn to think, to feel, to move boldly, when the time is right, and when to wait."

"They also need to believe in The Balance. We must defend it..." Alius' eyes filled with tears, "Can we go to the animals? Please?"

"Alright," said Adrian quietly, taking her hand and moving into the vectors.

The streaming colors were vibrant and there was no hint of the grating of the dark energies, as they passed into the plane of the animals and landed in the meadow.

Unis and the herd of unicorns were not in the pasture and, other than a warm wind blowing through the trees, there was only silence.

Alius whispered, "Not a creature was stirring..."

"This is strange," replied Adrian. "This world is always filled with the sounds of life."

"Maybe we should go to the cave," suggested Alius.

They levitated above the trees, up the side of the mountain, and landed on the path at the entrance to the cavern. Adrian smelled the smoke of a pinion fire wafting from the entrance, "That's the smoke from her fire!"

He took Alius' hand and led her into the darkness. After several turns they could see the glow of the flames and Adrian started walking faster but Alius grabbed him by the shoulder, "Wait! Look just in front of you!"

It took only a fraction of a second for his eyes to shift focus from the end of the tunnel to two inches in front of his nose. His breath moved an intricately woven silken web that stretched across the width and height of the passage. A surprisingly loud voice called from just above his head, "It would take years to devour something your size!"

Adrian looked up to find a rainbow-hued spider, it's feet glowed electric green, its hairy legs an ocean blue, the body was as yellow as the morning sun, and the eyes the intensity of two red beams in the darkness. "Why have you spun your web to close off Orana's cave?"

The glowing spider scampered across the web to face the boy, "To preserve her memory! Why?"

"Perhaps we should start over," said Adrian quietly.

Holding on to the web with its two hind feet, the spider leaned out to within an inch of Adrian's eyes, six of its legs clawed at the air between them. "Why would we want to do that?"

"Because...I'm Adrian, a student of Orana's. We were there when she died."

The spider leaned left and right, inspecting his eyes. "I believe that you are telling the truth, but why have you come here?"

"Because I...felt her...her energy, as if nothing had changed, as if she was still alive."

"What is it that you want?" asked the tiny predator, scurrying across the web to bundle up a moth that made an unfortunate turn in search of the flames.

"I guess I just need to sit by her fire and learn to believe that she is really gone."

"That shouldn't be any problem."

"But how do we pass into her chamber without destroying your beautiful web?"

"Oh, come now…that should be easy for a *seer!*"

Alius giggled and took his hand, moving into the vectors and back again on the other side of the barrier. Adrian turned around to find the spider waving with its four front legs and laughing raucously, "You are a *seer!*"

"I have a question. Where are all of the other animals?"

"Ah, you noticed, very good. They're having a meeting on the plain," said the spider, who stopped waving and stood very erect.

"What are they taking about?"

"They're discussing whether there is anything that the animals can do to stop man from destroying the Earth."

"What do you mean?"

"The flooding affected thousands of square miles of coastland, destroying the habitat of all sorts of creatures. It will be years before things get back to normal. Accommodations need to be found for them elsewhere and there's already a great migration. It's all so…unsettling."

"So, when Zepallo melted the polar ice, it affected the plane of the animals?"

"Obviously!"

"Are you saying that the weather is the same in both planes?"

"Of course, it is! The physical world is exactly the same…the ocean currents, the weather patterns, and the global warming. That's what they're talking about, how to stop the pollution that will destroy us all."

"I never thought about that," said Alius.

"Me neither," replied Adrian, "but it does make perfect sense."

They turned into the chamber to find a large, fresh fire burning in the pit. There were no coals and the flaming logs had yet to form ash. Songbirds provided music that echoed through the cavern and a long ray of sunlight filtered down through the smoke to the spot where Orana always sat, her hair fanned out around her, her aura glowing, a small knowing smile on her lips.

The two *seers* sat down on a blanket next to the fire and the silver tea service appeared before them. There were two cups, a tiny pot of honey, and the tea in the pitcher was hot. Alius poured the golden liquid into the cups, added a few drops of honey, and handed one to Adrian.

The flavor exploded inside his mouth, a rush of sweet and bitter followed the hot liquid as it coursed down his throat and seared his stomach. He had forgotten about Orana's tea. Slowly, the sensations and memories of his lessons crept through his body and overwhelmed his mind. He gazed with total focus at the emblem on the wall, was aware of the rippling sound of running water, the mesmerizing song of the birds, the sweet scent of the pinion smoke, and the determined thump of his heart beating in his chest. Allowing his senses to reach out, he knew that, other than the rainbow spider and Alius, of course, there was no other living creature nearby, except... the energy of Orana. The sensation was strong and, at first, he assumed that it was just being in her space but there was more to it than that. Some part of her was still here.

Adrian felt her eyes burning into his soul, her energy reaching out to embrace him, just as she had before his lessons started. He flashed through the white world and watched himself grow from an infant to a very old man, he flew through the jungle, out over the blue-green ocean, crashing down through its surface to the cold depths of the world before life began.

"What just happened," asked Alius, as he gasped for breath.

"I just went through a very fast version of the lessons that Orana provided for me. I can feel her. She's here...somewhere."

"I'm almost as sensitive as you are but I don't feel anything, other than a very strange numbness from this tea."

Adrian touched her hand gently, closed his eyes, and concentrated. His body lifted above the blanket and an electric blue aura radiated around him. The sunbeam moved across the fire and wrapped around the glowing egg surrounding the young *seer* like a snake constricting its prey, but gently...ever so gently, its light so intense that Alius shielded her eyes and turned away.

The cave filled with thousands of hummingbirds, the buzz of their wings droned behind the sharp echo of their chirping, as they swooped around the fire pit. A shimmering vision of Orana appeared, her white hair falling around her like a flaming shawl, her eyes gentle but strong, her lips curled into a curious smile, "What is it that you seek?"

Adrian spoke but felt as if he was hearing his own words from far away, "I felt you...I guess I couldn't...or didn't want to believe that you were really dead."

The ancient woman smiled, "I am here."

"But...are you...?"

"I am living but certainly not in the sense of being alive. There are some advantages..."

"I don't understand," replied Adrian quietly.

"You saw my body die but did you see my spirit or my energy disappear? No, you were too busy seeing with your eyes instead of with your heart!"

"But...I saw you..."

"You saw what I intended for everyone to see. I am far more powerful, if they presume that I'm dead, that I can no longer affect the battle one way or another!"

The young *seer* was confused. "I'm afraid you'll have to explain this to me."

A third cup of tea appeared and the old lady sipped from the tiny teacup and returned it to the china saucer. "Alright, I'm surprised that you haven't figured this out for yourself. Just as there are many planes in the real world, there are many realities in the spiritual world. Our energy never ceases, it just moves from one reality to another, just as you can move from the real world to the vectors or the plane of the animals. There are several other planes that you need to learn about when you've time.

Anyway, back to the subject…it is to our advantage for the Dark Forces and our own comrades, for that matter, to assume that I died in that collision with the flying saucer. What a wonderful way to go! Spectacular, certainly spectacular!" She snickered but her eyes were deadly serious, "As far as anyone else is concerned, I'm dead, but to you, my young student, I will make myself, my knowledge, and my talents available, whenever you might need me. There is much to do and little time to do it in."

"What do you mean?"

"Well, now that you mention it, I do suppose that time is a bit different on this side of the looking-glass…let's leave it at this…you won the battle. You managed to stop that maniac and to kill Alpha, as well as many of their troops, but Zepallo and the two surviving clones will be back. You inflicted heavy damage to one facility but they're already back in production at another and they're building more around the world."

"The Keepers are organizing themselves and they've started a school for *seers* and Keepers on Morgan's Knot, where they want to bring together all of the knowledge and technology in one place. Sort of a research library."

"It's about time, although I do blame myself for isolating various groups from each other. I always thought that it provided an additional layer of security…perhaps I was wrong. We're only a half-century behind the enemy, the Keepers have a lot of catching up to do."

"We got President Bartlett to be Chancellor of the school, to help organize everything."

The ancient *seer* smiled, "There are many powerful people in the real world, who would be more than willing to offer any assistance, if they're asked in the right way."

"We've got an attorney in Washington who's helping us fight against Zepallo's holdings in the financial markets."

"That one is the devil. If he can't steal it, he'll figure out a way to buy it. Either way, he won't be satisfied, until the world is transformed into a very dark place. I grew up a child of the Dark Ages and spent the better part of a thousand years fighting to see that those mistakes are never repeated. Now it's your time to lead the battle."

Adrian remained quiet, as the words resonated through his body and touched his soul, "I'm sure I'm not ready to take your place."

"You won't be taking my place. You'll be making your own. That's what your lessons were about, that's what your life has been about…learning to believe in yourself. As you will learn, there are many fine and talented *seers* in the world. You'll need their help but you will lead, you'll see the vision and the path and find the strength to follow it. I knew that from the first moment you entered this cave."

"But how…?"

"You've learned to listen and you're just beginning to learn to see. Seeing along the vectors is only a small part of the talent but that's why we're called *seers*. In time, you'll learn to see beyond the moment, into the future, as well as the past, through the planes and the various levels of reality. That vision is a heavy burden that you must carry with you like a sack of coal across your back and, once you begin the journey, you can never turn back."

"How do I find you?"

"You already know the answer to your question," smiled Orana. "You knew to come here, you felt it. Open your senses and I'll be there, always."

She closed her eyes and slowly disappeared, a wisp of smoke in a faint breeze, and Adrian settled back onto the blanket. Alius was in a deep sleep, lying on her side with her hand beneath her head. The young *seer* leaned over and kissed her forehead.

"What just happened?"

"I don't know. We were drinking tea and then you curled up for a little nap," said Adrian quietly. "I think we should be on our way."

He held her arm, as she struggled to her feet, brushed back her white hair, and rubbed her eyes. "I wonder what was in that tea? All I remember was a bright light and then you waking me."

"You didn't miss much," laughed Adrian.

"What did you do while I was asleep?"

"I meditated and learned that the Dark Forces were only bruised by our efforts. They're in full production again. Alpha is dead but the others survived."

Alius pressed her palms to her temples, "My head hurts. I don't think I'm quite myself at the moment but I do think that we need to inform our friends."

The children's battle to save mankind from our own worst impulses continues...